# The Guns of Shiloh
## A Story of the Great Western Campaign

Joseph A. Altsheler

**The Guns of Shiloh: A Story of the Great Western Campaign**

Copyright © 2019 Indo-European Publishing

The present edition is a reproduction of previous publication of this classic work. Minor typographical errors may have been corrected without note, however, for an authentic reading experience the spelling, punctuation, and capitalization have been retained from the original text.

ISBN: 978-1-64439-219-5

# CONTENTS

# FOREWORD

"The Guns of Shiloh," a complete story in itself, is the complement of "The Guns of Bull Run." In "The Guns of Bull Run" the Civil War and its beginnings are seen through the eyes of Harry Kenton, who is on the Southern side. In "The Guns of Shiloh" the mighty struggle takes its color from the view of Dick Mason, who fights for the North and who is with Grant in his first great campaign.

# CHAPTER I

## IN FLIGHT

Dick Mason, caught in the press of a beaten army, fell back slowly with his comrades toward a ford of Bull Run. The first great battle of the Civil War had been fought and lost. Lost, after it had been won! Young as he was Dick knew that fortune had been with the North until the very closing hour. He did not yet know how it had been done. He did not know how the Northern charges had broken in vain on the ranks of Stonewall Jackson's men. He did not know how the fresh Southern troops from the Valley of Virginia had hurled themselves so fiercely on the Union flank. But he did know that his army had been defeated and was retreating on the capital.

Cannon still thundered to right and left, and now and then showers of bursting shell sprayed over the heads of the tired and gloomy soldiers. Dick, thoughtful and scholarly, was in the depths of a bitterness and despair reached by few of those around him. The Union, the Republic, had appealed to him as the most glorious of experiments. He could not bear to see it broken up for any cause whatever. It had been founded with too much blood and suffering and labor to be dissolved in a day on a Virginia battlefield.

But the army that had almost grasped victory was retreating, and the camp followers, the spectators who had come out to see an easy triumph, and some of the raw recruits were running. A youth near Dick cried that the rebels fifty thousand strong with a hundred guns were hot upon their heels. A short, powerful man, with a voice like the roar of thunder, bade him hush or he would feel a rifle barrel across his back. Dick had noticed this man, a sergeant named Whitley, who had shown singular courage and coolness throughout the battle, and he crowded closer to him for companionship. The man observed the action and looked at him with blue eyes that twinkled out of a face almost black with the sun.

"Don't take it so hard, my boy," he said. "This battle's lost, but there are others that won't be. Most of the men were raw, but they did some mighty good fightin', while the regulars an' the cavalry are coverin' the retreat. Beauregard's army is not goin' to sweep us off the face of the earth."

His words brought cheer to Dick, but it lasted only a moment. He was to see many dark days, but this perhaps was the darkest of his life. His heart beat painfully and his face was a brown mask of mingled dust, sweat, and burned gunpowder. The thunder of the

1

Southern cannon behind them filled him with humiliation. Every bone in him ached after such fierce exertion, and his eyes were dim with the flare of cannon and rifles and the rolling clouds of dust. He was scarcely conscious that the thick and powerful sergeant had moved up by his side and had put a helping hand under his arm.

"Here we are at the ford!" cried Whitley. "Into it, my lad! Ah, how good the water feels!"

Dick, despite those warning guns behind him, would have remained a while in Bull Run, luxuriating in the stream, but the crowd of his comrades was pressing hard upon him, and he only had time to thrust his face into the water and to pour it over his neck, arms, and shoulders. But he was refreshed greatly. Some of the heat went out of his body, and his eyes and head ached less.

The retreat continued across the rolling hills. Dick saw everywhere arms and supplies thrown away by the fringe of a beaten army, the men in the rear who saw and who spread the reports of panic and terror. But the regiments were forming again into a cohesive force, and behind them the regulars and cavalry in firm array still challenged pursuit. Heavy firing was heard again under the horizon and word came that the Southern cavalry had captured guns and wagons, but the main division maintained its slow retreat toward Washington.

Now the cool shadows were coming. The sun, which had shown as red as blood over the field that day, was sinking behind the hills. Its fiery rays ceased to burn the faces of the men. A soft healing breeze stirred the leaves and grass. The river of Bull Run and the field of Manassas were gone from sight, and the echo of the last cannon shot died solemnly on the Southern horizon. An hour later the brigade stopped in the wood, and the exhausted men threw themselves upon the ground. They were so tired that their bodies were in pain as if pricked with needles. The chagrin and disgrace of defeat were forgotten for the time in the overpowering desire for rest.

Dick had enlisted as a common soldier. There was no burden of maintaining order upon him, and he threw himself upon the ground by the side of his new friend, Sergeant Whitley. His breath came at first in gasps, but presently he felt better and sat up.

It was now full night, thrice blessed to them all, with the heat and dust gone and no enemy near. The young recruits had recovered their courage. The terrible scenes of the battle were hid from their eyes, and the cannon no longer menaced on the horizon. The sweet, soothing wind blew gently over the hills among which they lay, and the leaves rustled peacefully.

Fires were lighted, wagons with supplies arrived, and the men began to cook food, while the surgeons moved here and there, binding up the wounds of the hurt. The pleasant odors of coffee and frying meat arose. Sergeant Whitley stood up and by the moonlight and the fires scanned the country about them with discerning eye. Dick looked at him with renewed interest. He was a man of middle years, but with all the strength and elasticity of youth. Despite his thick coat of tan he was naturally fair, and Dick noticed that his hands were the largest that he had ever seen on any human being. They seemed to the boy to have in them the power to strangle a bear. But the man was singularly mild and gentle in his manner.

"We're about half way to Washington, I judge," he said, "an' I expect a lot of our camp followers and grass-green men are all the way there by now, tellin' Abe Lincoln an' everybody else that a hundred thousand rebels fell hard upon us on the plain of Manassas."

He laughed deep down in his throat and Dick again drew courage and cheerfulness from one who had such a great store of both.

"How did it happen? Our defeat, I mean," asked Dick. "I thought almost to the very last moment that we had the victory won."

"Their reserves came an' ours didn't. But the boys did well. Lots worse than this will happen to us, an' we'll live to overcome it. I've been through a heap of hardships in my life, Dick, but I always remember that somebody else has been through worse. Let's go down the hill. The boys have found a branch an' are washin' up."

By "branch" he meant a brook, and Dick went with him gladly. They found a fine, clear stream, several feet broad and a foot deep, flowing swiftly between the slopes, and probably emptying miles further on into Bull Run. Already it was lined by hundreds of soldiers, mostly boys, who were bathing freely in its cool waters. Dick and the sergeant joined them and with the sparkle of the current fresh life and vigor flowed into their veins.

An officer took command, and when they had bathed their faces, necks, and arms abundantly they were allowed to take off their shoes and socks and put their bruised and aching feet in the stream.

"It seems to me, sergeant, that this is pretty near to Heaven," said Dick as he sat on the bank and let the water swish around his ankles.

"It's mighty good. There's no denyin' it, but we'll move still a step nearer to Heaven, when we get our share of that beef an' coffee, which I now smell most appetizin'. Hard work gives a fellow a ragin' appetite, an' I reckon fightin' is the hardest of all work. When I was

3

a lumberman in Wisconsin I thought nothin' could beat that, but I admit now that a big battle is more exhaustin'."

"You've worked in the timber then?"

"From the time I was twelve years old 'til three or four years ago. If I do say it myself, there wasn't a man in all Wisconsin, or Michigan either, who could swing an axe harder or longer than I could. I guess you've noticed these hands of mine."

He held them up, and they impressed Dick more than ever. They were great masses of bone and muscle fit for a giant.

"Paws, the boys used to call 'em," resumed Whitley with a pleased laugh. "I inherited big hands. Father had em an' mother had 'em, too. So mine were wonders when I was a boy, an' when you add to that years an' years with the axe, an' with liftin' an' rollin' big logs I've got what I reckon is the strongest pair of hands in the United States. I can pull a horseshoe apart any time. Mighty useful they are, too, as I'm likely to show you often."

The chance came very soon. A frightened horse, probably with the memory of the battle still lodged somewhere in his animal brain, broke his tether and came charging among the troops. Whitley made one leap, seized him by the bit in his mighty grasp and hurled him back on his haunches, where he held him until fear was gone from him.

"It was partly strength and partly sleight of hand, a trick that I learned in the cavalry," he said to Dick as they put on their shoes. "I got tired of lumberin' an' I wandered out west, where I served three years on horseback in the regular army, fightin' the Indians. Good fighters they are, too. Mighty hard to put your hand on 'em. Now they're there an' now they ain't. Now you see 'em before you, an' then they're behind you aimin' a tomahawk at your head. They taught us a big lot that I guess we can use in this war. Come on, Dick, I guess them banquet halls are spread, an' I know we're ready."

Not much order was preserved in the beaten brigade, which had become separated from the rest of the retreating army, but the spirits of all were rising and that, so Sergeant Whitley told Dick, was better just now than technical discipline. The Northern army had gone to Bull Run with ample supplies, and now they lacked for nothing. They ate long and well, and drank great quantities of coffee. Then they put out the fires and resumed the march toward Washington.

They stopped again an hour or two after midnight and slept until morning. Dick lay on the bare ground under the boughs of a great oak tree. It was a quarter of an hour before sleep came, because his nervous system had received a tremendous wrench that day. He closed his eyes and the battle passed again before them. He remembered, too, a lightning glimpse of a face, that of his cousin, Harry Kenton, seen but an instant and then gone. He tried to decide whether it was fancy or reality, and, while he was trying, he fell asleep and slept as one dead.

Dick was awakened early in the morning by Sergeant Whitley, who was now watching over him like an elder brother. The sun already rode high and there was a great stir and movement, as the brigade was forming for its continued retreat on the capital. The boy's body was at first stiff and sore, but the elasticity of youth returned fast, and after a brief breakfast he was fully restored.

Another hot day had dawned, but Dick reflected grimly that however hot it might be it could not be as hot as the day before had been. Scouts in the night had brought back reports that the Southern troops were on the northern side of Bull Run, but not in great force, and a second battle was no longer feared. The flight could be continued without interruption over the hot Virginia fields.

Much of Dick's depression returned as they advanced under the blazing sun, but Whitley, who seemed insensible to either fatigue or gloom, soon cheered him up again.

"They talk about the Southerners comin' on an' takin' Washington," he said, "but don't you believe it. They haven't got the forces, an' while they won the victory I guess they're about as tired as we are. Our boys talk about a hundred thousand rebels jumpin' on 'em, an' some felt as if they was a million, but they weren't any more than we was, maybe not as many, an' when they are all stove up themselves how can they attack Washington in its fortifications! Don't be so troubled, boy. The Union ain't smashed up yet. Just recollect whenever it's dark that light's bound to come later on. What do you say to that, Long Legs?"

He spoke to a very tall and very thin youth who marched about a half dozen feet away from them. The boy, who seemed to be about eighteen years of age, turned to them a face which was pale despite the Virginia sun. But it was the pallor of indoor life, not of fear, as the countenance was good and strong, long, narrow, the chin pointed, the nose large and bridged like that of an old Roman, the eyes full blue and slightly nearsighted. But there was a faint twinkle in those same nearsighted eyes as he replied in precise tones:

"According to all the experience of centuries and all the mathematical formulae that can be deduced therefrom night is bound to be followed by day. We have been whipped by the rebels, but it follows with arithmetical certainty that if we keep on fighting long enough we will whip them in time. Let x equal time and y equal

5

opportunity. Then when x and y come together we shall have x plus y which will equal success. Does my logic seem cogent to you, Mr. Big Shoulders and Big Hands?"

Whitley stared at him in amazement and admiration.

"I haven't heard so many big words in a long time," he said, "an' then, too, you bring 'em out so nice an' smooth, marchin' in place as regular as a drilled troop."

"I've been drilled too," said the tall boy, smiling. "My name is George Warner, and I come from Vermont. I began teaching a district school when I was sixteen years old, and I would be teaching now, if it were not for the war. My specialty is mathematics. X equals the war, y equals me and x plus y equals me in the war."

"Your name is Warner and you are from Vermont," said Dick eagerly. "Why, there was a Warner who struck hard for independence at Bennington in the Revolution."

"That's my family," replied the youth proudly. "Seth Warner delivered a mighty blow that helped to form this Union, and although I don't know much except to teach school I'm going to put in a little one to help save it. X equalled the occasion, y equalled my willingness to meet it, and x plus y have brought me here."

Dick told who he and Whitley were, and he felt at once that he and this long and mathematical Vermont lad were going to be friends. Whitley also continued to look upon Warner with much favor.

"I respect anybody who can talk in mathematics as you do," he said. "Now with me I never know what x equals an' I never know what y equals, so if I was to get x an' y together they might land me about ten thousand miles from where I wanted to be. But a fellow can bend too much over books. That's what's the matter with them eyes of yours, which I notice always have to take two looks where I take only one."

"You are undoubtedly right," replied Warner. "My relatives told me that I needed some fresh air, and I am taking it, although the process is attended with certain risks from bullets, swords, bayonets, cannon balls, and shells. Still, I have made a very close mathematical calculation. At home there is the chance of disease as well as here. At home you may fall from a cliff, you may be drowned in a creek or river while bathing, a tree may fall on you, a horse may throw you and break your neck, or you may be caught in a winter storm and freeze to death. But even if none of these things happens to you, you will die some day anyhow. Now, my figures show me that the chance of death here in the war is only twenty-five per cent greater than it was at home, but physical activity and an open air continuously increase my life chances thirty-five per cent. So, I make a net life gain of ten per cent."

Whitley put his hand upon Warner's shoulder.

"Boy," he said, "you're wonderful. I can cheer up the lads by talkin' of the good things to come, but you can prove by arithmetic, algebra an' every other kind of mathematics that they're bound to come. You're goin' to be worth a lot wherever you are."

"Thanks for your encomiums. In any event we are gaining valuable experience. Back there on the field of Bull Run I was able to demonstrate by my own hearing and imagination that a hundred thousand rebels could fire a million bullets a minute; that every one of those million bullets filled with a mortal spite against me was seeking my own particular person."

Whitley gazed at him again with admiration.

"You've certainly got a wonderful fine big bag of words," he said, "an' whenever you need any you just reach in an' take out a few a foot long or so. But I reckon a lot of others felt the way you did, though they won't admit it now. Look, we're nearly to Washington now. See the dome of the Capitol over the trees there, an' I can catch glimpses of roofs too."

Dick and George also saw the capital, and cheered by the sight, they marched at a swifter gait. Soon they turned into the main road, where the bulk of the army had already passed and saw swarms of stragglers ahead of them. Journalists and public men met them, and Dick now learned how the truth about Bull Run had come to the capital. The news of defeat had been the more bitter, because already they had been rejoicing there over success. As late as five o'clock in the afternoon the telegraph had informed Washington of victory. Then, after a long wait, had come the bitter despatch telling of defeat, and flying fugitives arriving in the night had exaggerated it tenfold.

The division to which Dick, Warner, and Whitley belonged marched over the Long Bridge and camped near the capital where they would remain until sent on further service. Dick now saw that the capital was in no danger. Troops were pouring into it by every train from the north and west. All they needed was leadership and discipline. Bull Run had stung, but it did not daunt them and they asked to be led again against the enemy. They heard that Lincoln had received the news of the defeat with great calmness, and that he had spent most of a night in his office listening to the personal narratives of public men who had gone forth to see the battle, and who at its conclusion had left with great speed.

"Lots of people have laughed at Abe Lincoln an' have called him only a rail-splitter," said Whitley, "but I heard him two or three times, when he was campaignin' in Illinois, an' I tell you he's a man."

"He was born in my state," said Dick, "and I mean to be proud of him. He'll have support, too. Look how the country is standing by him!"

More than once in the succeeding days Dick Mason's heart thrilled at the mighty response that came to the defeat of Bull Run. The stream of recruits pouring into the capital never ceased. He now saw men, and many boys, too, like himself, from every state north of the Ohio River and from some south of it. Dan Whitley met old logging friends from Wisconsin whom he had not seen in years, and George Warner saw two pupils of his as old as himself.

Dick had inherited a sensitive temperament, one that responded quickly and truthfully to the events occurring about him, and he foresaw the beginning of a mighty struggle. Here in the capital, resolution was hardening into a fight to the finish, and he knew from his relatives when he left Kentucky that the South was equally determined. There was an apparent pause in hostilities, but he felt that the two sections were merely gathering their forces for a mightier conflict.

His comrades and he had little to do, and they had frequent leaves of absence. On one of them they saw a man of imposing appearance pass down Pennsylvania Avenue. He would have caught the attention of anybody, owing to his great height and splendid head crowned with snow-white hair. He was old, but he walked as if he were one who had achieved greatly, and was conscious of it.

"It's Old Fuss and Feathers his very self," said Whitley.

"General Scott. It can be no other," said Dick, who had divined at once the man's identity. His eyes followed the retreating figure with the greatest interest. This was the young hero of the War of 1812 and the great commander who had carried the brilliant campaign into the capital of Mexico. He had been the first commander-in-chief of the Northern army, and, foreseeing the great scale of the coming war, had prepared a wide and cautious plan. But the public had sneered at him and had demanded instant action, the defeat at Bull Run being the result.

Dick felt pity for the man who was forced to bear a blame not his own, and who was too old for another chance. But he knew that the present cloud would soon pass away, and that he would be remembered as the man of Chippewa and Chapultepec.

"McClellan is already here to take his place," said Whitley. "He's the young fellow who has been winning successes in the western part of Virginia, an' they say he has genius."

Only a day or two later they saw McClellan walking down the

8

same avenue with the President. Dick had never beheld a more striking contrast. The President was elderly, of great height, his head surmounted by a high silk hat which made him look yet taller, while his face was long, melancholy, and wrinkled deeply. His collar had wilted with the heat and the tails of his long black coat flapped about his legs.

The general was clothed in a brilliant uniform. He was short and stocky and his head scarcely passed the President's shoulder. He was redolent of youth and self confidence. It showed in his quick, eager gestures and his emphatic manner. He attracted the two boys, but the sergeant shook his head somewhat solemnly.

"They say Scott was too old," he said, "and now they've gone to the other end of it. McClellan's too young to handle the great armies that are going into the field. I'm afraid he won't be a match for them old veterans like Johnston and Lee."

"Napoleon became famous all over the world when he was only twenty-six," said Warner.

"That's so," retorted Whitley, "but I never heard of any other Napoleon. The breed began and quit with him."

But the soldiers crowding the capital had full confidence in "Little Mac," as they had already begun to call him. Those off duty followed and cheered him and the President, until they entered the White House and disappeared within its doors. Dick and his friends were in the crowd that followed, although they did not join in the cheers, not because they lacked faith, but because all three were thoughtful. Dick had soon discovered that Whitley, despite his lack of education, was an exceedingly observant man, with a clear and reasoning mind.

"It was a pair worth seeing," said the sergeant, as they turned away, "but I looked a lot more at Old Abe than I did at 'Little Mac.' Did you ever think, boys, what it is to have a big war on your hands, with all sorts of men tellin' you all sorts of things an' tryin' to pull you in all sorts of directions?"

"I had not thought of it before, but I will think of it now," said Warner. "In any event, we are quite sure that the President has a great task before him. We hear that the South will soon have a quarter of a million troops in the field. Her position on the defensive is perhaps worth as many more men to her. Hence let x equal her troops, let y equal her defensive, and we have x plus y, which is equal to half a million men, the number we must have before we can meet the South on equal terms."

"An' to conquer her completely we'll need nigh on to a million," said the sergeant.

Shrewd and penetrating as was Sergeant Whitley he did not

dream that before the giant struggle was over the South would have tripled her defensive quarter of a million and the North would almost have tripled her invading million.

A few days later their regiment marched out of the capital and joined the forces on the hills around Arlington, where they lay for many days, impatient but inactive. There was much movement in the west, and they heard of small battles in which victory and defeat were about equal. The boys had shown so much zeal and ability in learning soldierly duties that they were made orderlies by their colonel, John Newcomb, a taciturn Pennsylvanian, a rich miner who had raised a regiment partly at his own expense, and who showed a great zeal for the Union. He, too, was learning how to be a soldier and he was not above asking advice now and then of a certain Sergeant Whitley who had the judgment to give it in the manner befitting one of his lowly rank.

The summer days passed slowly on. The heat was intense. The Virginia hills and plains fairly shimmered under the burning rays of the sun. But still they delayed. Congress had shown the greatest courage, meeting on the very day that the news of Bull Run had come, and resolving to fight the war to a successful end, no matter what happened. But while McClellan was drilling and preparing, the public again began to call for action. "On to Richmond!" was the cry, but despite it the army did not yet move.

European newspapers came in, and almost without exception they sneered at the Northern troops, and predicted the early dissolution of the Union. Monarchy and privileged classes everywhere rejoiced at the disaster threatening the great republic, and now that it was safe to do so, did not hesitate to show their delight. Sensitive and proud of his country, Dick was cut to the quick, but Warner was more phlegmatic.

"Let 'em bark," he said. "They bark because they dislike us, and they dislike us because they fear us. We threatened Privilege when our Revolution succeeded and the Republic was established. The fact of our existence was the threat and the threat has increased with our years and growth. Europe is for the South, but the reason for it is one of the simplest problems in mathematics. Ten per cent of it is admiration for the Southern victory at Bull Run, and ninety per cent of it is hatred—at least by their ruling classes—of republican institutions, and a wish to see them fall here."

"I suspect you're right," said Dick, "and we'll have to try all the harder to keep them from being a failure. Look, there goes our balloon!"

Every day, usually late in the afternoon, a captive balloon rose from the Northern camp, and officers with powerful glasses inspected the Southern position, watching for an advance or a new movement of any kind.

"I'm going up in it some day," said Dick, confidently. "Colonel Newcomb has promised me that he will take me with him when his turn for the ascension comes."

The chance was a week in coming, a tremendously long time it seemed to Dick, but it came at last. He climbed into the basket with Colonel Newcomb, two generals, and the aeronauts and sat very quiet in a corner. He felt an extraordinary thrill when the ropes were allowed to slide and the balloon was slowly going almost straight upward. The sensation was somewhat similar to that which shook him when he went into battle at Bull Run, but pride came to his rescue and he soon forgot the physical tremor to watch the world that now rolled beneath them, a world that they seemed to have left, although the ropes always held.

Dick's gaze instinctively turned southward, where he knew the Confederate army lay. A vast and beautiful panorama spread in a semi-circle before him. The green of summer, the green that had been stained so fearfully at Bull Run, was gone. The grass was now brown from the great heats and the promise of autumn soon to come, but—from the height at least—it was a soft and mellow brown, and the dust was gone.

The hills rolled far away southward, and under the horizon's rim. Narrow ribbons of silver here and there were the numerous brooks and creeks that cut the country. Groves, still heavy and dark with foliage, hung on the hills, or filled some valley, like green in a bowl. Now and then, among clumps of trees, colonial houses with their pillared porticoes appeared.

It was a rare and beautiful scene, appealing with great force to Dick. There was nothing to tell of war save the Northern forces just beneath them, and he would not look down. But he did look back, and saw the broad band of the Potomac, and beyond it the white dome of the Capitol and the roof of Washington. But his gaze turned again to the South, where his absorbing interest lay, and once more he viewed the quiet country, rolling away until it touched the horizon rim. The afternoon was growing late, and great terraces of red and gold were heaping above one another in the sky until they reached the zenith.

"Try the glasses for a moment, Dick," said Colonel Newcomb, as he passed them to the boy.

Dick swept them across the South in a great semi-circle, and now new objects rose upon the surface of the earth. He saw distinctly the long chain of the Blue Ridge rising on the west, then blurring in the distance into a solid black rampart. In the south he saw a long curving line of rising blue plumes. It did not need Colonel Newcomb to tell him that these were the campfires of the army that they had met on the field of Bull Run, and that the Southern troops were now cooking their suppers.

No doubt his cousin Harry was there and perhaps others whom he knew. The fires seemed to Dick a defiance to the Union. Well, in view of their victory, the defiance was justified, and those fires might come nearer yet. Dick, catching the tone of older men who shared his views, had not believed at first that the rebellion would last long, but his opinion was changing fast, and the talk of wise Sergeant Whitley was helping much in that change.

While he yet looked through the glasses he saw a plume of white smoke coming swiftly towards the Southern fires. Then he remembered the two lines of railroad that met on the battlefield, giving it its other name, Manassas Junction, and he knew that the smoke came from an engine pulling cars loaded with supplies for their foes.

He whispered of the train as he handed the glasses back to Colonel Newcomb, and then the colonel and the generals alike made a long examination.

"Beauregard will certainly have an abundance of supplies," said one of the generals. "I hear that arms and provisions are coming by every train from the South, and meanwhile we are making no advance."

"We can't advance yet," said the other general emphatically. "McClellan is right in making elaborate preparations and long drills before moving upon the enemy. It was inexperience, and not want of courage, that beat us at Bull Run."

"The Southerners had the same inexperience."

"But they had the defensive. I hear that Tom Jackson saved them, and that they have given him the name Stonewall, because he stood so firm. I was at West Point with him. An odd, awkward fellow, but one of the hardest students I have ever known. The boys laughed at him when he first came, but they soon stopped. He had a funny way of studying, standing up with his book on a shelf, instead of sitting down at a desk. Said his brain moved better that way. I've heard that he walked part of the way from Virginia to reach West Point. I hear now, too, that he is very religious, and always intends to pray before going into battle."

"That's a bad sign—for us," said the other general. "It's easy enough to sneer at praying men, but just you remember Cromwell. I'm a little shaky on my history, but I've an impression that when

Cromwell, the Ironsides, old Praise-God-Barebones, and the rest knelt, said a few words to their God, sang a little and advanced with their pikes, they went wherever they intended to go and that Prince Rupert and all the Cavaliers could not stop them."

"It is so," said the other gravely. "A man who believes thoroughly in his God, who is not afraid to die, who, in fact, rather favors dying on the field, is an awful foe to meet in battle."

"We may have some of the same on our side," said Colonel Newcomb. "We have at least a great Puritan population from which to draw."

One of the generals gave the signal and the balloon was slowly pulled down. Dick, grateful for his experience, thanked Colonel Newcomb and rejoined his comrades.

# CHAPTER II

## THE MOUNTAIN LIGHTS

When Dick left the balloon it was nearly night. Hundreds of campfires lighted up the hills about him, but beyond their circle the darkness enclosed everything. He still felt the sensations of one who had been at a great height and who had seen afar. That rim of Southern campfires was yet in his mind, and he wondered why the Northern commander allowed them to remain week after week so near the capital. He was fully aware, because it was common talk, that the army of the Union had now reached great numbers, with a magnificent equipment, and, with four to one, should be able to drive the Southern force away. Yet McClellan delayed.

Dick obtained a short leave of absence, and walked to a campfire, where he knew he would find his friend, George Warner. Sergeant Whitley was there, too, showing some young recruits how to cook without waste, and the two gave the boy a welcome that was both inquisitive and hearty.

"You've been up in the balloon," said Warner. "It was a rare chance."

"Yes," replied Dick with a laugh, "I left the world, and it is the only way in which I wish to leave it for the next sixty or seventy years. It was a wonderful sight, George, and not the least wonderful thing in it was the campfires of the Southern army, burning down there towards Bull Run."

"Burnin' where they ought not to be," said Whitley—no gulf was yet established between commissioned and non-commissioned officers in either army. "Little Mac may be a great organizer, as they say, but you can keep on organizin' an' organizin', until it's too late to do what you want to do."

"It's a sound principle that you lay down, Mr. Whitley," said Warner in his precise tones. "In fact, it may be reduced to a mathematical formula. Delay is always a minus quantity which may be represented by $y$. Achievement is represented by $x$, and, consequently, when you have achievement hampered by delay you have $x$ minus $y$, which is an extremely doubtful quantity, often amounting to failure."

"I travel another road in my reckonin's," said Whitley, "I don't know anything about $x$ and $y$, but I guess you an' me, George, come to the same place. It's been a full six weeks since Bull Run, an' we haven't done a thing."

Whitley, despite their difference in rank, could not yet keep from addressing the boys by their first names. But they took it as a matter of course, in view of the fact that he was so much older than they and vastly their superior in military knowledge.

"Dick," continued the sergeant, "what was it you was sayin' about a cousin of yours from the same town in Kentucky bein' out there in the Southern army?"

"He's certainly there," replied Dick, "if he wasn't killed in the battle, which I feel couldn't have happened to a fellow like Harry. We're from the same little town in Kentucky, Pendleton. He's descended straight from one of the greatest Indian fighters, borderers and heroes the country down there ever knew, Henry Ware, who afterwards became one of the early governors of the State. And I'm descended from Henry Ware's famous friend, Paul Cotter, who, in his time, was the greatest scholar in all the West. Henry Ware and Paul Cotter were like the old Greek friends, Damon and Pythias. Harry and I are proud to have their blood in our veins. Besides being cousins, there are other things to make Harry and me think a lot of each other. Oh, he's a grand fellow, even if he is on the wrong side!"

Dick's eyes sparkled with enthusiasm as he spoke of the cousin and comrade of his childhood.

"The chances of war bring about strange situations, or at least I have heard so," said Warner. "Now, Dick, if you were to meet your cousin face to face on the battlefield with a loaded gun in your hand what would you do?"

"I'd raise that gun, take deliberate aim at a square foot of air about thirty feet over his head and pull the trigger."

"But your duty to your country tells you to do otherwise. Before you is a foe trying to destroy the Union. You have come out armed to save that Union, consequently you must fire straight at him and not at the air, in order to reduce the number of our enemies."

"One enemy where there are so many would not count for anything in the total. Your arithmetic will show you that Harry's percentage in the Southern army is so small that it reaches the vanishing point. If I can borrow from you, George, x equals Harry's percentage, which is nothing, y equals the value of my hypothetical opportunity, which is nothing, then x plus y equals nothing, which represents the whole affair, which is nothing, that is, worth nothing to the Union. Hence I have no more obligation to shoot Harry if I meet him than he has to shoot me."

"Well spoken, Dick," said Sergeant Whitley. "Some people, I reckon, can take duty too hard. If you have one duty an' another an' bigger one comes along right to the same place you ought to 'tend to the bigger one. I'd never shoot anybody that was a heap to me just because he was one of three or four hundred thousand who was on the other side. I've never thought much of that old Roman father—I forget his name—who had his son executed just because he wasn't doin' exactly right. There was never a rule that oughtn't to have exceptions under extraordinary circumstances."

"If you can establish the principle of exceptions," replied the young Vermonter very gravely, "I will allow Dick to shoot in the air when he meets his cousin in the height of battle, but it is a difficult task to establish it, and if it fails Dick, according to all rules of logic and duty, must shoot straight at his cousin's heart."

The other two looked at Warner and saw his left eyelid droop slightly. A faint twinkle appeared in either eye and then they laughed.

"I reckon that Dick shoots high in the air," said the sergeant.

Dick, after a pleasant hour with his friends, went back to Colonel Newcomb's quarters, where he spent the entire evening writing despatches at dictation. He was hopeful that all this writing portended something, but more days passed, and despite the impatience of both army and public, there was no movement. Stories of confused and uncertain fighting still came out of the west, but between Washington and Bull Run there was perfect peace.

The summer passed. Autumn came and deepened. The air was crisp and sparkling. The leaves, turned into glowing reds and yellows and browns, began to fall from the trees. The advancing autumn contained the promise of winter soon to come. The leaves fell faster and sharp winds blew, bringing with them chill rains. Little Mac, or the Young Napoleon, as many of his friends loved to call him, continued his preparations, and despite all the urgings of President and Congress, would not move. His fatal defect now showed in all its destructiveness. To him the enemy always appeared threefold his natural size.

Reliable scouts brought back the news that the Southern troops at Manassas, a full two months after their victory there, numbered only forty thousand. The Northern commander issued statements that the enemy was before him with one hundred and fifty thousand soldiers. He demanded that his own forces should be raised to nearly a quarter of a million men and nearly five hundred cannon before he could move.

The veteran, Scott, full of triumphs and honors, but feeling himself out of place in his old age, went into retirement. McClellan, now in sole command, still lingered and delayed, while the South, making good use of precious months, gathered all her forces to meet him or whomsoever came against her.

Youth chafed most against the long waiting. It seemed to Dick and his mathematical Vermont friend that time was fairly wasting away under their feet, and the wise sergeant agreed with them.

The weather had grown so cold now that they built fires for warmth as well as cooking, and the two youths sat with Sergeant Whitley one cold evening in late October before a big blaze. Both were tanned deeply by wind, sun and rain, and they had grown uncommonly hardy, but the wind that night came out of the northwest, and it had such a sharp edge to it that they were glad to draw their blankets over their backs and shoulders.

Dick was re-reading a letter from his mother, a widow who lived on the outskirts of Pendleton. It had come that morning, and it was the only one that had reached him since his departure from Kentucky. But she had received another that he had written to her directly after the Battle of Bull Run.

She wrote of her gratitude because Providence had watched over him in that dreadful conflict, all the more dreadful because it was friend against friend, brother against brother. The state, she said, was all in confusion. Everybody suspected everybody else. The Southerners were full of victory, the Northerners were hopeful of victory yet to come. Colonel Kenton was with the Southern force under General Buckner, gathered at Bowling Green in that state, but his son, her nephew Harry, was still in the east with Beauregard. She had heard that the troops of the west and northwest were coming down the Ohio and Mississippi in great numbers, and people expected hard fighting to occur very soon in western and southern Kentucky. It was all very dreadful, and a madness seemed to have come over the land, but she hoped that Providence would continue to watch over her dear son.

Warner and the sergeant knew that the letter was from Dick's mother, but they had too much delicacy to ask him questions. The boy folded the sheets carefully and returned them to their place in the inside pocket of his coat. Then he looked for a while thoughtfully into the blaze and the great bed of coals that had formed beneath. As far as one could see to right and left like fires burned, but the night remained dark with promise of rain, and the chill wind out of the northwest increased in vigor. The words just read for the fifth time had sunk deep in his mind, and he was feeling the call of the west.

"My mother writes," he said to his comrades, "that the Confederate general, Buckner, whom I know, is gathering a large force around Bowling Green in the southern part of our state, and that fighting is sure to occur soon between that town and the Mississippi. An officer named Grant has come down from Illinois, and he is said to be pushing the Union troops forward with a lot of vigor. Sergeant, you are up on army affairs. Do you know this man Grant?"

Sergeant Whitley shook his head.

"Never heard of him," he replied. "Like as not he's one of the officers who resigned from the army after the Mexican War. There was so little to do then, and so little chance of promotion, that a lot of them quit to go into business. I suppose they'll all be coming back now."

"I want to go out there," said Dick. "It's my country, and the westerners at least are acting. But look at our army here! Bull Run was fought the middle of summer. Now it's nearly winter, and nothing has been done. We don't get out of sight of Washington. If I can get myself sent west I'm going."

"And I'm going with you," said Warner.

"Me, too," said the sergeant.

"I know that Colonel Newcomb's eyes are turning in that direction," continued Dick. "He's a war-horse, he is, and he'd like to get into the thick of it."

"You're his favorite aide," said the calculating young Vermonter. "Can't you sow those western seeds in his mind and keep on sowing them? The fact that you are from this western battle ground will give more weight to what you say. You do this, and I'll wager that within a week the Colonel will induce the President to send the whole regiment to the Mississippi."

"Can you reduce your prediction to a mathematical certainty?" asked Dick, a twinkle appearing in his eye.

"No, I can't do that," replied Warner, with an answering twinkle, "but you're the very fellow to influence Colonel Newcomb's mind. I'm a mathematician and I work with facts, but you have the glowing imagination that conduces to the creation of facts."

"Big words! Grand words!" said the sergeant.

"Never let Colonel Newcomb forget the west," continued Warner, not noticing the interruption. "Keep it before him all the time. Hint that there can be no success along the Mississippi without him and his regiment."

"I'll do what I can," promised Dick faithfully, and he did much. Colonel Newcomb had already formed a strong attachment for this zealous and valuable young aide, and he did not forget the words that Dick said on every convenient occasion about the west. He made urgent representations that he and his regiment be sent to the relief of the struggling Northern forces there, and he contrived also that these petitions should reach the President. One day the order came to go, but not to St. Louis, where Halleck, now in command, was. Instead they were to enter the mountains of West Virginia and Kentucky, and help the mountaineers who were loyal to the Union. If they accomplished that task with success, they were to proceed to the greater theatre in Western Kentucky and Tennessee. It was not all they wished, but they thought it far better than remaining at Washington, where it seemed that the army would remain indefinitely.

Colonel Newcomb, who was sitting in his tent bending over maps with his staff, summoned Dick.

"You are a Kentuckian, my lad," he said, "and I thought you might know something about this region into which we are going."

"Not much, sir," replied Dick. "My home is much further west in a country very different both in its own character and that of its people. But I have been in the mountains two or three times, and I may be of some help as a guide."

"I am sure you will do your best," said Colonel Newcomb. "By the way, that young Vermont friend of yours, Warner, is to be on my staff also, and it is very likely that you and he will go on many errands together."

"Can't we take Sergeant Whitley with us sometimes?" asked Dick boldly.

"So you can," replied the colonel, laughing a little. "I've noticed that man, and I've a faint suspicion that he knows more about war than any of us civilian officers."

"It's our task to learn as much as we can from these old regulars," said a Major Hertford, a man of much intelligence and good humor, who, previous to the war, had been a lawyer in a small town. Alan Hertford was about twenty-five and of fine manner and appearance.

"Well spoken, Major Hertford," said the thoughtful miner, Colonel Newcomb. "Now, Dick, you can go, and remember that we are to start for Washington early in the morning and take a train there for the north. It will be the duty of Lieutenant Warner and yourself, as well as others, to see that our men are ready to the last shoe for the journey."

Dick and Warner were so much elated that they worked all that night, and they did not hesitate to go to Sergeant Whitley for advice or instruction. At the first spear of dawn the regiment marched away in splendid order from Arlington to Washington, where the train that was to bear them to new fields and unknown fortunes was ready.

It was a long train of many coaches, as the regiment

19

numbered seven hundred men, and it also carried with it four guns, mounted on trucks. The coaches were all of primitive pattern. The soldiers were to sleep on the seats, and their arms and supplies were heaped in the aisles. It was a cold, drizzling day of closing autumn, and the capital looked sodden and gloomy. Cameron, the Secretary of War, came to see them off and to make the customary prediction concerning their valor and victory to come. But he was a cold man, and he was repellent to Dick, used to more warmth of temperament.

Then, with a ringing of bells, a heave of the engine, a great puffing of smoke, and a mighty rattling of wheels, the train drew out of Washington and made its noisy way toward Baltimore. Dick and Warner were on the same seat. It was only forty miles to Baltimore, but their slow train would be perhaps three hours in arriving. So they had ample opportunity to see the country, which they examined with the curious eyes of youth. But there was little to see. The last leaves were falling from the trees under the early winter rain. Bare boughs and brown grass went past their windows and the fields were deserted. The landscape looked chill and sullen.

Warner was less depressed than Dick. He had an even temperament based solidly upon mathematical calculations. He knew that while it might be raining today, the chances were several to one against its raining tomorrow.

"I've good cause to remember Baltimore," he said. "I was with the New England troops when they had the fight there on the way down to the capital. Although we hold it, it's really a Southern city, Dick. Most all the border cities are Southern in sympathy, and they're swarming with people who will send to the Southern leaders news of every movement we make. I state, and moreover I assert it in the face of all the world, that the knowledge of our departure from Washington is already in Southern hands. By close mathematical calculation the chances are at least ninety-five per cent in favor of my statement."

"Very likely," said Dick, "and we'll have that sort of thing to face all the time when we invade the South. We've got to win this war, George, by hard fighting, and then more hard fighting, and then more and more of the same."

"Guess you're right. Arithmetic shows at least one hundred per cent of probability in favor of your suggestion."

Dick looked up and down the long coach packed with young troops. Besides the commissioned officers and the sergeants, there was not one in the coach who was twenty-five. Most of them were nineteen or twenty, and it was the same in the other coaches. After the first depression their spirits rose. The temper of youth showed strongly. They were eager to see Baltimore, but the train stopped there only a few minutes, and they were not allowed to leave the coaches.

Then the train turned towards the west. The drizzle of rain had now become a pour, and it drove so heavily that they could see but little outside. Food was served at noon and afterward many slept in the cramped seats. Dick, despite his stiff position, fell asleep too. By the middle of the afternoon everybody in their coach was slumbering soundly except Sergeant Whitley, who sat by the door leading to the next car.

All that afternoon and into the night the train rattled and moved into the west. The beautiful rolling country was left behind, and they were now among the mountains, whirling around precipices so sharply that often the sleeping boys were thrown from the seats of the coaches. But they were growing used to hardships. They merely climbed back again upon the seats, and were asleep once more in half a minute.

The rain still fell and the wind blew fiercely among the somber mountains. A second engine had been added to the train, and the speed of the train was slackened. The engineer in front stared at the slippery rails, but he could see only a few yards. The pitchy darkness closed in ahead, hiding everything, even the peaks and ridges. The heart of that engineer, and he was a brave man, as brave as any soldier on the battlefield, had sunk very low. Railroads were little past their infancy then and this was the first to cross the mountains. He was by no means certain of his track, and, moreover, the rocks and forest might shelter an ambush.

The Alleghanies and their outlying ridges and spurs are not lofty mountains, but to this day they are wild and almost inaccessible in many places. Nature has made them a formidable barrier, and in the great Civil War those who trod there had to look with all their eyes and listen with all their ears. The engineer was not alone in his anxiety this night. Colonel Newcomb rose from an uneasy doze and he went with Major Hertford into the engineer's cab. They were now going at the rate of not more than five or six miles an hour, the long train winding like a snake around the edges of precipices and feeling its way gingerly over the trestles that spanned the deep valleys. All trains made a great roar and rattle then, and the long ravines gave it back in a rumbling and menacing echo. Gusts of rain were swept now and then into the faces of the engineer, the firemen and the officers.

"Do you see anything ahead, Canby?" said Colonel Newcomb to the engineer.

"Nothing. That's the trouble, sir. If it were a clear night I shouldn't be worried. Then we wouldn't be likely to steam into danger with our eyes shut. This is a wild country. The mountaineers in the main are for us, but we are not far north of the Southern line, and if they know we are crossing they may undertake to raid in here."

"And they may know it," said the colonel. "Washington is full of Southern sympathizers. Stop the train, Canby, when we come to the first open and level space, and we'll do some scouting ahead."

The engineer felt great relief. He was devoutly glad that the colonel was going to take such a precaution. At that moment he, more than Colonel Newcomb, was responsible for the lives of the seven hundred human beings aboard the train, and his patriotism and sense of responsibility were both strong.

The train, with much jolting and clanging, stopped fifteen minutes later. Both Dick and Warner, awakened by the shock, sat up and rubbed their eyes. Then they left the train at once to join Colonel Newcomb, who might want them immediately. Wary Sergeant Whitley followed them in silence.

The boys found Colonel Newcomb and the remaining members of his staff standing near, and seeking anxiously to discover the nature of the country about them. The colonel nodded when they arrived, and gave them an approving glance. The two stood by, awaiting the colonel's orders, but they did not neglect to use their eyes.

Dick saw by the engineer's lantern that they were in a valley, and he learned from his words that this valley was about three miles long with a width of perhaps half a mile. A little mountain river rushed down its center, and the train would cross the stream about a mile further on. It was still raining and the cold wind whistled down from the mountains. Dick could see the somber ridges showing dimly through the loom of darkness and rain. He was instantly aware, too, of a tense and uneasy feeling among the officers. All of them carried glasses, but in the darkness they could not use them. Lights began to appear in the train and many heads were thrust out at the windows.

"Go through the coaches, Mr. Mason and Mr. Warner," said Colonel Newcomb, "and have every light put out immediately. Tell them, too, that my orders are for absolute silence."

Dick and the Vermonter did their work rapidly, receiving many curious inquiries, as they went from coach to coach, all of which they were honestly unable to answer. They knew no more than the other boys about the situation. But when they left the last coach and returned to the officers near the engine, the train was in total darkness, and no sound came from it. Colonel Newcomb again gave them an approving nod. Dick noticed that the fires in the engine were now well covered, and that no sparks came from the smoke-stack. Standing by it he could see the long shape of the train running back in the darkness, but it would have been invisible to any one a hundred yards away.

"You think we're thoroughly hidden now, Canby?" said the colonel.

"Yes, sir. Unless they've located us precisely on advance information. I don't see how they could find us among the mountains in all this darkness and rain."

"But they've had the advance information! Look there!" exclaimed Major Hertford, pointing toward the high ridge that lay on their right.

A beam of light had appeared on the loftiest spur, standing out at first like a red star in the darkness, then growing intensely brighter, and burning with a steady, vivid light. The effect was weird and powerful. The mountain beneath it was invisible, and it seemed to burn there like a real eye, wrathful and menacing. The older men, as well as the boys, were held as if by a spell. It was something monstrous and eastern, like the appearance of a genie out of the Arabian Nights.

The light, after remaining fixed for at least a minute, began to move slowly from side to side and then faster.

"A signal!" exclaimed Colonel Newcomb. "Beyond a doubt it is the Southerners. Whatever they're saying they're saying it to somebody. Look toward the south!"

"Ah, there they are answering!" exclaimed Major Hertford.

All had wheeled simultaneously, and on another high spur a mile to the south a second red light as vivid and intense as the first was flashing back and forth. It, too, the mountain below invisible, seemed to swing in the heavens. Dick, standing there in the darkness and rain, and knowing that imminent and mortal danger was on either side, felt a frightful chill creeping slowly down his spine. It is a terrible thing to feel through some superior sense that an invisible foe is approaching, and not be able to know by any kind of striving whence he came.

The lights flashed alternately, and presently both dropped from the sky, seeming to Dick to leave blacker spots on the darkness in their place. Then only the heavy night and the rain encompassed them.

"What do you think it is?" asked Colonel Newcomb of Major Hertford.

"Southern troops beyond a doubt. It is equally certain that they were warned in some manner from Washington of our departure."

"I think so, too. It is probable that they saw the light and have been signalling their knowledge to each other. It seems likely to me that they will wait at the far end of the valley to cut us off. What force do you think it is?"

"Perhaps a cavalry detachment that has ridden hurriedly to intercept us. I would say at a guess that it is Turner Ashby and his men. A skillful and dangerous foe, as you know."

Already the fame of this daring Confederate horseman was spreading over Virginia and Maryland.

"If we are right in our guess," said Major Hertford, "they will dismount, lead their horses along the mountain side, and shut down the trap upon us. Doubtless they are in superior force, and know the country much better than we do. If they get ahead of us and have a little time to do it in they will certainly tear up the tracks."

"I think you are right in all respects," said Colonel Newcomb. "But it is obvious that we must not give them time to destroy the road ahead of us. As for the rest, I wonder."

He pulled uneasily at his short beard, and then he caught sight of Sergeant Whitley standing silently, arms folded, by the side of the engine. Newcomb, the miner colonel, was a man of big and open mind. A successful business man, he had the qualities which made him a good general by the time the war was in its third year. He knew Whitley and he knew, too, that he was an old army regular, bristling with experience and shrewdness.

"Sergeant Whitley," he said, "in this emergency what would you do, if you were in my place?"

The sergeant saluted respectfully.

"If I were in your place, sir, which I never will be," he replied, "I would have all the troops leave the train. Then I would have the engineers take the train forward slowly, while the troops marched on either side of it, but at a sufficient distance to be hidden in the darkness. Then, sir, our men could not be caught in a wreck, but with their feet on solid earth they would be ready, if need be, for a fight, which is our business."

"Well spoken, Sergeant Whitley," said Colonel Newcomb, while the other officers also nodded approval. "Your plan is excellent and we will adopt it. Get the troops out of the train quickly but in silence and do you, Canby, be ready with the engine."

Dick and Warner with the older officers turned to the task. The young soldiers were out of the train in two minutes and were forming in lines on either side, arms ready. There were many whisperings among these boys, but none loud enough to be heard twenty yards away. All felt intense relief when they left the train and stood upon the solid, though decidedly damp earth.

But the cold rain sweeping upon their faces was a tonic, both mental and physical, after the close heat of the train. They did not know why they had disembarked, but they surmised with good reason that an attack was threatened and they were eager to meet it.

Dick and Warner were near the head of the line on the right of the tracks, and Sergeant Whitley was with them. The train began to puff heavily, and in spite of every precaution some sparks flew from the smoke-stack. Dick knew that it was bound to rumble and rattle when it started, but he was surprised at the enormous amount of noise it made, when the wheels really began to turn. It seemed to him that in the silence of the night it could be heard three or four miles. Then he realized that it was merely his own excitement and extreme tension of both mind and body. Canby was taking the train forward so gently that its sounds were drowned two hundred yards away in the swirl of wind and rain.

The men marched, each line keeping abreast of the train, but fifty yards or more to one side. The young troops were forbidden to speak and their footsteps made no noise in the wet grass and low bushes. Dick and Warner kept their eyes on the mountains, turning them alternately from north to south. Nothing appeared on either ridge, and no sound came to tell of an enemy near.

Dick began to believe that they would pass through the valley and out of the trap without a combat. But while a train may go two or three miles in a few minutes it takes troops marching in the darkness over uncertain ground a long time to cover the same distance. They marched a full half hour and then Dick suppressed a cry. The light, burning as intensely red as before, appeared again on the mountain to the right, but further toward the west, seeming to have moved parallel to the Northern troops. As Dick looked it began to flash swiftly from side to side and that chill and weird feeling again ran down his spine. He looked toward the south and there was the second signal, red and intense, replying to the first.

Dick heard a deep "Ah!" run along the line of young troops, and he knew now that they understood as much as he or any of the officers did. He now knew, too, that they would not pass out of the valley without a combat. The Southern forces, beyond a doubt, would try to shut them in at the western mouth of the valley, and a battle in the night and rain was sure to follow.

The train continued to move slowly forward. Had Colonel Newcomb dared he would have ordered Canby to increase his speed in order that he might reach the western mouth of the valley before the Southern force had a chance to tear up the rails, but there was no use for the train without the troops and they were already marching as fast as they could.

The gorge was now not more than a quarter of a mile away. Dick was able to discern it, because the darkness there was not quite so dark as that which lay against the mountains on either side. He was hopeful that they might yet reach it before the Southern force could close down upon them, but before they went many yards further he heard the beat of horses' feet both to right and left and knew that the enemy was at hand.

"Take the train on through the pass, Canby!" shouted Colonel Newcomb. "We'll cover its retreat, and join you later—if we can."

The train began to rattle and roar, and its speed increased. Showers of sparks shot from the funnels of the two engines, and gleamed for an instant in the darkness. The beat of horses' feet grew to thunder. Colonel Newcomb with great presence of mind drew the two parallel lines of his men close together, and ordered them to lie down on either side of the railroad track and face outward with cocked rifles. Dick, the Vermonter, and Sergeant Whitley lay close together, and the three faced the north.

"See the torches!" said Whitley.

Dick saw eight or ten torches wavering and flickering at a height of seven or eight feet above the ground, and he knew that they were carried by horsemen, but he could not see either men or horses beneath. Then the rapid beat of hoofs ceased abruptly at a distance that Dick thought must be about two hundred yards.

"Lie flat!" cried Whitley. "They're about to fire!"

# CHAPTER III

## THE TELEGRAPH STATION

The darkness to the north was suddenly split apart by a solid sheet of flame. Dick by the light saw many men on horseback and others on foot, bridle rein over arm. It was well for the seven hundred boys that they had pressed themselves against the solid earth. A sheet of bullets swept toward them. Most passed over their heads, but many struck upon bones and flesh, and cries of pain rose from the lines of men lying along the railroad track.

The seven hundred pulled trigger and fired at the flash. They fired so well that Dick could hear Southern horses neighing with pain, and struggling in the darkness. He felt sure that many men, too, had been hit. At least no charge came. The seven hundred shouted with exultation and, leaping to their feet, prepared to fire a second volley. But the swift command of their officers quickly put them down again.

"Don't forget the other Confederate column to the south of us," whispered Whitley. "They did not fire at first for fear their bullets would pass over our heads and strike their own comrades. For the same reason they must have dropped back a little in order to avoid the fire of their friends. Their volley will come from an angle about midway between our left and rear."

Just as he spoke the last words the rifles flashed at the surmised angle and again the bullets beat among the young troops or swept over their heads. A soldier was killed only a few feet from Dick. The boy picked up his rifle and ammunition and began to fire whenever he saw the flash of an opposing weapon. But the fire of both Confederate columns ceased in a minute or two, and not a shot nor the sound of a single order came out of the darkness. But Dick with his ear to the soft earth, could hear the crush of hoofs in the mud, and with a peculiar ability to discern whence sound came he knew that the force on the left and rear was crossing the railroad track in order to join their comrades on the north. He whispered his knowledge to Whitley, who whispered back:

"It's the natural thing for them to do. They could not afford to fight on in the darkness with two separate forces. The two columns would soon be firing into each other."

Colonel Newcomb now gave an order for the men to rise and follow the railroad track, but also to fire at the flash of the rifles whenever a volley was poured upon them. He must not only beat off the Southern attack, but also continue the journey to those points in the west where they were needed so sorely. Some of his men had been killed, and he was compelled to leave their bodies where they had fallen. Others were wounded, but without exception they were helped along by their comrades.

Warner also had secured a rifle, with which he fired occasionally, but he and Dick, despite the darkness, kept near to Colonel Newcomb in order that they might deliver any orders that he should choose to give. Sergeant Whitley was close to them. Dick presently heard the rush of water.

"What is that?" he exclaimed.

"It's the little river that runs down the valley," replied Warner. "There's a slope here and it comes like a torrent. A bridge or rather trestle is only a little further, and we've got to walk the ties, if we reach the other side. They'll make their heaviest rush there, I suppose, as beyond a doubt they are thoroughly acquainted with the ground."

The Northern troops left the track which here ran along an embankment several feet high, and took shelter on its southern side. They now had an advantage for a while, as they fired from a breastwork upon their foes, who were in the open. But the darkness, lit only by the flashes of the rifles, kept the fire of both sides from being very destructive, the bullets being sent mainly at random.

Dick dimly saw the trestle work ahead of them, and the roaring of the little river increased. He did not know how deep the water was, but he was sure that it could not be above his waist as it was a small stream. An idea occurred to him and he promptly communicated it to Colonel Newcomb.

"Suppose, sir," he said, "that we ford the river just below the trestle. It will deceive them and we'll be half way across before they suspect the change."

"A good plan, Mr. Mason," said Colonel Newcomb. "We'll try it."

Word was quickly passed along the line that they should turn to the left as they approached the trestle, march swiftly down the slope, and dash into the stream. As fast as they reached the other side of the ford the men should form upon the bank there, and with their rifles cover the passage of their comrades.

The skeleton work of the trestle now rose more clearly into view. The rain had almost ceased and faint rays of moonlight showed through the rifts where the clouds had broken apart. The boys distinctly heard the gurgling rush of waters, and they also saw the clear, bluish surface of the mountain stream. The same quickening of light disclosed the Southern force on their right flank and rear, only four or five hundred yards away. Dick's hasty glance backward lingered for a moment on a powerful man on a white horse just in advance of the Southern column. He saw this man raise his hand and then command the men to fire. He and twenty others under the impulse of excitement shouted to the regiment to drop down, and the Northern lads did so.

Most of the volley passed over their heads. Rising they sent back a return discharge, and then the head of the columns rushed into the stream. Dick felt swift water whirling about him and tugging at his body, but it rose no higher than his waist, although foam and spray were dashed into his face. He heard all around him the splashing of his comrades, and their murmurs of satisfaction. They realized now that they were not only able to retreat before a much superior force, but this same stream, when crossed, would form a barrier behind which they could fight two to one.

The Confederate leader, whoever he might be, and Dick had no doubt that he was the redoubtable Turner Ashby, also appreciated the full facts and he drove his whole force straight at the regiment. It was well for the young troops that part of them were already across, and, under the skillful leadership of Colonel Newcomb, Major Hertford, and three or four old, regular army sergeants, of whom the best was Whitley, were already forming in line of battle.

"Kneel," shouted the colonel, "and fire over the heads of your comrades at the enemy!"

The light was still growing brighter. The rain came only in slight flurries. The clouds were trooping off toward the northeast, and the moon was out. Dick clearly saw the black mass of the Southern horsemen wheeling down upon them. At least three hundred of the regiment were now upon the bank, and, with fairly steady aim, they poured a heavy volley into the massed ranks of their foe. Dick saw horses fall while others dashed away riderless. But the Southern line wavered only for a moment and then came on again with many shouts. There were also dismounted men on either flank who knelt and maintained a heavy fire upon the defenders.

The lads in blue were suffering many wounds, but a line of trees and underbrush on the western shore helped them. Lying there partly protected they loaded and pulled trigger as fast as they could, while the rest of their comrades emerged dripping from the stream to join them. The Confederates, brave as they were, had no choice but to give ground against such strong defense, and the miner colonel, despite his reserve and his middle years, gave vent to his exultation.

"We can hold this line forever!" he exclaimed to his aides. "It's one thing to charge us in the open, but it's quite another to get at us across a deep and rushing stream. Major Hertford, take part of the men to the other side of the railroad track and drive back any attempt at a crossing there. Lieutenant Mason, you and Lieutenant Warner go ahead and see what has become of the train. You can get back here in plenty time for more fighting."

Dick and Warner hurried forward, following the line of the railroad. Their blood was up and they did not like to leave the defense of the river, but orders must be obeyed. As they ran down the railroad track a man came forward swinging a lantern, and they saw the tall gaunt figure of Canby, the chief engineer. Behind him the train stretched away in the darkness.

"I guess that our men have forded the river and are holding the bank," said Canby. "Do they need the train crew back there to help?"

He spoke with husky eagerness. Dick knew that he was longing to be in the middle of the fight, but that his duty kept him with the train.

"No," he replied. "The river bank, and the road along its shore give us a great position for defense, and I know we can hold it. Colonel Newcomb did not say so, but perhaps you'd better bring the train back nearer us. It's not our object to stay in this valley and fight, but to go into the west. Is all clear ahead?"

"No enemy is there. Some of the brakemen have gone on a mile or two and they say the track hasn't been touched. You tell Colonel Newcomb that I'm bringing the train right down to the battle line."

Dick and Warner returned quickly to Colonel Newcomb, who appreciated Canby's courage and presence of mind. As the train approached the four cannon were unloaded from the trucks, and swept the further shore with shell and shrapnel. After a scattered fire the Southern force withdrew some distance, where it halted, apparently undecided. The clouds rolled up again, the feeble moon disappeared, and the river sank into the dark.

"May I make a suggestion, Colonel Newcomb?" said Major Hertford.

"Certainly."

"The enemy will probably seek an undefended ford much higher up, cross under cover of the new darkness and attack us in heavy force on the flank. Suppose we get aboard the train at once, cannon and all, and leave them far behind."

"Excellent. If the darkness covers their movements it also covers ours. Load the train as fast as possible and see that no wounded are left behind."

He gave rapid orders to all his officers and aides, and in fifteen minutes the troops were aboard the train again, the cannon were lifted upon the trucks, Canby and his assistants had all steam up, and the train with its usual rattle and roar resumed its flight into the west.

Dick and Warner were in the first coach near Colonel Newcomb, ready for any commands that he might give. Both had come through the defense of the ford without injury, although a bullet had gone through Dick's coat without touching the skin. Sergeant Whitley, too, was unharmed, but the regiment had suffered. More than twenty dead were left in the valley for the enemy to bury.

Despite all the commands and efforts of the officers there was much excited talk in the train. Boys were binding up wounds of other boys and were condoling with them. But on the whole they were exultant. Youth did not realize the loss of those who had been with them so little. Scattered exclamations came to Dick:

"We beat 'em off that time, an' we can do it again."

"Lucky though we had that little river before us. Guess they'd have rode us right down with their horses if it hadn't been for the stream an' its banks."

"Ouch, don't draw that bandage so tight on my arm. It ain't nothin' but a flesh wound."

"I hate a battle in the dark. Give me the good sunshine, where you can see what's goin' on. My God, that you Bill! I'm tremendous glad to see you! I thought you was lyin' still, back there in the grass!"

Dick said nothing. He was in a seat next to the window, and his face was pressed against the rain-marked pane. The rifle that he had picked up and used so well was still clutched, grimed with smoke, in his hands. The train had not yet got up speed. He caught glimpses of the river behind which they had fought, and which had served them so well as a barrier. In fact, he knew that it had saved them. But they had beaten off the enemy! The pulses in his temples still throbbed from exertion and excitement, but his heart beat exultantly. The bitterness of Bull Run was deep and it had lasted long, but here they were the victors.

The speed of the train increased and Dick knew that they were safe from further attack. They were still running among mountains, clad heavily in forest, but a meeting with a second Southern force was beyond probability. The first had made a quick raid on information supplied by spies in Washington, but it had failed and the way was now clear.

Ample food was served somewhat late to the whole regiment, the last wounds were bound up, and Dick, having put aside the rifle, fell asleep at last. His head lay against the window and he slept heavily all through the night. Warner in the next seat slept in the same way. But the wise old sergeant just across the aisle remained awake much longer. He was summing up and he concluded that the seven hundred lads had done well. They were raw, but they were being whipped into shape.

He smiled a little grimly as the unspoken words, "whipped into shape," rose to his lips. The veteran of many an Indian battle foresaw something vastly greater than anything that had occurred on the plains. "Whipped into shape!" Why, in the mighty war that was gathering along a front of two thousand miles no soldier could escape being whipped into shape, or being whipped out of it.

But the sergeant's own eyes closed after a while, and he, too, slept the sleep of utter mental and physical exhaustion. The train rumbled on, the faithful Canby in the first engine aware of his great responsibility and equal to it. Not a wink of sleep for him that night. The darkness had lightened somewhat more. The black of the skies had turned to a dusky blue, and the bolder stars were out. He could always see the shining rails three or four hundred yards ahead, and he sent his train steadily forward at full speed, winding among the gorges and rattling over the trestles. The silent mountains gave back every sound in dying echoes, but Canby paid no heed to them. His eyes were always on the track ahead, and he, too, was exultant. He had brought the regiment through, and while it was on the train his responsibility was not inferior to that of Colonel Newcomb.

When Dick awoke, bright light was pouring in at the car windows, but the car was cold and his body was stiff and sore. His military overcoat had been thrown over him in the night and Warner had been covered in the same way. They did not know that Sergeant Whitley had done that thoughtful act.

Dick stretched himself and drew deep breaths. Warm youth soon sent the blood flowing in a full tide through his veins, and the stiffness and soreness departed. He saw through the window that they were still running among the mountains, but they did not seem to be so high here as they were at the river by which they had fought in the night. He knew from his geography and his calculation of time that they must be far into that part of Virginia which is now West Virginia.

There was no rain now, at least where the train was running, but the sun had risen on a cold world. Far up on the higher peaks he saw a fine white mist which he believed to be falling snow. Obviously it was winter here and putting on the big military coat he drew it tightly about him. Others in the coach were waking up and some of them, grown feverish with their wounds, were moving restlessly on their seats, where they lay protected by the blankets of their fellows.

Dick now and then saw a cabin nestling in the lee of a hill, with the blue smoke rising from its chimney into the clear, wintry air, and small and poor as they were they gave him a singular sense of peace and comfort. His mind felt for a few moments a strong reaction from war and its terrors, but the impulse and the strong purpose that bore him on soon came back.

The train rushed through a pass and entered a sheltered valley a mile or two wide and eight or ten miles long. A large creek ran through it, and the train stopped at a village on its banks. The whole population of the village and all the farmers of the valley were there to meet them. It was a Union valley and by some system of mountain telegraphy, although there were no telegraph wires, news of the battle at the ford had preceded the train.

"Come, lads," said Colonel Newcomb to his staff. "Out with you! We're among friends here!"

Dick and Warner were glad enough to leave the train. The air, cold as it was, was like the breath of heaven on their faces, and the cheers of the people were like the trump of fame in their ears. Pretty girls with their faces in red hoods or red comforters were there with food and smoking coffee. Medicines for the wounded, as much as the village could supply, had been brought to the train, and places were already made for those hurt too badly to go on with the expedition.

The whole cheerful scene, with its life and movement, the sight of new faces and the sound of many voices, had a wonderful effect upon young Dick Mason. He had a marvellously sensitive temperament, a direct inheritance from his famous border ancestor, Paul Cotter. Things were always vivid to him. Either they glowed with color, or they were hueless and dead. This morning the long strain of the night and its battle was relaxed completely. The grass in the valley was brown with frost, and the trees were shorn of their leaves by the winter winds, but to Dick it was the finest village that he had ever seen, and these were the friendliest people in the world.

He drank a cup of hot coffee handed to him by the stalwart wife of a farmer, and then, when she insisted, drank another.

"You're young to be fightin'," she said sympathetically.

"We all are," said Dick with a glance at the regiment, "but however we may fight you'll never find anybody attacking a breakfast with more valor and spirit than we do."

She looked at the long line of lads, drinking coffee and eating ham, bacon, eggs, and hot biscuits, and smiled.

"I reckon you tell the truth, young feller," she said, "but it's good to see 'em go at it."

She passed on to help others, and Dick, summoned by Colonel Newcomb, went into a little railroad and telegraph station. The telegraph wires had been cut behind them, but ten miles across the mountains the spur of another railroad touched a valley. The second railroad looped toward the north, and it was absolutely sure that it was beyond the reach of Southern raiders. Colonel Newcomb wished to send a message to the Secretary of War and the President, telling of the night's events and his triumphant passage through the ordeal. These circumstances might make them wish to change his orders, and at any rate the commander of the regiment wished to be sure of what he was doing.

"You're a Kentuckian and a good horseman," said Colonel Newcomb to Dick. "The villagers have sent me a trusty man, one Bill Petty, as a guide. Take Sergeant Whitley and you three go to the station. I've already written my dispatches, and I put them in your care. Have them sent at once, and if necessary wait four hours for an answer. If it comes, ride back as fast as you can. The horses are ready and I rely upon you."

"Thank you, sir, I'll do my best," said Dick, who deeply appreciated the colonel's confidence. He wasted no time in words, but went at once to Sergeant Whitley, who was ready in five minutes. Warner, who heard of the mission, was disappointed because he was not going too. But he was philosophical.

"I've made a close calculation," he said, "and I have demonstrated to my own satisfaction that our opportunities are sixty per cent energy and ability, twenty per cent manners, and twenty per cent chance. In this case chance, which made the Colonel better acquainted with you than with me, was in your favor. We won't discuss the other eighty per cent, because this twenty is enough. Besides it looks pretty cold on the mountains, and its fine here in the village. But luck with you, Dick."

He gave his comrade's hand a strong grasp and walked away toward the little square of the village, where the troops were encamped for the present. Dick sprang upon a horse which Bill Petty was holding for him. Whitley was already up, and the three rode swiftly toward a blue line which marked a cleft between two ridges. Dick first observed their guide. Bill Petty was a short but very stout man, clad in a suit of home-made blue jeans, the trousers of which were thrust into high boots with red tops. A heavy shawl of dark red was wrapped around his shoulders, and beneath his broad-brimmed hat a red woolen comforter covered his ears, cheeks, and chin. His thick hair and a thick beard clothing his entire face were a

34

flaming red. The whole effect of the man was somewhat startling, but when he saw Dick looking at him in curiosity his mouth opened wide in a grin of extreme good nature.

"I guess you think I'm right red," he said. "Well, I am, an' as you see I always dress to suit my complexion. Guess I'll warm up the road some on a winter day like this."

"Would you mind my callin' you Red Blaze?" asked Sergeant Whitley gravely.

"Not-a-tall! Not-a-tall! I'd like it. I guess it's sorter pictorial an' 'maginative like them knights of old who had fancy names 'cordin' to their qualities. People 'round here are pretty plain, an' they've never called me nothin' but Bill. Red Blaze she is."

"An' Blaze for short. Well, then, Blaze, what kind of a road is that we're goin' to ride on?"

"Depends on the kind of weather in which you ask the question. As it's the fust edge of winter here in the mountains, though it ain't quite come in the lowlands, an' as it's rained a lot in the last week, I reckon you'll find it bad. Mebbe our hosses will go down in the road to thar knees, but I guess they won't sink up to thar bodies. They may stumble an' throw us, but as we'll hit in soft mud it ain't likely to hurt us. It may rain hard, 'cause I see clouds heapin' up thar in the west. An' if it rains the cold may then freeze a skim of ice over the road, on which we could slip an' break our necks, hosses an' all. Then thar are some cliffs close to the road. If we was to slip on that thar skim of ice which we've reckoned might come, then mebbe we'd go over one of them cliffs and drop down a hundred feet or so right swift. If it was soft mud down below we might not get hurt mortal. But it ain't soft mud. We'd hit right in the middle of sharp, hard rocks. An' if a gang of rebel sharpshooters has wandered up here they may see us an' chase us 'way off into the mountains, where we'd break our necks fallin' off the ridges or freeze to death or starve to death."

Whitley stared at him.

"Blaze," he exclaimed, "what kind of a man are you anyway?"

"Me? I'm the happiest man in the valley. When people are low down they come an' talk to me to get cheered up. I always lay the worst before you first an' then shove it out of the way. None of them things that I was conjurin' up is goin' to happen. I was just tellin' you of the things you was goin' to escape, and now you'll feel good, knowin' what dangers you have passed before they happened."

Dick laughed. He liked this intensely red man with his round face and twinkling eyes. He saw, too, that the mountaineer was a fine horseman, and as he carried a long slender-barreled rifle over his shoulder, while a double-barreled pistol was thrust in his belt, it was likely that he would prove a formidable enemy to any who sought to stop him.

"Perhaps your way is wise," said the boy. "You begin with the bad and end with the good. What is the name of this place to which we are going?"

"Hubbard. There was a pioneer who fit the Injuns in here in early times. I never heard that he got much, 'cept a town named after him. But Hubbard is a right peart little place, with a bank, two stores, three churches, an' nigh on to two hundred people. Are you wrapped up well, Mr. Mason, 'cause it's goin' to be cold on the mountains?"

Dick wore heavy boots, and a long, heavy military coat which fell below his knees and which also had a high collar protecting his ears. He was provided also with heavy buckskin gloves. The sergeant was clad similarly.

"I think I'm clothed against any amount of cold," he replied.

"Well, you need to be," said Petty, "'cause the pass through which we're goin' is at least fifteen hundred feet above Townsville—that's our village—an' I reckon it's just 'bout as high over Hubbard. Them fifteen hundred feet make a pow'ful difference in climate, as you'll soon find out. It's not only colder thar, but the winds are always blowin' hard through the pass. Jest look back at Townsville. Ain't she fine an' neat down thar in the valley, beside that clear creek which higher up in the mountains is full of the juiciest an' sweetest trout that man ever stuck a tooth into."

Dick saw that Petty was talkative, but he did not mind. In fact, both he and Whitley liked the man's joyous and unbroken run of chatter. He turned in his saddle and looked back, following the stout man's pointing finger. Townsville, though but a little mountain town built mainly of logs, was indeed a jewel, softened and with a silver sheen thrown over it by the mountain air which was misty that morning. He dimly saw the long black line of the train standing on the track, and here and there warm rings of smoke rose from the chimneys and floated up into the heavens, where they were lost.

He thought he could detect little figures moving beside the train and he knew that they must be those of his comrades. He felt for a moment a sense of loneliness. He had not known these lads long, but the battle had bound them firmly together. They had been comrades in danger and that made them comrades as long as they lived.

"Greatest town in the world," said Petty, waving toward it a huge hand, encased in a thick yarn glove. "I've traveled from it as much as fifty miles in every direction, north, south, east, an' west, an' I ain't never seed its match. I reckon I'm somethin' of a traveler, but every time I come back to Townsville, I think all the more of it, seein' how much better it is than anything else."

Dick glanced at the mountaineer, and saw that there could be no doubt of his sincerity.

"You're a lucky man, Mr. Petty," he said, "to live in the finest place in the world."

"Yes, if I don't get drug off to the war. I'm not hankerin' for fightin' an' I don't know much what the war's about though I'm for the Union, fust to last, an' that's the way most of the people 'bout here feel. Turn your heads ag'in, friends, an' take another look at Townsville."

Dick and Whitley glanced back and saw only the blank gray wall of the mountain. Petty laughed. He was the finest laugher that Dick had ever heard. The laugh did not merely come from the mouth, it was also exuded, pouring out through every pore. It was rolling, unctuous, and so strong that Petty not only shook with it, but his horse seemed to shake also. It was mellow, too, with an organ note that comes of a mighty lung and throat, and of pure air breathed all the year around.

"Thought I'd git the joke on you," he said, when he stopped laughing. "The road's been slantin' into the mountains, without you knowin' it, and Townsville is cut off by the cliffs. You'll find it gettin' wilder now 'till we start down the slope on the other side. Lucky our hosses are strong, 'cause the mud is deeper than I thought it would be."

It was not really a road that they were following, merely a path, and the going was painful. Under Petty's instructions they stopped their mounts now and then for a rest, and a mile further on they began to feel a rising wind.

"It's the wind that I told you of," said Petty. "It's sucked through six or seven miles of pass, an' it will blow straight in our faces all the way. As we'll be goin' up for a long distance you'll find it growin' colder, too. But you've got to remember that after you pass them cold winds an' go down the slope you'll strike another warm little valley, the one in which Hubbard is layin' so neat an' so snug."

Dick had already noticed the increasing coldness and so had the sergeant. Whitley, from his long experience on the plains, had the keenest kind of an eye for climatic changes. He noticed with some apprehension that the higher peaks were clothed in thick, cold fog, but he said nothing to the brave boy whom he had grown to love like a son. But both he and Dick drew their heavy coats closer and were thankful for the buckskin gloves, without which their hands would have stiffened on the reins.

Now they rode in silence with their heads bent well forward, because the wind was becoming fiercer and fiercer. Over the peaks the fogs were growing thicker and darker and after a while the sharp edge of the wind was wet with rain. It stung their faces, and they drew their hat brims lower and their coat collars higher to protect themselves from such a cutting blast.

"Told you we might have trouble," called Petty, cheerfully, "but if you ride right on through trouble you'll leave trouble behind. Nor this ain't nothin' either to what we kin expect before we git to the top of the pass. Cur'us what a pow'ful lot human bein's kin stand when they make up their minds to it."

"Are the horses well shod?" asked Whitley.

"Best shod in the world, 'cause I done it myself. That's my trade, blacksmith, an' I'm a good one if I do say it. I heard before we started that you had been a soldier in the west. I s'pose that you had to look mighty close to your hosses then. A man couldn't afford to be ridin' a hoss made lame by bad shoein' when ten thousand yellin' Sioux or Blackfeet was after him."

"No, you couldn't," replied the sergeant. "Out there you had to watch every detail. That's one of the things that fightin' Indians taught. You had to be watchin' all the time an' I reckon the trainin' will be of value in this war. Are we mighty near to the top of the pass, Mr. Petty?"

"Got two or three miles yet. The slope is steeper on the other side. We rise a lot more before we hit the top."

The wind grew stronger with every rod they ascended, and the horses began to pant with their severe exertions. At Petty's suggestion the three riders dismounted and walked for a while, leading their horses. The rain turned to a fine hail and stung their faces. Had it not been for his two good comrades Dick would have found his situation inexpressibly lonely and dreary. The heavy fog now enveloped all the peaks and ridges and filled every valley and chasm. He could see only fifteen or twenty yards ahead along the muddy path, and the fine hail which gave every promise of becoming a storm of sleet stung continually. The wind confined in the narrow gorge also uttered a hideous shrieking and moaning.

"Tests your nerve!" shouted Petty to Dick. "There are hard things besides battles to stand, an' this is goin' to be one of the hard ones, but if you go through it all right you kin go through any number of the same kind all right, too. Likely the sleet will be so thick that it will make a sheet of slippery ice for us comin' back. Now, hosses that ain't got calks on thar shoes are pretty shore to slip an' fall, breakin' a leg or two, an' mebbe breakin' the necks of thar riders."

Dick looked at him with some amazement. Despite his

announcement of dire disaster the man's eyes twinkled merrily and the round, red outline of his bushy head in the scarlet comforter made a cheerful blaze.

"It's jest as I told you," said Petty, meeting the boy's look. "Without calks on thar shoes our hosses are pretty shore to slip on the ice and break theirselves up, or fall down a cliff an' break themselves up more."

"Then why in thunder, Blaze," exclaimed Whitley, "did we start without calks on the shoes of our horses?"

Red Blaze broke into a deep mellow laugh, starting from the bottom of his diaphragm, swelling as it passed through his chest, swelling again as it passed through throat and mouth, and bursting upon the open air in a mighty diapason that rose cheerfully above the shrieking and moaning of the wind.

"We didn't start without em," he replied. "The twelve feet of these three hosses have on 'em the finest calked shoes in all these mountains. I put 'em on myself, beginnin' the job this mornin' before you was awake, your colonel, on the advice of the people of Townsville who know me as one of its leadin' an' trusted citizens, havin' selected me as the guide of this trip. I was jest tellin' you what would happen to you if I didn't justify the confidence of the people of Townsville."

"I allow, Red Blaze," said the sergeant with confidence, "that you ain't no fool, an' that you're lookin' out for our best interests. Lead on."

Red Blaze's mellow and pleased laugh rose once more above the whistling of the wind.

"You kin ride ag'in now, boys," he said. "The hosses are pretty well rested."

They resumed the saddle gladly and now mounted toward the crest of the pass. The sleet turned to snow, which was a relief to their faces, and Dick, with the constant beating of wind and snow, began to feel a certain physical exhilaration. He realized the truth of Red Blaze's assertion that if you stiffen your back and push your way through troubles you leave troubles behind.

They rode now in silence for quite a while, and then Red Blaze suddenly announced:

"We're at the top, boys."

# CHAPTER IV

## THE FIGHT IN THE PASS

The three halted their horses and stood for a minute or two on the very crest of the pass. The fierce wind out of the northwest blew directly in their faces and both riders and horses alike were covered with snow. But Dick felt a wonderful thrill as he gazed upon the vast white wilderness. East and west, north and south he saw the driving snow and the lofty peaks and ridges showing through it, white themselves. The towns below and the cabins that snuggled in the coves were completely hidden. They could see no sign of human life on slope or in valley.

"Looks as wild as the Rockies," said the sergeant tersely.

"But you won't find any Injuns here to ambush you," said Red Blaze, "though I don't make any guarantee against bushwhackers and guerillas, who'll change sides as often as two or three times a day, if it will suit their convenience. They could hide in the woods along the road an' pick us off as easy as I'd shoot a squirrel out of a tree. They'd like to have our arms an' our big coats. I tell you what, friends, a mighty civil war like ours gives a tremenjeous opportunity to bad men. They're all comin' to the top. Every rascal in the mountains an' in the lowlands, too, I guess, is out lookin' for plunder an' wuss."

"You're right, Red Blaze," said the sergeant with emphasis, "an' it won't be stopped until the generals on both sides begin to hang an' shoot the plunderers an' murderers."

"But they can't ketch 'em all," said Red Blaze. "A Yankee general with a hundred thousand men will be out lookin' for what? Not for a gang of robbers, not by a jugful. He'll be lookin' for a rebel general with another hundred thousand men, an' the rebel general with a hundred thousand men will be lookin' for that Yankee general with his hundred thousand. So there you are, an' while they're lookin' for each other an' then fightin' each other to a standstill, the robbers will be plunderin' an' murderin'. But don't you worry about bein' ambushed. I was jest tellin' you what might happen, but wouldn't happen. We kin go down hill fast now, and we'll soon be in Hubbard, which is the other side of all that fallin' snow."

The road down the mountain was also better than the one by which they had ascended, and as the horses with their calked shoes

40

were swift of foot they made rapid progress. As they descended, the wind lowered fast and there was much less snow. Red Blaze said it was probably not snowing in the valley at all.

"See that shinin' in the sun," he said. "That's the tin coverin' on the steeple of the new church in Hubbard. The sun strikes squar'ly on it, an' now I know I'm right 'bout it not snowin' down thar. Wait 'til we turn 'roun' this big rock. Yes, thar's Hubbard, layin' out in the valley without a drop of snow on her. It looks good, don't it, friends, with the smoke comin' out of the chimneys. That little red house over thar is the railroad an' telegraph station, an' we'll go straight for it, 'cause we ain't got no time to waste."

They emerged into the valley and rode rapidly for the station. Farmers on the outskirts and villagers looked wonderingly at them, but they did not pause to answer questions. They galloped their tired mounts straight for the little red building, which was the station. Dick sprang first from his horse, and leaving it to stand at the door, ran inside. A telegraph instrument was clicking mournfully in the corner. A hot stove was in another corner, and sitting near it was a lad of about Dick's age, clad in mountain jeans, and lounging in an old cane-bottomed chair. But Dick's quick glance saw that the boy was bright of face and keen of eye. He promptly drew out his papers and said:

"I'm an aide from the Northern regiment of Colonel Newcomb at Townsville. Here are duplicate dispatches, one set for the President of the United States and the other for the Secretary of War. They tell of a successful fight that we had last night with Southern troops, presumably the cavalrymen of Turner Ashby. I wish you to send them at once."

"He's speakin' the exact truth, Jim," said Red Blaze, who had come in behind Dick, "an' I've brought him an' the sergeant here over the mountains to tell about it."

The boy sprang to his instrument. But he stopped a moment to ask one question.

"Did you really beat 'em off?" he asked as he looked up with shining eye.

"We certainly did," replied Dick.

"I'll send it faster than I ever sent anything before," said the boy. "To think of me, Jim Johnson, sending a dispatch to Abraham Lincoln, telling of a victory!"

"I reckon you're right, Jim, it's your chance," said Red Blaze.

Jim bent over the instrument which now began to click steadily and fast.

"You're to wait for answers," said Dick.

The boy nodded, but his shining eyes remained bent over the instrument. Dick went to the door, brushed off the snow, came back and sat down by the stove. Sergeant Whitley, who had tied the horses to hitching posts, came in, pulled up an empty box and sat down by him. Red Blaze slipped away unnoticed. But he came back very soon, and men and women came with him, bringing food and smoking coffee. There was enough for twenty.

Red Blaze had spread among the villagers, every one of whom he knew, the news that the Union arms had won a victory. Nor had it suffered anything in the telling. Colonel Newcomb's regiment, by the most desperate feats of gallantry, had beaten off at least ten thousand Southerners, and the boy and the man in uniform, who were resting by the fire in the station, had been the greatest two heroes of a battle waged for a whole night.

Curious eyes gazed at Dick and the sergeant as they sat there by the stove. Dick himself, warm, relaxed, and the needs of his body satisfied, felt like going to sleep. But he watched the boy operator, who presently finished his two dispatches and then lifted his head for the first time.

"They've gone straight into Washington," he said. "We ought to get an answer soon."

"We'll wait here for it," said Dick.

The three messengers were now thoroughly warmed at the stove, they had eaten heartily of the best the village could furnish, and a great feeling of comfort pervaded them. While they were waiting for the reply that they hoped would come from Washington, Dick Mason and Sergeant Whitley went outside. No snow was falling in the valley, but off on the mountain crest they still saw the white veil, blown by the wind.

Red Blaze joined them and was everywhere their guide and herald. He ascribed to them such deeds of skill and valor that they were compelled to call him the best romancer they had met in a long time.

"I suppose that if Mr. Warner were here," said the sergeant, "he would reduce these statements to mathematics, ten per cent fact an' ninety per cent fancy."

"Just about that," said Dick.

Red Blaze came to them presently, bristling with news.

"A farmer from a hollow further to the west," he said, "has just come in, an' he says that a band of guerillas is ridin' through the hills. 'Bout twenty of them, he said, led by a big dark fellow, his face covered with black beard. They've been liftin' hosses an' takin' other things, but they're strangers in these parts. Tom Sykes, who was held up by them an' robbed of his hoss, says that the rest of 'em called their leader Skelly. Tom seemed to think that mebbe they came from somewhere in the Kentucky mountains. They called themselves a scoutin' party of the Southern army."

Dick started violently.

"Why, I know this man Skelly," he said. "He lives in the mountains to the eastward of my home in Kentucky. He organized a band at the beginning of the war, but over there he said he was fightin' for the North."

"He'll be fightin' for his own hand," said the sergeant sternly. "But he can't play double all the time. That sort of thing will bring a man to the end of a rope, with clear air under his feet."

"I'm glad you've told me this," said Red Blaze. "Skelly might have come ridin' in here, claimin' that he an' his men was Northern troops, an' then when we wasn't suspectin' might have held up the whole town. I'll warn 'em. Thar ain't a house here that hasn't got two or three rifles an' shotguns in it, an' with the farmers from the valley joinin' in Hubbard could wipe out the whole gang."

"Tell them to be on guard all the time, Red Blaze," said Whitley with strong emphasis. "In war you've got to watch, watch, watch. Always know what the other fellow is doin', if you can."

"Let's go back to the station," said Dick. "Maybe we'll have an answer soon."

They found the young operator hanging over his instrument, his eyes still shining. He had been in that position ever since they left him, and Dick knew that his eagerness to get an answer from Washington kept him there, mind and body waiting for the tick of the key.

Dick, the sergeant, and Red Blaze sat down by the stove again, and rested there quietly for a quarter of an hour. Red Blaze was thinking that it would be another cold ride back over the pass. The sergeant, although he was not sleepy, closed his eyes and saw again the vast rolling plains, the herds of buffalo spreading to the horizon, and the bands of Sioux and Cheyennes galloping down, their great war bonnets making splashes of color against the thin blue sky. Dick was thinking of Pendleton, the peaceful little town in Kentucky that was his home, and of his cousin, Harry Kenton. He did not know now where Harry was, and he did not even know whether he was dead or alive.

Dick sighed a little, and just at that moment the telegraph key began to click.

"The answer is coming!" exclaimed the young operator excitedly and then he bent closer over the key to take it. The three chairs straightened up, and they, too, bent toward the key. The boy wrote rapidly, but the clicking did not go on long. When it ceased he straightened up with his finished message in his hand. His face was flushed and his eyes still shining. He folded the paper and handed it to Dick.

"It's for you, Mr. Mason," he said.

Dick unfolded it and read aloud:

"Colonel John D. Newcomb:

"Congratulations on your success and fine management of your troops. Victory worth much to us. Read dispatch to regiment and continue westward to original destination.

A. LINCOLN."

Dick's face glowed, and the sergeant's teeth came together with a little click of satisfaction.

"When I saw that it was to be read to the regiment I thought it no harm to read it to the rest of you," said Dick, as he refolded the precious dispatch and put it in his safest pocket. "Now, sergeant, I think we ought to be off at full speed."

"Not a minute to waste," said Sergeant Whitley.

Their horses had been fed and were rested well. The three bade farewell to the young operator, then to almost all of Hubbard and proceeded in a trot for the pass. They did not speak until they were on the first slope, and then the sergeant, looking up at the heights, asked:

"Shall we have snow again on our return, Red Blaze? I hope not. It's important for us to get back to Townsville without any waste of time."

"I hate to bring bad news," replied Red Blaze, "but we'll shore have more snow. See them clouds, sailin' up an' always sailin' up from the southwest, an' see that white mist 'roun' the highest peaks. That's snow, an' it'll hit the pass just as it did when we was comin' over. But we've got this in favor of ourselves an' our hosses now: The wind is on our backs."

They rode hard now. Dick had received the precious message from the President, and it would be a proud moment for him when he put it in the hands of the colonel. He did not wish that moment to be delayed. Several times he patted the pocket in which the paper lay.

As they ascended, the wind increased in strength, but being

44

on their backs now it seemed to help them along. They were soon high up on the slopes and then they naturally turned for a parting look at Hubbard in its valley, a twin to that of Townsville. It looked from afar neat and given up to peace, but Dick knew that it had been stirred deeply by the visit of his comrades and himself.

"It seems," he said, "that the war would pass by these little mountain nests."

"But it don't," said Red Blaze. "War, I guess, is like a mad an' kickin' mule, hoofs lashin' out everywhar, an' you can't tell what they're goin' to hit. Boys, we're makin' good time. That wind on our backs fairly lifts us up the mountain side."

Petty had all the easy familiarity of the backwoods. He treated the boy and man who rode with him as comrades of at least a year's standing, and they felt in return that he was one of them, a man to be trusted. They retained all the buoyancy which the receipt of the dispatch had given them, and Dick, his heart beating high, scarcely felt the wind and cold.

"In another quarter of an hour we'll be at the top," said Petty. Then he added after a moment's pause: "If I'm not mistook, we'll have company. See that path, leadin' out of the west, an' runnin' along the slope. It comes into the main road, two or three hundred yards further on, an' I think I can see the top of a horseman's head ridin' in it. What do you say, sergeant?"

"I say that you are right, Red Blaze. I plainly see the head of a big man, wearing a fur cap, an' there are others behind him, ridin' in single file. What's your opinion, Mr. Mason?"

"The same as yours and Red Blaze's. I, too, can see the big man with the fur cap on his head and at least a dozen following behind. Do you think it likely, Red Blaze, that they'll reach the main road before we pass the mouth of the path?"

A sudden thought had leaped up in Dick's mind and it set his pulses to beating hard. He remembered some earlier words of Red Blaze's.

"We'll go by before they reach the main road," replied Red Blaze, "unless they make their hosses travel a lot faster than they're travelin' now."

"Then suppose we whip up a little," said Dick.

Both Red Blaze and the sergeant gave him searching glances.

"Do you mean—" began Whitley.

"Yes, I mean it. I know it. The man in front wearing the fur cap is Bill Skelly. He and his men made an attack upon the home of my uncle, Colonel Kenton, who is a Southern leader in Kentucky. He

45

and his band were Northerners there, but they will be Southerners here, if it suits their purpose."

"An' it will shorely suit their purpose to be Southerners now," said Red Blaze. "We three are ridin' mighty good hoss flesh. Me an' the sergeant have good rifles an' pistols, you have good pistols, an' we all have good, big overcoats. This is a lonely mountain side with war flyin' all about us. Easy's the place an' easy's the deed. That is if we'd let 'em, which we ain't goin' to do."

"Not by a long shot," said Sergeant Whitley, resting his rifle across the pommel of his saddle. "They've got to follow straight behind. The ground is too rough for them to ride around an' flank us."

Dick said nothing, but his gauntleted hand moved down to the butt of one of his pistols. His heart throbbed, but he preserved the appearance of coolness. He was fast becoming inured to danger. Owing to the slope they could not increase the speed of their horses greatly, but they were beyond the mouth of the path before they were seen by Skelly and his band. Then the big mountaineer uttered a great shout and began to wave his hand at them.

"The road curves here a little among the rocks," said the sergeant, who unconsciously took command. "Suppose we stop, sheltered by the curve, and ask them what they want."

"The very thing to do," said Dick.

"Sass 'em, sergeant! Sass 'em!" said Red Blaze.

They drew their horses back partially in the shadow of the rocky curve, but the sergeant was a little further forward than the others. Dick saw Skelly and a score of men emerge into the road and come rapidly toward them. They were a wild-looking crew, mounted on tough mountain ponies, all of them carrying loot, and all armed heavily.

The sergeant threw up his rifle, and with a steady hand aimed straight at Skelly's heart.

"Halt!" he cried sharply, "and tell me who you are!"

The whole crew seemed to reel back except Skelly, who, though stopping his horse, remained in the center of the road.

"What do you mean?" he cried. "We're peaceful travelers. What business is it of yours who we are?"

"Judgin' by your looks you're not peaceful travelers at all. Besides these ain't peaceful times an' we take the right to demand who you are. If you come on another foot, I shoot."

The sergeant's tones were sharp with resolve.

"Your name!" he continued.

46

"Ramsdell, David Ramsdell," replied the leader of the band.

"That's a lie," said Sergeant Whitley. "Your name is Bill Skelly, an' you're a mountaineer from Eastern Kentucky, claimin' to belong first to one side and then to the other as suits you."

"Who says so?" exclaimed Skelly defiantly.

The sergeant beckoned Dick, who rode forward a little.

"I do," said the boy in a loud, clear voice. "My name is Dick Mason, and I live at Pendleton in Kentucky. I saw you more than once before the war, and I know that you tried to burn down the house of Colonel Kenton there, and kill him and his friends. I'm on the other side, but I'm not for such things as that."

Skelly distinctly saw Dick sitting on his horse in the pass, and he knew him well. Rage tore at his heart. Although on "the other side" this boy, too, was a lowlander and in a way a member of that vile Kenton brood. He hated him, too, because he belonged to those who had more of prosperity and education than himself. But Skelly was a man of resource and not a coward.

"You're right," he cried, "I'm Bill Skelly, an' we want your horses an' arms. We need 'em in our business. Now, just hop down an' deliver. We're twenty to three."

"You come forward at your own risk!" cried the sergeant, and Skelly, despite the numbers at his back, wavered. He saw that the man who held the rifle aimed at his heart had nerves of steel, and he did not dare advance knowing that he would be shot at once from the saddle. A victory won by Skelly's men with Skelly dead was no victory at all to Skelly.

The guerilla reined back his horse, and his men retreated with him. But the three knew well that it was no withdrawal. The mountaineers rode among some scrub that grew between the road and the cliff; and Whitley exclaimed to his two comrades:

"Come boys, we must ride for it! It's our business to get back with the dispatches to Colonel Newcomb as soon as possible, an' not let ourselves be delayed by this gang."

"That is certainly true," said Dick. "Lead on, Mr. Petty, and we'll cross the mountain as fast as we can."

Red Blaze started at once in a gallop, and Dick and the sergeant followed swiftly after. But Sergeant Whitley held his cocked rifle in hand and he cast many backward glances. A great shout came from Skelly and his band when they saw the three take to flight, and the sergeant's face grew grimmer as the sound reached his ears.

"Keep right in the middle of the road, boys," he said. "We can't afford to have our horses slip. I'll hang back just a little and send in a bullet if they come too near. This rifle of mine carries pretty far, farther, I expect, than any of theirs."

"I'm somethin' on the shoot myself," said Red Blaze. "I love peace, but it hurts my feelin's if anybody shoots at me. Them fellers are likely to do it, an' me havin' a rifle in my hands I won't be able to stop the temptation to fire back."

As he spoke the raiders fired. There was a crackling of rifles, little curls of blue smoke rose in the pass, and bullets struck on the frozen earth, while two made the snow fly from bushes by the side of the road. The sergeant raised his own rifle, longer of barrel than the average army weapon, and pulled the trigger. He had aimed at Skelly, but the leader swerved, and a man behind him rolled off his horse. The others, although slowing their speed a little, in order to be out of the range of that deadly rifle, continued to come.

The pursuit at first seemed futile to Dick, because they would soon descend into Townsville's valley, and the raiders could not follow them into the midst of an entire regiment. But presently he saw their plan. The pass now widened out with a few hundred yards of level space on either side of the road thickly covered with forest. The branches of the trees were bare, but the undergrowth was so dense that horsemen could be hidden in it. Bands of the raiders darted into the woods both to right and left, and he knew that advancing on a straight line one or the other of the parties expected to catch the fugitives who must follow the curves of the road.

The advantage of the pursuit was soon shown as a shot from the right whistled by them. Red Blaze, quick as lightning, fired at the flash of the rifle.

"I don't know whether I hit him or not," he said, judicially, "but the chances are pow'ful good that I did. Still it looks as if they meant to hang on an' likely we kin soon expect shots from the other side, too. Then if they know the country as well as they 'pear to do they'll have us clamped in a vise."

As he spoke his eyes twinkled cheerfully out of his flaming countenance.

"You certainly seem to take it easy," said Dick.

"I take it easy, 'cause the jaws of that vise ain't goin' to clamp down. Bein' somewhat interested in a run for your life you haven't noticed how dark it's gettin' up here on the heights an' how hard it's snowin'. It's comin' down a lot thicker than it was when we crossed the first time."

It was true. Dick noticed now that the snow was pouring

down, and that all the peaks and ridges were lost in the white whirlwind.

"I told you that I had been a traveler," said Red Blaze. "I've been as far as fifty miles from Townsville, and I know all the country in every direction, twenty miles from it, inch by inch. Inside five minutes the snowstorm will be on us full blast, an' we won't be able to see more'n twenty yards away. An' that crowd that's follerin' won't be able to see either. An' me knowin' the ground inch by inch I'll take you straight back to your regiment while they'll get lost in the storm."

There was room now in the road for the three to ride abreast, and they kept close together. They heard once a shout behind them and saw the flash of a firearm in the white hurricane, but no bullet struck them, and they kept steadily on their course, Red Blaze directing with the sure instinct that comes of long use and habit.

Heavier and heavier grew the snow. There was but little wind now, and it came straight down. It seemed to Dick that the whole earth was blotted out by the white fall. He and the sergeant resigned themselves completely to the guidance of Red Blaze, who never veered an inch from the right path.

"If I didn't know the way my hoss would," he said. "I'd just give him his head an' he'd take us straight to his warm stable in Townsville, an' the two bundles of oats that I mean to give him. I reckon it was pretty smart of me, wasn't it, to order a snowstorm an' have it come just when it was needed."

Again the cheerful eyes twinkled in the flaming face.

"You're certainly a winner," said Dick, "and you win for us all."

The snow was now so deep in the pass that they could not proceed at great speed, but they did the best they could, and, as Red Blaze said, their best, although it might be somewhat slow, was certainly better than that of Skelly and his men. Dick believed in fact that the raiders had been compelled to abandon the pursuit.

When they reached a lower level, where the snow was far less dense, they stopped and listened. The sergeant's ears had been trained to uncommon keenness by his life on the plains, and he could hear nothing but the sigh of the falling snow. Nor could Petty, who had fine ears himself.

They descended still further, and made another stop. It was snowing here also, but it was merely an ordinary fall, and they could get a long view back up the pass. They saw nothing there but earth and trees covered with snow. Looking in the other direction they saw the sunshine gleaming for a moment on a roof in Townsville.

"We're all safe now," said Red Blaze, "an' we'll be with the soldiers in another half hour. But just you two remember that mebbe the next time I couldn't call up a snowstorm to cover us an' save our lives."

"Once is enough," said Dick, "and, Mr. Petty, Sergeant Whitley and I want to thank you."

Mittened hands met buckskinned ones in the strong grasp of friendship, and now, as they rode on, the whole village emerged into sight. There was the long train standing on the track, the smoke rising in spires from the neat houses, and then the figures of human beings.

The fall of snow was light in the valley and as soon as they reached the levels the three proceeded at a gallop. Dick saw Colonel Newcomb standing by the train, and springing from his horse he handed him the dispatch. The colonel opened it, and as he read Dick saw the glow appear upon his face.

"Fire up!" he said to Canby, the engineer, who stood near. "We start at once!"

The troops who were ready and waiting were hurried into the coaches, and the engine whistled for departure.

# CHAPTER V

## THE SINGER OF THE HILLS

As the engine whistled for the last time Dick sprang upon a car-step, one hand holding to the rail while with the other he returned the powerful grip of Red Blaze, who with his own unconfined hand grasped the bridles of the three horses, which had served them so well. Petty had received a reward thrust upon him by Colonel Newcomb, but Dick knew that the mountaineer's chief recompense was the success achieved in the perilous task chosen for him.

"Good-bye, Mr. Mason," said Red Blaze, "I'm proud to have knowed you an' the sergeant, an' to have been your comrade in a work for the Union."

"Without you we should have failed."

"It jest happened that I knowed the way. It seems to me that there's a heap, a tremenjeous heap, in knowin' the way. It gives you an awful advantage. Now you an' your regiment are goin' down thar in them Kentucky mountains. They're mighty wild, winter's here an' the marchin' will be about as bad as it could be. Them's mostly Pennsylvania men with you, an' they don't know a thing 'bout that thar region. Like as not you'll be walkin' right straight into an ambush, an' that'll be the end of you an' them Pennsylvanians."

"You're a cheerful prophet, Red Blaze."

"I meant if you didn't take care of yourselves an' keep a good lookout, which I know, of course, that you're goin' to do. I was jest statin' the other side of the proposition, tellin' what would happen to keerless people, but Colonel Newcomb an' Major Hertford ain't keerless people. Good-bye, Mr. Mason. Mebbe I'll see you ag'in before this war is over."

"Good-bye, Red Blaze. I truly hope so."

The train was moving now and with a last powerful grasp of a friendly hand Dick went into the coach. It was the first in the train. Colonel Newcomb and Major Hertford sat near the head of it, and Warner was just sitting down not far behind them. Dick took the other half of the seat with the young Vermonter, who said, speaking in a whimsical tone:

"You fill me with envy, Dick. Why wasn't it my luck to go with you, Sergeant Whitley, and the man they call Red Blaze on that errand and help bring back with you the message of President Lincoln? But I heard what our red friend said to you at the car-step.

There's a powerful lot in knowing the way, knowing where you're going, and what's along every inch of the road. My arithmetic tells me that it is often fifty per cent of marching and fighting."

"I think you are right," said Dick.

A little later he was sound asleep in his seat, and at the command of Colonel Newcomb he was not disturbed. His had been a task, taxing to the utmost both body and mind, and, despite his youth and strength, it would take nature some time to replace what had been worn away.

He slept on while the boys in the train talked and laughed. Stern discipline was not yet enforced in either army, nor did Colonel Newcomb consider it necessary here. These lads, so lately from the schools and farms, had won a victory and they had received the thanks of the President. They had a right to talk about it among themselves and a little vocal enthusiasm now might build up courage and spirit for a greater crisis later.

The colonel, moreover, gave glances of approval and sympathy to his gallant young aide, who in the seat next to the window with his head against the wall slept so soundly. All the afternoon Dick slept on, his breathing regular and steady. The train rattled and rumbled through the high mountains, and on the upper levels the snow was falling fast.

Darkness came, and supper was served to the troops, but at the colonel's command Dick was not awakened. Nature had not yet finished her task of repairing. There was worn tissue still to be replaced, and the nerves had not yet recovered their full steadiness.

So Dick slept on, while the night deepened and the snow continued to drive against the window panes. Nor did he awake until morning, when the train stopped at a tiny station in the hills. There was no snow here, but the sun, just rising, threw no heat, and icicles were hanging from every cliff. Dispatches were waiting for Colonel Newcomb, and after breakfast he announced to his staff:

"I have orders from Washington to divide my regiment. The Southern forces are operating at three points in Kentucky. They are gathering at Columbus on the Mississippi, at Bowling Green in the south, and here in the mountains there is a strong division under an officer named Zollicoffer. Scattered forces of our men, the principal one led by a Virginian named Thomas, are endeavoring to deal with Zollicoffer. The Secretary of War regrets the division of the regiment, but he thinks it necessary, as all our detached forces must be strengthened. I go on with the main body of the regiment to join Grant, near the mouth of the Ohio. You, Major Hertford, will take three companies and march south in search of Thomas, but be careful that you are not snapped up by the rebels on the way. And if you can get volunteers and join Thomas with your force increased threefold, so much the better."

"I shall try my best, sir," said Major Hertford, "and thank you for this honor."

Dick and Warner stood by without a word, but Dick cast an appealing look at Colonel Newcomb.

"Yes, I know," said the Colonel, who caught the glance. "This is your state, and you wish to go with Major Hertford. You are to do so. So is your friend, Lieutenant Warner, and, Major Hertford, I also lend to you Sergeant Whitley, who is a man of much experience and who has already proved himself to be of great value."

The three saluted and were grateful. They longed for action, which they believed would come more quickly with Major Hertford's column. A little later, when military form permitted it, the two boys thanked Colonel Newcomb in words.

"Maybe you won't thank me a few days from now," said the colonel a little grimly, "but I am hopeful that our plans here in Eastern Kentucky will prove successful, and that before long you will be able to join the great forces in the western part of the state. You are both good boys and now, good-bye."

The preparations for the mountain column, as Dick and Warner soon called it, had been completed. They were on foot, but they were well armed, well clothed, and they had supplies loaded in several wagons, purchased hastily in the village. A dozen of the strong mountaineers volunteered to be drivers and guides, and the major was glad to have them. Later, several horses were secured for the officers, but, meanwhile, the train was ready to depart.

Colonel Newcomb waved them farewell, the faithful and valiant Canby opened the throttle, and the train steamed away. The men in the little column, although eager for their new task, watched its departure with a certain sadness at parting with their comrades. The train became smaller and smaller, then it was only a spiral of smoke, and that, too, soon died on the clear western horizon.

"And now to find Thomas!" said Major Hertford, who retained Dick and Warner on his staff, practically its only members, in fact. "It looks odd to hunt through the mountains for a general and his army, but we've got it to do, and we'll do it."

The horses for the officers were obtained at the suggestion of Sergeant Whitley, and the little column turned southward through the wintry forest. Dick and Warner were riding strong mountain ponies, but at times, and in order to show that they considered themselves no better than the others, they dismounted and walked over the frozen ground. The greatest tasks were with the wagons containing the ammunition and supplies. The mountain roads were little more than trails, sometimes half blocked with ice or snow and then again deep in mud. The winter was severe. Storms of rain, hail, sleet and snow poured upon them, but, fortunately, they were marching through continuous forests, and the skilled mountaineers, under any circumstances, knew how to build fires, by the side of which they could dry themselves, and sleep warmly at night.

They also heard much gossip as they advanced to meet General Thomas, who had been sent from Louisville to command the Northern troops in the Kentucky mountains. Thomas was a Virginian, a member of the old regular army, a valiant, able, and cautious man, who chose to abide by the Union. Many other Virginians, some destined to be as famous as he, and a few more so, wondered why he had not gone with his seceding state, and criticised him much, but Thomas, chary of speech, hung to his belief, and proved it by action.

Dick learned, too, that the Southern force operating against Thomas, while actively led by Zollicoffer, was under the nominal command of one of his own Kentucky Crittendens. Here he saw again how terribly his beloved state was divided, like other border states. General Crittenden's father was a member of the Federal Congress at Washington, and one of his brothers was a general also, but on the other side. But he was to see such cases over and over again, and he was to see them to a still greater and a wholesale degree, when the First Maryland regiment of the North and the First Maryland regiment of the South, recruited from the same district, should meet face to face upon the terrible field of Antietam.

But Antietam was far in the future, and Dick's mind turned from the cases of brother against brother to the problems of the icy wilderness through which they were moving, in a more or less uncertain manner. Sometimes they were sent on false trails, but their loyal mountaineers brought them back again. They also found volunteers, and Major Hertford's little force swelled from three hundred to six hundred. In the main, the mountaineers were sympathetic, partly through devotion to the Union, and partly through jealousy of the more prosperous lowlanders.

One day Major Hertford sent Dick, Warner, and Sergeant Whitley, ahead to scout. He had recognized the ability of the two lads, and also their great friendship for Sergeant Whitley. It seemed fitting to him that the three should be nearly always together, and he watched them with confidence, as they rode ahead on the icy mountain trail and then disappeared from sight.

Dick and his friends had learned, at mountain cabins which they had passed, that the country opened out further on into a fine little valley, and when they reached the crest of a hill somewhat

54

higher than the others, they verified the truth of the statement. Before them lay the coziest nook they had yet seen in the mountains, and in the center of it rose a warm curl of smoke from the chimney of a house, much superior to that of the average mountaineer. The meadows and corn lands on either side of a noble creek were enclosed in good fences. Everything was trim and neat.

The three rode down the slope toward the house, but halfway to the bottom they reined in their ponies and listened. Some one was singing. On the thin wintry air a deep mellow voice rose and they distinctly heard the words:

Soft o'er the fountain, ling'ring falls the southern moon,
Far o'er the mountain breaks the day too soon.
In thy dark eyes' splendor, where the warm light loves to dwell,
Weary looks yet tender, speak their fond farewell.
'Nita, Juanita!  Ask thy soul if we should part,
'Nita, Juanita!  Lean thou on my heart.

It was a wonderful voice that they heard, deep, full, and mellow, all the more wonderful because they heard it there in those lone mountains. The ridges took up the echo, and gave it back in tones softened but exquisitely haunting.

The three paused and looked at one another. They could not see the singer. He was hidden from them by the dips and swells of the valley, but they felt that here was no common man. No common mind, or at least no common heart, could infuse such feeling into music. As they listened the remainder of the pathetic old air rose and swelled through the ridges:

When in thy dreaming, moons like these shall shine again,
And daylight beaming prove thy dreams are vain,
Wilt thou not, relenting, for thy absent lover sigh?
In thy heart consenting to a prayer gone by!
'Nita, Juanita!  Let me linger by thy side!
'Nita, Juanita!  Be thou my own fair bride.

"I'm curious to see that singer," said Warner. "I heard grand opera once in Boston, just before I started to the war, but I never heard anything that sounds finer than this. Maybe time and place help to the extent of fifty per cent, but, at any rate, the effect is just the same."

"Come on," said Dick, "and we'll soon find our singer, whoever he is."

The three rode at a rapid pace until they reached the valley.

There they drew rein, as they saw near them a tall man, apparently about forty years of age, mending a fence, helped by a boy of heavy build and powerful arms. The man glanced up, saw the blue uniforms worn by the three horsemen, and went peacefully on with his fence-mending. He also continued to sing, throwing his soul into the song, and both work and song proceeded as if no one was near.

He lifted the rails into place with mighty arms, but never ceased to sing. The boy who helped him seemed almost his equal in strength, but he neither sang nor spoke. Yet he smiled most of the time, showing rows of exceedingly strong, white teeth.

"They seem to me to be of rather superior type," said Dick. "Maybe we can get useful information from them."

"I judge that the singer will talk about almost everything except what we want to know," said the shrewd and experienced sergeant, "but we can certainly do no harm by speaking to him. Of course they have seen us. No doubt they saw us before we saw them."

The three rode forward, saluted politely and the fence-menders, stopping their work, saluted in the same polite fashion. Then they stood expectant.

"We belong to a detachment which is marching southward to join the Union army under General Thomas," said Dick. "Perhaps you could tell us the best road."

"I might an' ag'in I mightn't, stranger. If you don't talk much you never have much to take back. If I knew where that army is it would be easy for me to tell you, but if I didn't know I couldn't. Now, the question is, do I know or don't I know? Do you think you can decide it for me stranger?"

It was impossible for Dick or the sergeant to take offense. The man's gaze was perfectly frank and open and his eyes twinkled as he spoke. The boy with him smiled widely, showing both rows of his powerful white teeth.

"We can't decide it until we know you better," said Dick in a light tone.

"I'm willin' to tell you who I am. My name is Sam Jarvis, an' this lunkhead here is my nephew, Ike Simmons, the son of my sister, who keeps my house. Now I want to tell you, young stranger, that since this war began and the Yankees and the Johnnies have taken a notion to shoot up one another, people who would never have thought of doin' it before, have come wanderin' into these mountains. But you can get a hint about 'em sometimes. Young man, do you want me to tell you your name?"

"Tell me my name!" responded Dick in astonishment. "Of course you can't do it! You never saw or heard of me before."

56

"Mebbe no," replied Jarvis, with calm confidence, "but all the same your name is Dick Mason, and you come from a town in Kentucky called Pendleton. You've been serving with the Yanks in the East, an' you've a cousin, named Harry Kenton, who's been servin' there also, but with the Johnnies. Now, am I a good guesser or am I just a plum' ignorant fool?"

Dick stared at him in deepening amazement.

"You do more than guess," he replied. "You know. Everything that you said is true."

"Tell me this," said Jarvis. "Was that cousin of yours, Harry Kenton, killed in the big battle at Bull Run? I've been tremenjeously anxious about him ever since I heard of that terrible fight."

"He was not. I have not seen him since, but I have definite news now that he passed safely through the battle."

Sam Jarvis and his nephew Ike breathed deep sighs of relief.

"I'm mighty glad to hear it," said Jarvis, "I shorely liked that boy, Harry, an' I think I'll like you about as well. It don't matter to me that you're on different sides, bein' as I ain't on any side at all myself, nor is this lunkhead, Ike, my nephew."

"How on earth did you know me?"

"'Light, an' come into the house an' I'll tell you. You an' your pardners look cold an' hungry. There ain't danger of anybody taking your hosses, 'cause you can hitch 'em right at the front door. Besides, I've got an old grandmother in the house, who'd like mighty well to see you, Mr. Mason."

Dick concluded that it was useless to ask any more questions just yet, and he, Warner and the sergeant, dismounting and leading their horses, walked toward the house with Jarvis and Ike. Jarvis, who seemed singularly cheerful, lifted up his voice and sang:

> Thou wilt come no more, gentle Annie,
> Like a flower, thy spirit did depart,
> Thou art gone, alas! like the many
> That have bloomed in the summer of my heart.
> Shall we never more behold thee?
> Never hear thy winning voice again?
> When the spring time comes, gentle Annie?
> When the wild flowers are scattered o'er the plain?

It seemed to Dick that the man sang spontaneously, and the deep, mellow voice always came back in faint and dying echoes that moved him in a singular manner. All at once the war with its passions and carnage floated away. Here was a little valley fenced in from the battle-world in which he had been living. He breathed

57

deeply and as the eyes of Jarvis caught his a sympathetic glance passed between them.

"Yes," said Jarvis, as if he understood completely, "the war goes around us. There is nothing to fight about here. But come into the house. This is my sister, the mother of that lunkhead, Ike, and here is my grandmother."

He paused before the bent figure of an old, old woman, sitting in a rocking chair beside the chimney, beside which a fire glowed and blazed. Her chin rested on one hand, and she was staring into the coals.

"Grandmother," said Jarvis very gently, "the great-grandson of the great Henry Ware that you used to know was here last spring, and now the great-grandson of his friend, Paul Cotter, has come, too."

The withered form straightened and she stood up. Fire came into the old, old eyes that regarded Dick so intently.

"Aye," she said, "you speak the truth, grandson. It is Paul Cotter's own face. A gentle man he was, but brave, and the greatest scholar. I should have known that when Henry Ware's great-grandson came Paul Cotter's, too, would come soon. I am proud for this house to have sheltered you both."

She put both her hands on his shoulders, and stood up very straight, her face close to his. She was a tall woman, above the average height of man, and her eyes were on a level with Dick's.

"It is true," she said, "it is he over again. The eyes are his, and the mouth and the nose are the same. This house is yours while you choose to remain, and my grandchildren and my great-grandson will do for you whatever you wish."

Dick noticed that her grammar and intonation were perfect. Many of the Virginians and Marylanders who emigrated to Kentucky in that far-off border time were people of cultivation and refinement.

After these words of welcome she turned from him, sat down in her chair and gazed steadily into the coals. Everything about her seemed to float away. Doubtless her thoughts ran on those dim early days, when the Indians lurked in the canebrake and only the great borderers stood between the settlers and sure death.

Dick began to gather from the old woman's words a dim idea of what had occurred. Harry Kenton must have passed there, and as they went into the next room where food and coffee were placed before them, Jarvis explained.

"Your cousin, Harry Kenton, came through here last spring on his way to Virginia," he said. "He came with me an' this lunkhead, Ike, all the way from Frankfort and mostly up the Kentucky River.

Grandmother was dreaming and she took him at first for Henry Ware, his very self. She saluted him and called him the great governor. It was a wonderful thing to see, and it made me feel just a little bit creepy for a second or two. Mebbe you an' your cousin, Harry Kenton, are Henry Ware an' Paul Cotter, their very selves come back to earth. It looks curious that both of you should wander to this little place hid deep in the mountains. But it's happened all the same. I s'pose you've just been moved 'round that way by the Supreme Power that's bigger than all of us, an' that shifts us about to suit plans made long ago. But how I'm runnin' on! Fall to, friends—I can't call you strangers, an' eat an' drink. The winter air on the mountains is powerful nippin' an' your blood needs warmin' often."

The boys and the sergeant obeyed him literally and with energy. Jarvis sat by approvingly, taking an occasional bite or drink with them. Meanwhile they gathered valuable information from him. A Northern commander named Garfield had defeated the Southern forces under Humphrey Marshall in a smart little battle at a place called Middle Creek. Dick knew this Humphrey Marshall well. He lived at Louisville and was a great friend of his uncle, Colonel Kenton. He had been a brilliant and daring cavalry officer in the Mexican War, doing great deeds at Buena Vista, but now he was elderly and so enormously stout that he lacked efficiency.

Jarvis added that after their defeat at Middle Creek the Southerners had gathered their forces on or near the Cumberland River about Mill Spring and that they had ten thousand men. Thomas with a strong Northern force, coming all the way from the central part of the state, was already deep in the mountains, preparing to meet him.

"Remember," said Jarvis, "that I ain't takin' no sides in this war myself. If people come along an' ask me to tell what I know I tell it to 'em, be they Yank or Reb. Now, I wish good luck to you, Mr. Mason, an' I wish the same to your cousin, Mr. Kenton."

Dick, Warner and the sergeant finished the refreshments and rose for the return journey. They thanked Jarvis, and when they saw that he would take no pay, they did not insist, knowing that it would offend him. Dick said good-bye to the ancient woman and once again she rose, put her hands on his shoulders and looked into his eyes.

"Paul Cotter was a good man," she said, "and you who have his blood in your veins are good, too. I can see it in something that lies back in your eyes."

She said not another word, but sat down in the chair and stared once more into the coals, dreaming of the far day when the great borderers saved her and others like her from the savages, and thinking little of the mighty war that raged at the base of her hills.

The boys and the sergeant rode fast on the return trail. They knew that Major Hertford would push forward at all speed to join Thomas, whom they could now locate without much difficulty. Jarvis and Ike had resumed their fence-mending, but when the trees hid the valley from them a mighty, rolling song came to the ears of Dick, Warner and the sergeant:

> They bore him away when the day had fled,
>   And the storm was rolling high,
>   And they laid him down in his lonely bed
>   By the light of an angry sky.
>   The lightning flashed, and the wild sea lashed
>   The shore with its foaming wave,
>   And the thunder passed on the rushing blast
>   As it howled o'er the rover's grave.
> "That man's no fool," said Dick.

"No, he ain't," said the sergeant, with decision, "nor is that nephew Ike of his that he calls a lunkhead. Did you notice, Mr. Mason, that the boy never spoke a word while we was there? Them that don't say anything never have anything to take back."

They rode hard now, and soon reached Major Hertford with their news. On the third day thereafter they entered a strong Union camp, commanded by a man named Garfield, the young officer who had won the victory at Middle Creek.

# CHAPTER VI

## MILL SPRING

Garfield's camp was on a little group of hills in a very strong position, and his men, flushed with victory, were eager for another encounter with the enemy. They had plenty of good tents to fend them from the winter weather which had often been bitter. Throughout the camp burned large fires for which they had an almost unbroken wilderness to furnish fuel. The whole aspect of the place was pleasing to the men who had marched far and hard.

Major Hertford and his aides, Richard Mason and George Warner, were received in Colonel Garfield's tent. A slim young man, writing dispatches at a rude little pine table, rose to receive them. He did not seem to Dick to be more than thirty, and he had the thin, scholarly face of a student. His manner was attractive, he shook hands warmly with all three of them and said:

"Reinforcements are most welcome indeed. My own work here seems to be largely done, but you will reach General Thomas in another day, and he needs you. Take my chair, Major Hertford. To you two lads I can offer only stumps."

The tent had been pitched over a spot where three stumps had been smoothed off carefully until they made acceptable seats. One end of the tent was entirely open, facing a glowing fire of oak logs. Dick and Warner sat down on the stumps and spread out their hands to the blaze. Beyond the flames they saw the wintry forest and mountains, seemingly as wild as they were when the first white man came.

The usual coffee and food were brought, and while they ate and drank Major Hertford answered the numerous and pertinent questions of Colonel Garfield. He listened attentively to the account of the fight in the mountains, and to all the news that they could tell him of Washington.

"We have been cut off in these mountains," he said. "I know very little of what is going on, but what you say only confirms my own opinion. The war is rapidly spreading over a much greater area, and I believe that its scope will far exceed any of our earlier calculations."

A grave and rather sad expression occupied for a moment the mobile face. He interested Dick greatly. He seemed to him scholar and thinker as well as soldier. He and Warner long afterward attended the inauguration of this man as President of the United States.

After a brief rest, and good wishes from Garfield, Major Hertford and his command soon reached the main camp under Thomas. Here they were received by a man very different in appearance and manner from Garfield.

General George H. Thomas, who was to receive the famous title, "The Rock of Chickamauga," was then in middle years. Heavily built and bearded, he was chary of words. He merely nodded approval when Major Hertford told of their march.

"I will assign your troops to a brigade," he said, "and I don't think you'll have long to wait. We're expecting a battle in a few days with Crittenden and Zollicoffer."

"Not much to say," remarked Dick to Warner, as they went away.

"That's true," said Warner, thoughtfully, "but didn't you get an impression of strength from his very silence? I should say that in his make-up he is five per cent talk, twenty-five per cent patience and seventy per cent action; total, one hundred per cent."

The region in which they lay was west of the higher mountains, which they had now crossed, but it was very rough and hilly. Not far from them was a little town called Somerset, which Dick had visited once, and near by, too, was the deep and swift Cumberland River, with much floating ice at its edges. When the two lads lay by a campfire that night Sergeant Whitley came to them with the news of the situation, which he had picked up in his usual deft and quiet way.

"The Southern army is on the banks of the Cumberland," he said. "It has not been able to get its provisions by land through Cumberland Gap. Instead they have been brought by boats on the river. As I hear it, Crittenden and Zollicoffer are afraid that our general will advance to the river an' cut off these supplies. So they mean to attack us as soon as they can. If I may venture to say so, Mr. Mason, I'd advise that you and Lieutenant Warner get as good a rest as you can, and as soon as you can."

They ate a hearty supper and being told by Major Hertford that they would not be wanted until the next day, they rolled themselves in heavy blankets, and, pointing their feet toward a good fire, slept on the ground. The night was very cold, because it was now the middle of January, but the blankets and fire kept them warm.

Dick did not fall to sleep for some time, because he knew that he was going into battle again in a few days. He was on the soil of his native state now. He had already seen many Kentuckians in the army of Thomas and he knew that they would be numerous, too, in that of Crittenden and Zollicoffer. To some extent it would be a battle of brother against brother. He was glad that Harry Kenton was in the east. He did not wish in the height of battle to see his own cousin again on the opposite side.

But when he did fall asleep his slumber was sound and restful, and he was ready and eager the next morning, when the sergeant, Warner, and he were detached for duty in a scouting party.

"The general has asked that you be sent owing to your experience in the mountains," said Major Hertford, "and I have agreed gladly. I hope that you're as glad as I am."

"We are, sir," said the two boys together. The sergeant stood quietly by and smiled.

The detachment numbered a hundred men, all young, strong, and well mounted. They were commanded by a young captain, John Markham, in whom Dick recognized a distant relative. In those days nearly all Kentuckians were more or less akin. The kinship was sufficient for Markham to keep the two boys on either side of him with Sergeant Whitley just behind. Markham lived in Frankfort and he had marched with Thomas from the cantonments at Lebanon to their present camp.

"John," said Dick, addressing him familiarly and in right of kinship, "you've been for months in our own county. You've surely heard something from Pendleton?"

He could not disguise the anxiety in his voice, and the young captain regarded him with sympathy.

"I had news from there about a month ago, Dick," he replied. "Your mother was well then, as I have no doubt she is now. The place was not troubled by guerillas who are hanging on the fringe of the armies here in Eastern, or in Southern and Western Kentucky. The war for the present at least has passed around Pendleton. Colonel Kenton was at Bowling Green with Albert Sidney Johnston, and his son, Harry, your cousin, is still in the East."

It was a rapid and condensed statement, but it was very satisfying to Dick who now rode on for a long time in silence. The road was as bad as a road could be. Snow and ice were mixed with the deep mud which pulled hard at the hoofs of their horses. The country was rough, sterile, and inhabited but thinly. They rode many miles without meeting a single human being. About the third hour they saw a man and a boy on a hillside several hundred yards away, but when Captain Markham and a chosen few galloped towards them they disappeared so deftly among the woods that not a trace of them could be found.

"People in this region are certainly bashful," said Captain Markham with a vexed laugh. "We meant them no harm, but they wouldn't stay to see us."

"But they don't know that," said Dick with the familiarity of kinship, even though distant. "I fancy that the people hereabouts wish both Northerners and Southerners would go away."

Two miles further on they came to a large, double cabin standing back a little distance from the road. Smoke was rising from the chimney, and Captain Markham felt sure that they could obtain information from its inmates. Dick, at his direction, beat on the door with the butt of a small riding whip. There was no response. He beat again rapidly and heavily, and no answer coming he pushed in the door.

A fire was burning on the hearth, but the house was abandoned. Nor had the owners been gone long. Besides the fire to prove it, clothing was hanging on hooks in the wall, and there was food in the cupboard. Captain Markham sighed.

"Again they're afraid of us," he said. "I've no doubt the signal has been passed ahead of us, and that we'll not get within speaking distance of a single native. Curious, too, because this region in the main is for the North."

"Perhaps somebody has been robbing and plundering in our name," said Dick. "Skelly and his raiders have been through these parts."

"That's so," said Markham, thoughtfully. "I'm afraid those guerillas who claim to be our allies are going to do us a great deal of harm. Well, we'll turn back into the road, if you can call this stream of icy mud a road, and go on."

Another mile and they caught the gleam of water among the wintry boughs. Dick knew that it was the Cumberland which was now a Southern artery, bringing stores and arms for the army of Crittenden and Zollicoffer. Even here, hundreds of miles from its mouth, it was a stream of great depth, easily navigable, and far down its current they saw faintly the smoke of two steamers.

"They bear supplies for the Southern army," said Captain Markham. "We can cut off the passage of boats on this river and for that reason, so General Thomas concludes, the Southern army is going to attack us. What do you think of his reasoning, sergeant?"

"Beggin' your pardon, sir, for passin' an opinion upon my general," replied Sergeant Whitley, "but I think his reasons are good. Here it is the dead of winter, with more mud in the roads than I ever saw before anywhere, but there's bound to be a battle right away. Men will fight, sir, to keep from losin' their grub."

A man rode forward from the ranks, saluted and asked leave to speak. He was a native of the next county and knew that region well. Two miles east of them and running parallel with the road over which they had come was another and much wider road, the one that they called the big road.

"Which means, I suppose, that it contains more mud than this one," said Captain Markham.

"True, sir," replied the man, "but if the rebel army is advancing it is likely to be on that road."

"That is certainly sound logic. At least we'll go there and see. Can you lead us through these woods to it?"

"I can take you straight across," replied the man whose name was Carpenter. "But on the way we'll have to ford a creek which is likely to be pretty deep at this time of the year."

"Show the way," said Captain Markham briskly.

They plunged into the deep woods, and Carpenter guided them well. The creek, of which he had told, was running bankful of icy water, but their horses swam it and they kept straight ahead until Carpenter, who was a little in advance, held up a warning hand.

Captain Markham ordered his whole troop to stop and keep as quiet as possible. Then he, Dick, Warner, Sergeant Whitley and Carpenter rode slowly forward. Before they had gone many yards Dick heard the heavy clank of metal, the cracking of whips, the swearing of men, and the sound of horses' feet splashing in the mud. He knew by the amount and variety of the noises that a great force was passing.

They advanced a little further and reined into a clump of bushes which despite their lack of leaves were dense enough to shelter them from observation. As the bushes grew on a hillock they had a downward and good look into the road, which was fairly packed with men in the gray of the Confederate army, some on horseback, but mostly afoot, their cannon, ammunition and supply wagons sinking almost to the hub in the mud. As far as Dick could see the gray columns extended.

"There must be six or seven thousand men here," he said to Captain Markham.

"Undoubtedly," replied Markham, "this is the main Confederate army advancing to attack ours, but the badness of the roads operates against the offense. We shall reach General Thomas with the word that they are coming long before they are there."

They watched the marching army for a half hour longer in order to be sure of everything, and then turning they rode as fast as they could toward Thomas, elated at their success. They swam the creek again, but at another point. Carpenter told them that the Southern army would cross it on a bridge, and Markham lamented that he could not turn and destroy this bridge, but such an attempt would have been folly.

They finally turned into the main road along which the Southern army was coming, although they were now miles ahead of it, and, covered from head to foot with the red mud of the hills, they urged on their worn horses toward the camp of Thomas.

"I haven't had much experience in fighting, but I should imagine that complete preparation had a great deal to do with success," said Captain Markham.

"I'd put it at sixty per cent," said Warner.

"I should say," added Dick, "that the road makes at least eighty per cent of our difficulty in getting back to Thomas."

In fact, the road was so bad that they were compelled after a while to ride into the woods and let their ponies rest. Here they were fired upon by Confederate skirmishers from a hill two or three hundred yards away. Their numbers were small, however, and Captain Markham's force charging them drove them off without loss.

Then they resumed their weary journey, but the rest had not fully restored the horses and they were compelled at times to walk by the side of the road, leading their mounts. Sergeant Whitley, with his age and experience, was most useful now in restraining the impatient young men. Although of but humble rank he kept them from exhausting either themselves or their horses.

"It will be long after dark before we can reach camp," said Captain Markham, sighing deeply. "Confound such roads. Why not call them morasses and have done with it!"

"No, we can't make it much before midnight," said Dick, "but, after all, that will be early enough. If I judge him right, even midnight won't catch General Thomas asleep."

"You've judged him right," said Markham. "I've been with 'Pap' Thomas some time—we call him 'Pap' because he takes such good care of us—and I think he is going to be one of the biggest generals in this war. Always silent, and sometimes slow about making up his mind he strikes like a sledge-hammer when he does strike."

"He'll certainly have the opportunity to give blow for blow," said Dick, as he remembered that marching army behind them. "How far do you think it is yet to the general's camp?"

"Not more than a half dozen miles, but it will be dark in a few minutes, and at the rate we're going it will take us two full hours more to get there."

The wintry days were short and the sun slid down the gray, cold sky, leaving forest and hills in darkness. But the little band toiled patiently on, while the night deepened and darkened, and a chill wind whistled down from the ridges. The officers were silent now, but they looked eagerly for the first glimpse of the campfires of Thomas. At last they saw the little pink dots in the darkness, and then they pushed forward with new zeal, urging their weary horses into a run.

When Captain Markham, Dick and Warner galloped into camp, ahead of the others, a thickset strong figure walked forward to meet them. They leaped from their horses and saluted.

"Well?" said General Thomas.

"The enemy is advancing upon us in full force, sir," replied Captain Markham.

"You scouted thoroughly?"

"We saw their whole army upon the road."

"When do you think they could reach us?"

"About dawn, sir."

"Very good. We shall be ready. You and your men have done well. Now, find food and rest. You will be awakened in time for the battle."

Dick walked away with his friends. Troopers took their horses and cared for them. The boy glanced back at the thickset, powerful figure, standing by one of the fires and looking gravely into the coals. More than ever the man with the strong, patient look inspired confidence in him. He was sure now that they would win on the morrow. Markham and Warner felt the same confidence.

"There's a lot in having a good general," said Warner, who had also glanced back at the strong figure. "Do you remember, Dick, what it was that Napoleon said about generals?"

"A general is everything, an army nothing or something like that."

"Yes, that was it. Of course, he didn't mean it just exactly as he said it. A general can't be one hundred per cent and an army none. It was a figure of speech so to say, but I imagine that a general is about forty per cent. If we had had such leadership at Bull Run we'd have won."

Dick and Warner, worn out by their long ride, soon slept but there was movement all around them during the late hours of the night. Thomas with his cautious, measuring mind was rectifying his lines in the wintry darkness. He occupied a crossing of the roads, and he posted a strong battery of artillery to cover the Southern approach. Around him were men from Kentucky, the mountains of Tennessee, Ohio, Indiana, and Minnesota. The Minnesota troops were sun-tanned men who had come more than a thousand miles from an Indian-infested border to defend the Union.

All through the night Thomas worked. He directed men with spades to throw up more intrenchments. He saw that the guns of the battery were placed exactly right. He ordered that food should be ready for all very early in the morning, and then, when nothing more remained to be done, save to wait for the decree of battle, he sat before his tent wrapped in a heavy military overcoat, silent and watchful. Scouts had brought in additional news that the Southern army was still marching steadily along the muddy roads, and that Captain Markham's calculation of its arrival about dawn would undoubtedly prove correct.

Dick awoke while it was yet dark, and throwing off the heavy blankets stood up.

Although the dawn had not come, the night was now fairly light and Dick could see a long distance over the camp which stretched to left and right along a great front. Near him was the battery with most of the men sleeping beside their guns, and not far away was the tent. Although he could not see the general, he knew instinctively that he was not asleep.

It was cold and singularly still, considering the presence of so many thousands of men. He did not hear the sound of human voices and there was no stamp of horses' feet. They, too, were weary and resting. Then Dick was conscious of a tall, thin figure beside him. Warner had awakened, too.

"Dick," he said, "it can't be more than an hour till dawn."

"Just about that I should say."

"And the scene, that is as far as we can see it, is most peaceful."

Dick made no answer, but stood a long time listening. Then he said:

"My ears are pretty good, George, and sound will carry very far in this silence just before the dawn. I thought I heard a faint sound like the clank of a cannon."

"I think I hear it, too," said Warner, "and here is the dawn closer at hand than we thought. Look at those cold rays over there, behind that hill in the east. They are the vanguard of the sun."

"So they are. And this is the vanguard of the Southern army!"

He spoke the last words quickly and with excitement.

In front of them down the road they heard the crackle of a dozen rifle shots. The Southern advance undoubtedly had come into contact with the Union sentinels and skirmishers. After the first shots there was a moment's breathless silence, and then came a scattered and rapid fire, as if at least a hundred rifles were at work.

Dick's pulse began to beat hard, and he strained his eyes through the darkness, but he could not yet see the enemy. He saw instead little jets of fire like red dots appearing on the horizon, and then the sound of the rifles came again. Warner was with him and both stood by the side of Major Hertford, ready to receive and deliver his orders. Dick now heard besides the firing in front the confused murmur and moving of the Union army.

Few of these troops had been in battle before—the same could be said of the soldiers on the other side—and this attack in the half-light troubled them. They wished to see the men who were going to shoot at them, in order that they might have a fair target in return. Fighting in the night was scarcely fair. One never knew what to do. But Thomas, the future "Rock of Chickamauga," was already showing himself a tower of strength. He reassured his nervous troops, he borrowed Dick and Warner and sent them along the line with messages from himself that they had nothing to do but stand firm and the victory was theirs.

Meanwhile the line of red dots in front was lengthening. It stretched farther to left and right than Dick could see, and was rapidly coming nearer. Already the sentinels and skirmishers were waging a sharp conflict, and the shouts of the combatants increased in volume. Then the cold sun swung clear of the earth, and its wintry beams lighted up both forest and open. The whole Southern army appeared, advancing in masses, and Dick, who was now with Major Hertford again, saw the pale rays falling on rifles and bayonets, and the faces of his own countrymen as they marched upon the Union camp.

"There's danger for our army! Lots of it!" said Warner, as he watched the steady advance of the Southern brigades.

Dick remembered Bull Run, but his thoughts ran back to the iron general who commanded now.

"Thomas will save us," he said.

The skirmishers on both sides were driven in. Their scattered fire ceased, but a moment later the whole front of the Southern army burst into flame. It seemed to Dick that one vast sheet of light like a sword blade suddenly shot forward, and then a storm of lead, bearing many messengers of death, beat upon the Northern army, shattering its front lines and carrying confusion among its young troops. But the officers and a few old regulars like Sergeant Whitley steadied them and they returned the fire.

Major Hertford, Dick and Warner were all on foot, and their own little band, already tried in battle, yielded not an inch. They formed a core of resistance around which others rallied and Thomas himself was passing along the line, giving heart to the lads fresh from the farms.

But the Southern army fired again, and shouting the long fierce rebel yell, charged with all its strength. Dick saw before him a vast cloud of smoke, through which fire flashed and bullets whistled. He heard men around him uttering short cries of pain, and he saw others fall, mostly sinking forward on their faces. But those who stood, held fast and loaded and fired until the barrels of their rifles burned to the touch.

Dick felt many tremors at first, but soon the passion of battle seized him. He carried no rifle, but holding his officer's small sword in his hand he ran up and down the line crying to the men to stand firm, that they would surely beat back the enemy. That film of fire and smoke was yet before his eyes, but he saw through it the faces of his countrymen still coming on. He heard to his right the thudding of the great guns that Thomas had planted on a low hill, but the rifle fire was like the beat of hail, a crackling and hissing that never ceased.

The farm lads, their rifles loaded afresh, fired anew at the enemy, almost in their faces, and the Southern line here reeled back against so firm and deadly a front.

But an alarming report ran down the line that their left was driven back, and it was true. The valiant Zollicoffer leading his brigade in person, had rushed upon this portion of the Northern army which was standing upon another low hill and struck it with great violence. It was wavering and would give way soon. But Thomas, showing the singular calm that always marked him in battle, noticed the weak spot. The general was then near Major Hertford. He quickly wrote a dispatch and beckoned to Dick:

70

"Here," he said, "jump on the horse that the sergeant is holding for me, and bring up our reserve, the brigade under General Carter. They are to meet the attack there on the hill, where our troops are wavering!"

Dick, aflame with excitement, leaped into the saddle, and while the roar of battle was still in his ears reached the brigade of Carter, already marching toward the thick of the conflict. One entire regiment, composed wholly of Kentuckians, was detached to help the Indiana troops who were being driven fiercely by Zollicoffer.

Dick rode at the head of the Kentuckians, but a bullet struck his horse in the chest. The boy felt the animal shiver beneath him, and he leaped clear just in time, the horse falling heavily and lying quite still. But Dick alighted on his feet, and still brandishing his sword, and shouting at the top of his voice, ran on.

In an instant they reached the Indiana troops, who turned with them, and the combined forces hurled themselves upon the enemy. The Southerners, refusing to yield the ground they had gained, received them, and there began a confused and terrible combat, shoulder to shoulder and hand to hand. Elsewhere the battle continued, but here it raged the fiercest. Both commanders knew that they were to win or lose upon this hill, and they poured in fresh troops who swelled the area of conflict and deepened its intensity.

Dick saw Warner by his side, but he did not know how he had come there, and just beyond him the thick and powerful figure of Sergeant Whitley showed through the hot haze of smoke. The back of Warner's hand had been grazed by a bullet. He had not noticed it himself, but the slow drip, drip of the blood held Dick for a moment with a sort of hideous fascination. Then he broke his gaze violently away and turned it upon the enemy, who were pouring upon them in all their massed strength.

Thomas had sent the Kentuckians to the aid of the Indiana men just in time. The hill was a vast bank of smoke and fire, filled with whistling bullets and shouts of men fighting face to face. Some one reeled and fell against Dick, and for a moment, he was in horror lest it should be Warner, but a glance showed him that it was a stranger. Then he rushed on again, filled with a mad excitement, waving his small sword, and shouting to the men to charge.

From right to left the roar of battle came to his ears, but on the hill where he stood the struggle was at its height. The lines of Federals and Confederates, face to face at first, now became mixed, but neither side gained. In the fiery struggle a Union officer, Fry, saw Zollicoffer only a few feet away. Snatching out his pistol he shot him dead. The Southerners seeing the fall of the general who was so popular among them hesitated and then gave back. Thomas, watching everything with keen and steady gaze, hurled an Ohio regiment from the right flank upon the Southern center, causing it to give way yet further under the shock.

"We win! We win!" shouted Dick in his ardor, as he saw the Southern line yielding. But the victory was not yet achieved. Crittenden, who was really Zollicoffer's superior in the command, displayed the most heroic courage throughout the battle. He brought up fresh troops to help his weakened center. He reformed his lines and was about to restore the battle, but Thomas, silent and ever watchful, now rushed in a brigade of Tennessee mountaineers, and as they struck with all their weight, the new line of the South was compelled to give way. Success seen and felt filled the veins of the soldiers with fresh fire. Dick and the men about him saw the whole Southern line crumble up before them. The triumphant Union army rushed forward shouting, and the Confederates were forced to give way at all points.

Dick and Warner, with the watchful sergeant near, were in the very front of the advance. The two young aides carried away by success and the fire of battle, waved their swords continually and rushed at the enemy's lines.

Dick's face was covered with smoke, his lips were burnt, and his throat was raw from so much shouting. But he was conscious only of great elation. "This is not another Bull Run!" he cried to Warner, and Warner cried back: "Not by a long shot!"

Thomas, still cool, watchful, and able to judge of results amid all the thunder and confusion of battle, hurried every man into the attack. He was showing upon this, his first independent field, all the great qualities he was destined later to manifest so brilliantly in some of the greatest battles of modern times.

The Southern lines were smashed completely by those heavy and continuous blows. Driven hard on every side they now retreated rapidly, and their triumphant enemies seized prisoners and cannon.

The whole Confederate army continued its swift retreat until it reached its intrenchments, where the officers rallied the men and turned to face their enemy. But the cautious Thomas stopped. He had no intention of losing his victory by an attack upon an intrenched foe, and drew off for the present. His army encamped out of range and began to attend to the wounded and bury the dead.

Dick, feeling the reaction after so much exertion and

excitement, sat down on a fallen tree trunk and drew long, panting breaths. He saw Warner near and remembered the blood that had been dripping from his hand.

"Do you know that you are wounded, George?" he said. "Look at the back of your hand."

Warner glanced at it and noticed the red stripe. It had ceased to bleed.

"Now, that's curious," he said. "I never felt it. My blood and brain were both so hot that the flick of a bullet created no sensation. I have figured it out, Dick, and I have concluded that seventy per cent of our bravery in battle is excitement, leaving twenty per cent to will and ten per cent to chance."

"I suppose your calculation is close enough."

"It's not close merely. It's exact."

Both sprang to their feet and saluted as Major Hertford approached. He had escaped without harm and he saw with pleasure that the lads were alive and well, except for Warner's slight wound.

"You can rest now, boys," he said, "I won't need you for some time. But I can tell you that I don't think General Thomas means to quit. He will follow up his victory."

But Dick and Warner had been sure of that already. The army, flushed with triumph, was eager to be led on, even to make a night attack on the intrenchments of the enemy, but Thomas held them, knowing that another brigade of Northern troops was marching to his aid. The brigade came, but it was now dark and he would not risk a night attack. But some of the guns were brought up and they sent a dozen heavy cannon shot into the intrenchments of the enemy. There was no reply and neither of the boys, although they strained ears, could hear anything in the defeated camp.

"I shouldn't be surprised if we found them gone in the morning," said Major Hertford to Dick. "But I think our general is right in not making any attack upon their works. What do you say to that, Sergeant Whitley? You've had a lot of experience."

Sergeant Whitley was standing beside them, also trying to pierce the darkness with trained eyes, although he could not see the Confederate intrenchments.

"If a sergeant may offer an opinion I agree with you fully, sir," he said. "A night attack is always risky, an' most of all, sir, when troops are new like ours, although they're as brave as anybody. More'n likely if we was to rush on 'em our troops would be shootin' into one another in the darkness."

"Good logic," said Major Hertford, "and as it is quite certain that they are not in any condition to come out and attack us we'll stand by and wait till morning. So the general orders."

They walked back toward the place where the victorious troops were lighting the fires, out of the range of the cannon in the Confederate intrenchments. They were exultant, but they were not boasting unduly. Night, cold and dark, had shut down upon them and was taking the heat out of their blood. Hundreds of men were at work building fires, and Dick and Warner, with the permission of Major Hertford, joined them.

Both boys felt that the work would be a relief. Wood was to be had in abundance. The forest stretched on all sides of them in almost unbroken miles, and the earth was littered with dead wood fallen a year or years before. They merely kept away from the side on which the Confederate intrenchments lay, and brought in the wood in great quantities. A row of lights a half mile long sprang up, giving forth heat and warmth. Then arose the cheerful sound of tin and iron dishes and cups rattling against one another. A quarter of an hour later they were eating a victorious supper, and a little later most of them slept.

But in the night the Confederate troops abandoned their camp, leaving in it ten cannon and fifteen hundred wagons and crossed the river in boats, which they destroyed when they reached the other side. Then, their defeat being so severe, and they but volunteers, they scattered in the mountains to seek food and shelter for the remainder of the winter.

This army of the South ceased to exist.

# CHAPTER VII

# THE MESSENGER

Victory, overwhelming and complete, had been won, but General Thomas could not follow into the deep mountains where his army might be cut off. So he remained where he was for a little while and on the second day he sent for Dick.

The general was seated alone in a tent, an open end of which faced a fire, as it was now extremely cold. General Thomas had shown no undue elation over his victory. He was as silent as ever, and now, as always, he made upon Dick the impression of strength and indomitable courage.

"Sit down," he said, waving his hand toward a camp stool.

Dick, after saluting, sat down in silence.

"I hear," said the general, "that you behaved very well in the battle, and that you are a lad of courage and intelligence. Courage is common, intelligence, real intelligence, is rare. You were at Bull Run also, so I hear."

"I was, and the army fought well there too, but late in the day it was seized with a sudden panic."

"Something that may happen at any time to raw troops. But we'll pass to the question in hand. The campaign here in the mountains is ended for this winter, but great matters are afoot further west. A courier arrived last night stating that General Grant and Commodore Foote were preparing to advance by water from Cairo, Illinois, and attempt the reduction of the Confederate forts on the Cumberland and Tennessee. General Buell, one of your own Kentuckians, is advancing southward with a strong Union force, and in a few days his outposts will be on Green River. It will be of great advantage to Buell to know that the Confederate army in the eastern part of the state is destroyed. He can advance with freedom and, on the other hand, the Southern leader, Albert Sidney Johnston, will be compelled to throw a portion of his force to the eastward to protect his flank which has been uncovered by our victory at Mill Spring. Do you understand?"

"I do, sir."

"Then you are to carry dispatches of the utmost importance from me to General Buell. After you reach his camp—if you reach it—you will, of course, be subject to his orders. I have learned that you know the country well between here and Green River. Because of that, and because of your intelligence, real intelligence, I mean,

75

you are chosen for this task. You are to change to citizen's clothes at once, and a horse of great power and endurance has been selected for you. But you must use all your faculties all the time. I warn you that the journey is full of danger."

"I can carry it out," replied Dick with quiet confidence, "and I thank you for choosing me."

"I believe you will succeed," said the general, who liked his tone. "Return here in an hour with all your preparations made, and I will give you the dispatches."

Warner was filled with envy that his comrade was to go on a secret mission of great importance, but he generously wished him a full measure of success.

"Remember," he said, "that on an errand like yours, presence of mind counts for at least fifty per cent. Have a quick tongue. Always be ready with a tale that looks true."

"An' remember, too," said Sergeant Whitley, "that however tight a place you get into you can get into one tighter. Think of that and it will encourage you to pull right out of the hole."

The two wrung his hand and Major Hertford also gave him his warmest wishes. The horse chosen for him was a bay of tremendous power, and Dick knew that he would serve him well. He carried double blankets strapped to the saddle, pistols in holsters with another in his belt, an abundance of ammunition, and food for several days in his saddle bags. Then he returned to General Thomas, who handed him a thin strip of tissue paper.

"It is written in indelible ink," he said, "and it contains a statement of our forces and their positions here in the eastern part of the state. It also tells General Buell what reinforcements he can expect. If you are in imminent danger of capture destroy the paper, but to provide for such a chance, in case you escape afterward, I will read the dispatches to you."

He read them over several times and then questioned Dick. But the boy's memory was good. In fact, every word of the dispatches was burnt into his brain, and nothing could make him forget them.

"And now, my lad," said General Thomas, giving him his hand, "you may help us greatly. I would not send a boy upon such an errand, but the demands of war are terrible and must be obeyed."

The strong grasp of the general's hand imparted fresh enthusiasm to Dick, and for the present he did not have the slightest doubt that he would get safely through. He wore a strong suit of home-made brown jeans, a black felt cap with ear-flaps, and high boots. The dispatch was pinned into a small inside pocket of his vest.

He rode quickly out of camp, giving the sentinels the pass word, and the head of the horse was pointed west slightly by north. The ground was now frozen and he did not have the mud to hold him back.

The horse evidently had been longing for action. Such thews and sinews as his needed exercise. He stretched out his long neck, neighed joyously, and broke of his own accord into an easy canter. It was a lonely road, and Dick was glad that it was so. The fewer people he met the better it was in every way for him.

He shared the vigor and spirit of his horse. His breath turned to smoke, but the cold whipped his blood into a quicker torrent. He hummed snatches of the songs that he had heard Samuel Jarvis sing, and went on mile after mile through the high hills toward the low hills of Kentucky.

Dick did not pass many people. The ancient name of his state—the Dark and Bloody Ground—came back to him. He knew that war in one of its worst forms existed in this wild sweep of hills. Here the guerillas rode, choosing their sides as suited them best, and robbing as paid them most. Nor did these rough men hesitate at murder. So he rode most of the time with his hand on the butt of the pistol at his belt, and whenever he went through woods, which was most of the time, he kept a wary watch to right and to left.

The first person whom he passed was a boy riding on a sack of grain to mill. Dick greeted him cheerfully and the boy with the fearlessness of youth replied in the same manner.

"Any news your way?" asked Dick.

"Nothin' at all," replied the boy, his eyes enlarging with excitement, "but from the way you are comin' we heard tell there was a great battle, hundreds of thousands of men on each side an' that the Yankees won. Is it so, Mister?"

"It is true," replied Dick. "A dozen people have told me of it, but the armies were not quite so large as you heard. It is true also that the Yankees won."

"I'll tell that at the mill. It will be big news to them. An' which way be you goin', Mister?" said the boy with all the frankness of the hills.

"I'm on my way to the middle part of the state. I've been looking after some land that my people own in the mountains. Looks like a lonesome road, this. Will I reach any house soon?"

"Thar's Ben Trimble's three miles further on, but take my advice an' don't stop thar. Ben says he ain't goin' to be troubled in these war times by visitors, an' he's likely to meet you at the door with his double-barreled shotgun."

"I won't knock on Ben's door, so he needn't take down his double-barreled shotgun. What's next beyond Ben's house?"

"A half mile further on you come to Hungry Creek. It ain't much in the middle of summer, but right now it's full of cold water, 'nough of it to come right up to your hoss's body. You go through it keerful."

"Thank you for your good advice," said Dick. "I'll follow it, too. Good-bye."

He waved his gauntleted hand and rode on. A hundred yards further and he glanced back. The boy had stopped on the crest of a hill, and was looking at him. But Dick knew that it was only the natural curiosity of the hills and he renewed his journey without apprehension.

At the appointed time he saw the stout log cabin of Ben Trimble by the roadside with the warm smoke rising from the chimney, but true to his word he gave Ben and his shotgun no trouble, and continued straight ahead over the frozen road until he came to the banks of Hungry Creek. Here, too, the words of the boy came true. The water was both deep and cold, and Dick looked at it doubtfully.

He urged his great horse into the stream at last, and it appeared that the creek had risen somewhat since the boy had last seen it. In the middle the horse was compelled to swim, but it was no task for such a powerful animal, and Dick, holding his feet high, came dry to the shore that he sought.

The road led on through high hills, covered with oak and beech and cedar and pine, all the deciduous trees bare of leaves, their boughs rustling dryly whenever the wind blew. He saw the smoke of three cabins nestling in snug coves, but it was a full three hours before he met anybody else in the road. Then he saw two men riding toward him, but he could not tell much about them as they were wrapped in heavy gray shawls, and wore broad brimmed felt hats, pulled well down over their foreheads.

Dick knew that he could not exercise too much caution in this debatable land, and his right hand dropped cautiously to the butt of his pistol in such a manner that it was concealed by his heavy overcoat. His left hand rested lightly on the reins as he rode forward at an even pace. But he did not fail to take careful note of the two men who were now examining him in a manner that he did not like.

Dick saw that the strangers openly carried pistols in their belts, which was not of overwhelming significance in such times in such a region, but they did not have the look of mountaineers riding on peaceful business, and he reined his horse to the very edge of the road that he might pass them.

He noted with rising apprehension that they checked the pace of their horses as they approached, and that they reined to either side of the road to compel him to go between them. But he pulled his own horse out still further, and as they could not pass on both sides of him without an overt act of hostility they drew together again in the middle of the road.

"Mornin' stranger," they said together, when they were a few yards away.

"Good morning," said Dick, riding straight on, without checking his speed. But one of the men drew his horse across the road and said:

"What's your hurry? It ain't friendly to ride by without passin' the time o' day."

Now at close range, Dick liked their looks less than ever. They might be members of that very band of Skelly's which had already made so much trouble for both sides, and he summoned all his faculties in order to meet them at any game that they might try to play.

"I've been on land business in the mountains," he said, "and I'm anxious to get back to my home. Besides the day is very cold, and the two facts deprive me of the pleasure of a long conversation with you, gentlemen. Good-day."

"Wait just a little," said the spokesman, who still kept his horse reined across the road. "These be war times an' it's important to know what a fellow is. Be you for the Union or are you with the Scccsh?"

Dick was quite sure that whatever he answered they would immediately claim to be on the opposite side. Then would follow robbery and perhaps murder.

"Which is your side?" he asked.

"But we put the question first," the fellow replied.

Dick no longer had any doubts. The second man was drawing his horse up by the side of him, as if to seize him, while the first continued to bar the way. He was alarmed, deeply alarmed, but he lost neither his courage nor his presence of mind. Luckily he had already summoned every faculty for instant action, and now he acted. He uttered a sudden shout, and raked the side of his horse with both spurs.

His horse was not only large and powerful but of a most high spirit. When he heard that shout and felt the burning slash of the spurs he made a blind but mighty leap forward. The horse of the first stranger, smitten by so great a weight, fell in the road and his rider went down with him. The enraged horse then leaped clear of both and darted forward at headlong speed.

As his horse sprang Dick threw himself flat upon his neck, and the bullet that the second man fired whistled over his head. By impulse he drew his own pistol and fired back. He saw the man's pistol arm fall as if broken, and he heard a loud cry. That was a lucky shot indeed, and rising a little in his saddle he shouted again and again to the great horse that served him so well.

The gallant animal responded in full. He stretched out his long neck and the road flew fast behind him. Sparks flashed from the stones where the shod hoofs struck, and Dick exulting felt the cold air rush past. Another shot was fired at long range, but the bullet did not strike anywhere near.

Dick took only a single backward glance. He saw the two men on their horses, but drooping as if weak from hurts, and he knew that for the present at least he was safe from any hurt from them. But he allowed his horse his head for a long time, and then he gradually slowed him down. No human being was in sight now and he spoke to the noble animal soothingly.

"Good old boy," he said; "the strongest, the swiftest, the bravest, and the truest. I was sorry to make those red stripes on your sides, but it had to be done. Only quickness saved us."

The horse neighed. He was still quivering from excitement and exertion. So was Dick for that matter. The men might have been robbers merely—they were at least that bad—but they might have deprived him also of his precious dispatch. He was proud of the confidence put in him by General Thomas, and he meant to deserve it. It was this sense of responsibility and pride that had attuned his faculties to so high a pitch and that had made his action so swift, sudden and decisive.

But he steadied himself presently. The victory, for victory it certainly was, increased his strength and confidence. He stopped soon at a brook—they seemed to occur every mile—and bathed with cold water the red streaks his spurs had made on either side of his horse. Again he spoke soothing words and regretted the necessity that had caused him to make such wounds, slight though they were.

He also bathed his own face and hands and, as it was now about noon, ate of the cold ham and bread that he carried in his knapsack, meanwhile keeping constant watch on the road over which he had come. But he did not believe that the men would pursue, and he saw no sign of them. Mounting again he rode forward.

The remainder of the afternoon went by without interruption. He passed three or four people, but they were obviously natives of that region, and they asked him only innocent questions. The wintry day was short, and the twilight was soon at hand. He was riding over one of the bare ridges, when first he noticed how late the day had grown. All the sky was gray and chill and the cold sun was setting behind the western mountains. A breeze sprang up, rustling among the leafless branches, and Dick shivered in the saddle. A new necessity was pressed suddenly upon him. He must find shelter for the night. Even with his warm double blankets he could not sleep in the forest on such a night. Besides the horse would need food.

He rode on briskly for a full hour, anxiously watching both sides of the road for a cabin or cabin smoke. By that time night had come fully, though fortunately it was clear but very cold. He saw then on the right a faint coil of smoke rising against the dusky sky and he rode straight for it.

The smoke came from a strong double cabin, standing about four hundred yards from the road, and the sight of the heavy log walls made Dick all the more anxious to get inside them. The cold had grown bitter and even his horse shivered.

As he approached two yellow curs rushed forth and began to bark furiously, snapping at the horse's heels, the usual mountain welcome. But when a kick from the horse grazed the ear of one of them they kept at a respectful distance.

"Hello! Hello!" called Dick loudly.

This also was the usual mountain notification that a guest had come, and the heavy board door of the house opened inward. A man, elderly, but dark and strong, with the high cheek bones of an Indian stood in the door, the light of a fire blazing in the fireplace on the opposite side of the wall throwing him in relief. His hair was coal black, long and coarse, increasing his resemblance to an Indian.

Dick rode close to the door, and, without hesitation, asked for a night's shelter and food. This was his inalienable right in the hills or mountains of his state, and he would be a strange man indeed who would refuse it.

The man sharply bade the dogs be silent and they retreated behind the house, their tails drooping. Then he said to Dick in a tone that was not without hospitality:

"'Light, stranger, an' we'll put up your horse. Mandy will have supper ready by the time we finish the job."

Dick sprang down gladly, but staggered a little at first from the stiffness of his legs.

"You've rid far, stranger," said the man, who Dick knew at once had a keen eye and a keen brain, "an' you're young, too."

"But not younger than many who have gone to the war," replied Dick. "In fact, you see many who are not older than fifteen or sixteen."

He had spoken hastily and incautiously and he realized it at once. The man's keen gaze was turned upon him again.

"You've seen the armies, then?" he said. "Mebbe you're a sojer yourself?"

"I've been in the mountains, looking after some land that belongs to my family," said Dick. "My name is Mason, Richard Mason, and I live near Pendleton, which is something like a hundred miles from here."

He deemed it best to give his right name, as it would have no significance there.

"You must have seen armies," persisted the man, "or you wouldn't hev knowed 'bout so many boys of fifteen or sixteen bein' in them."

"I saw both the Federal and Confederate armies in Eastern Kentucky. My business took me near them, but I was always glad to get away from them, too."

"I heard tell today that there was a big battle."

"You heard right. It was fought near a little place called Mill Spring, and resulted in a complete victory for the Northern forces under General Thomas."

"That was what I heard. It will be good news to some, an' bad news to others. 'Pears to me, Mr. Mason, that you can't fight a battle that will suit everybody."

"I never heard of one that did."

"An' never will, I reckon. Mighty good hoss that you're ridin'. I never seed one with better shoulders. My name's Leffingwell, Seth Leffingwell, an' I live here alone, 'ceptin' my old woman, Mandy. All we ask of people is to let us be. Lots of us in the mountain feel that way. Let them lowlanders shoot one another up ez long ez they please, but up here there ain't no slaves, an' there ain't nothin' else to fight about."

The stable was a good one, better than usual in that country. Dick saw stalls for four horses, but no horses. They put his own horse in one of the stalls, and gave him corn and hay. Then they walked back to the house, and entered a large room, where a stalwart woman of middle age had just finished cooking supper.

"Whew, but the night's goin' to be cold," said Leffingwell, as he shut the door behind them, and cut off an icy blast. "It'll make the fire an' supper all the better. We're just plain mountain people, but you're welcome to the best we have. Ma, this is Mr. Mason, who has been on lan' business in the mountains, an' is back on his way to his home at Pendleton."

Leffingwell's wife, a powerful woman, as large as her husband,

and with a pleasant face, gave Dick a large hand and a friendly grasp.

"It's a good night to be indoors," she said. "Supper's ready, Seth. Will you an' the stranger set?"

She had placed the pine table in the middle of the room, and Dick noticed that it was large enough for five or six persons. He put his saddle bags and blankets in a corner and he and the man drew up chairs.

He had seldom beheld a more cheerful scene. In a great fireplace ten feet wide big logs roared and crackled. Corn cakes, vegetables, and two kinds of meat were cooking over the coals and a great pot of coffee boiled and bubbled. No candles had been lighted, but they were not needed. The flames gave sufficient illumination.

"Set, young man," said Leffingwell heartily, "an' see who's teeth are sharper, yourn or mine."

Dick sat down gladly, and they fell to. The woman alternately waited on them and ate with them. For a time the two masculine human beings ate and drank with so much vigor that there was no time for talk. Leffingwell was the first to break silence.

"I kin see you growin'," he said.

"Growing?"

"Yes, growin', you're eatin' so much, you're enjoyin' it so much, an' you're digestin' it so fast. You are already taller than you was when you set, an' you're broader 'cross the chest. No, 'tain't wuth while to 'pologize. You've got a right to be hungry, an' you mustn't forget Ma's cookin' either. She's never had her beat in all these mountains."

"Shut up, Seth," said Mrs. Leffingwell, genially, "you'll make the young stranger think you're plum' foolish, which won't be wide of the mark either."

"I'm grateful," said Dick falling into the spirit of it, "but what pains me, Mrs. Leffingwell, is the fact that Mr. Leffingwell will only nibble at your food. I don't understand it, as he looks like a healthy man."

"'Twouldn't do for me to be too hearty," said Leffingwell, "or I'd keep Mandy here cookin' all the time."

They seemed pleasant people to Dick, good, honest mountain types, and he was glad that he had found their house. The room in which they sat was large, apparently used for all purposes, kitchen, dining-room, sitting-room, and bedroom. An old-fashioned squirrel rifle lay on hooks projecting from the wall, but there was no other sign of a weapon. There was a bed at one end of the room and another at the other, which could be hidden by a rough woolen curtain running on a cord. Dick surmised that this bed would be assigned to him.

Their appetites grew lax and finally ceased. Then Leffingwell yawned and stretched his arms.

"Stranger," he said, "we rise early an' go to bed early in these parts. Thar ain't nothin' to keep us up in the evenin's, an' as you've had a hard, long ride I guess you're just achin' fur sleep."

Dick, although he had been unwilling to say so, was in fact very sleepy. The heavy supper and the heat of the room pulled so hard on his eyelids that he could scarcely keep them up. He murmured his excuses and said he believed he would like to retire.

"Don't you be bashful about sayin' so," exclaimed Leffingwell heartily, "'cause I don't think I could keep up more'n a half hour longer."

Mrs. Leffingwell drew the curtain shutting off one bed and a small space around it. Dick, used to primitive customs, said goodnight and retired within his alcove, taking his saddle bags. There was a small window near the foot of the room, and when he noticed it he resolved to let in a little air later on. The mountaineers liked hot rooms all the time, but he did not. This window contained no glass, but was closed with a broad shutter.

The boy undressed and got into bed, placing his saddle bags on the foot of it, and the pistol that he carried in his belt under his head. He fell asleep almost immediately and had he been asked beforehand he would have said that nothing could awake him before morning. Nevertheless he awoke before midnight, and it was a very slight thing that caused him to come out of sleep. Despite the languor produced by food and heat a certain nervous apprehension had been at work in the boy's mind, and it followed him into the unknown regions of sleep. His body was dead for a time and his mind too, but this nervous power worked on, almost independently of him. It had noted the sound of voices nearby, and awakened him, as if he had been shaken by a rough hand.

He sat up in his bed and became conscious of a hot and aching head. Then he remembered the window, and softly drawing two pegs that fastened it in order that he might not awaken his good hosts, he opened it inward a few inches.

The cold air poured in at the crevice and felt like heaven on his face. His temples quit throbbing and his head ceased to ache. He had not noticed at first the cause that really awakened him, but as he settled back into bed, grateful for the fresh air, the same mysterious power gave him a second warning signal.

He heard the hum of voices and sat up again. It was merely the Leffingwells in the bed at the far end of the room, talking!

Perhaps he had not been asleep more than an hour, and it was natural that they should lie awake a while, talking about the coming of this young stranger or any other event of the day that interested them. Then he caught a tone or an inflection that he did not remember to have been used by either of the Leffingwells. A third signal of alarm was promptly registered on his brain.

He leaned from the bed and pulling aside the curtain a half an inch or so, looked into the room. The fire had died down except a few coals which cast but a faint light. Yet it was sufficient to show Dick that the two Leffingwells had not gone to bed. They were sitting fully clothed before the fireplace, and three other persons were with them.

As Dick stared his eyes grew more used to the half dusk and he saw clearly. The three strangers were young men, all armed heavily, and the resemblance of two of them to the Leffingwells was so striking that he had no doubt they were their sons. Now he understood about those empty stalls. The third man, who had been sitting with his shoulder toward Dick, turned his face presently, and the boy with difficulty repressed an exclamation. It was the one who had reined his horse across the road to stop him. A fourth and conclusive signal of alarm was registered upon his brain.

He began to dress rapidly and without noise. Meanwhile he listened intently and could hear the words they spoke. The woman was pleading with them to let him go. He was only a harmless lad, and while these were dark days, a crime committed now might yet be punished.

"A harmless boy," said the strange man. "He's quick, an' strong enough, I tell you. You should have seen how he rode me down, and then shot Garmon in the arm."

"I'd like to have that hoss of his," said the elder Leffingwell. "He's the finest brute I ever laid eyes on. Sech power an' sech action. I noticed him at once, when Mason come ridin' up. S'pose we jest take the hoss and send the boy on."

"A hoss like that would be knowed," protested the woman. "What if sojers come lookin' fur him!"

"We could run him off in the hills an' keep him there a while," said Leffingwell. "I know places where sojers wouldn't find that hoss in a thousand years. What do you say to that, Kerins?"

"Good as fur as it goes," replied Kerins, "but it don't go fur enough by a long shot. The Yanks whipped the Johnnies in a big battle at Mill Spring. Me an' my pardners have been hangin' 'roun' in the woods, seein' what would happen. Now, we know that this boy rode straight from the tent of General Thomas hisself. He's a Union sojer, an' young as he is, he's an officer. He wouldn't be sent

85

out by General Thomas hisself 'less it was on big business. He's got messages, dispatches of some kind that are worth a heap to somebody. With all the armies gatherin' in the south an' west of the state it stands to reason that them dispatches mean a lot. Now, we've got to get 'em an' get the full worth of 'em from them to whom they're worth the most."

"He's got a pistol," said the elder Leffingwell, "I seed it in his belt. If he wakes before we grab him he'll shoot."

The man Kerins laughed.

"He'll never get a chance to shoot," he said. "Why, after all he went through today, he'll sleep like a log till mornin'."

"That's so," said one of the young Leffingwells, "an' Kerins is right. We ought to grab them dispatches. Likely in one way or another we kin git a heap fur 'em."

"Shut up, Jim, you fool," said his mother sharply. "Do you want murder on your hands? Stealin' hosses is bad enough, but if that boy has got the big dispatches you say he has, an' he's missin', don't you think that sojers will come after him? An' they'll trace him to this house, an' I tell you that in war trials don't last long. Besides, he's a nice boy an' he spoke nice all the time to pap an' me."

But her words did not seem to make any impression upon the others, except her husband, who protested again that it would be enough to take the horse. As for the dispatches it wasn't wise for them to fool with such things. But Kerins insisted on going the whole route and the young Leffingwells were with him.

Meanwhile Dick had dressed with more rapidity than ever before in his life, fully alive to the great dangers that threatened. But his fear was greatest lest he might lose the precious dispatches that he bore. For a few moments he did not know what to do. He might take his pistols and fight, but he could not fight them all with success. Then that pleasant flood of cold air gave him the key.

While they were still talking he put his saddle bags over his arm, opened the shutter its full width, and dropped quietly to the ground outside, remembering to take the precaution of closing the shutter behind him, lest the sudden inrush of cold startle the Leffingwells and their friends.

It was an icy night, but Dick did not stop to notice it. He ran to the stable, saddled and bridled his horse in two minutes, and in another minute was flying westward over the flinty road, careless whether or not they heard the beat of his horse's hoofs.

# CHAPTER VIII

## A MEETING AT NIGHT

Dick heard above the thundering hoofbeats only a single shout, and then, as he glanced backward, the house was lost in the moonlight. When he secured his own horse he had noticed that all the empty stalls were now filled, no doubt by the horses of the young Leffingwells and Kerins, but he was secure in his confidence that none could overtake the one he rode.

He felt of that inside pocket of his vest. The precious dispatch was there, tightly pinned into its hidden refuge, and as for himself, refreshed, warm, and strong after food, rest, and sleep, he felt equal to any emergency. He had everything with him. The stout saddle bags were lying across the saddle. He had thrust the holster of pistols into them, but he took it out now, and hung it in its own place, also across the saddle.

Although he was quite sure there would be no pursuit—the elder Leffingwells would certainly keep their sons from joining it— he sent his great horse straight ahead at a good pace for a long time, the road being fairly good. His excitement and rapid motion kept him from noticing at first the great bitterness of the cold.

When he had gone five or six miles he drew his horse down to a walk. Then, feeling the intensity of the cold as the mercury was far below zero, he dismounted, looped the reins over his arms, and walked a while. For further precaution he took his blanket-roll and wrapped the two blankets about his body, especially protecting his neck and ears.

He found that the walking, besides keeping him warmer, took all the stiffness out of his muscles, and he continued on foot several miles. He passed two brooks and a creek, all frozen over so solidly that the horse passed on them without breaking the ice. It was an extremely difficult task to make the animal try the ice, but after much delicate coaxing and urging he always succeeded.

He saw two more cabins at the roadside, but he did not think of asking hospitality at either. The night was now far advanced and he wished to put many more miles between him and the Leffingwell home before he sought rest again.

He mounted his horse once more, and increased his speed. Now the reaction came after so much exertion and excitement. He began to feel depressed. He was very young and he had no comrade. The loneliness of the winter night in a country full of dangers was appalling. It seemed to him, as his heart sank, that all things had conspired against him. But the moment of despair was brief. He summoned his courage anew and rode on bravely, although the sense of loneliness in its full power remained.

The moonlight was quite bright. The sky was a deep silky blue, in which myriads of cold stars shone and danced. By and by he skirted for a while the banks of a small river, which he knew flowed southward into the Cumberland, and which would not cross his path. The rays of the moonlight on its frozen surface looked like darts of cold steel.

He left the river presently and the road bent a little toward the north. Then the skies darkened somewhat but lightened again as the dawn began to come. The red but cold edge of the sun appeared above the mountains that he had left behind, and then the morning came, pale and cold.

Dick stopped at a little brook, broke the ice and drank, letting his horse drink after him. Then he ate heartily of the cold bread and meat in his knapsack. Pitying his horse he searched until he found a little grass not yet killed by winter in the lee of the hill, and waited until he cropped it all.

He mounted and resumed his journey through a country in which the hills were steadily becoming lower, with larger stretches of level land appearing between them. By night he should be beyond the last low swell of the mountains and into the hill region proper. As he calculated distances his heart gave a great thump. He was to locate Buell some distance north of Green River, and his journey would take him close to Pendleton.

The boy was torn by great and conflicting emotions. He would carry out with his life the task that Thomas had assigned to him, and yet he wished to stop near Pendleton, if only for an hour.

Yes an hour would do! And it could not interfere with his duty! But Pendleton was a Southern stronghold. Everybody there knew him, and they all knew, too, that he was in the service of the North. How could he pass by without being seen and what might happen then? The terrible conflict went on in his mind, and it was stilled only when he decided to leave it to time and chance.

He rode that day almost without interruption, securing an ample dinner, where no one chose to ask questions, accepting him at his own statement of himself and probably believing it. He heard that a small Southern force was to the southward, probably marching toward Bowling Green, where a great Confederate army under Albert Sidney Johnston was said to be concentrated. But the news gave him no alarm. His own road was still leading west slightly by north.

When night came he was in the pleasant and fertile hill country, dotted with double brick houses, and others of wood, all with wide porticos, supported by white pillars. It looked smiling and prosperous even in winter. The war had done no ravages here, and he saw men at work about the great barns.

He slept in the house of a big farmer, who liked the frank voice and eyes of the lad, and who cared nothing for any errand upon which he might be riding. He slept, too, without dreams, and without awakening until the morning, when he shared a solid breakfast with the family.

Dick obtained at the farmhouse a fresh supply of cold food for his saddle bags, to be held against an emergency, although it was likely now that he could obtain all he needed at houses as he passed. Receiving the good wishes of his hosts he rode on through the hills. The intense cold which kept troops from marching much really served him, as the detachments about the little towns stayed in their camps.

The day was quite clear, with the mercury still well below zero, but his heavy clothing kept him warm and comfortable. His great horse showed no signs of weariness. Apparently his sinews were made of steel.

Noon came, but Dick did not seek any farmhouse for what was called dinner in that region. Instead he ate from his saddle bags as he rode on. He did not wish to waste time, and, moreover, he had taken his resolution. He would go near Pendleton. It was on his most direct route, but he would pass in the night.

As the cold twilight descended he came into familiar regions. Like all other young Kentuckians he was a great horseman, and with Harry Kenton and other lads of his age he had ridden nearly everywhere in a circuit of thirty miles around Pendleton.

It was with many a throb of the heart that he now recognized familiar scenes. He knew the fields, the forests and the houses. But he was glad that the night had come. Others would know him, and he did not wish to be seen when he rode on such an errand. He had been saving his horse in the afternoon, but now he pushed him forward at a much faster gait. The great horse responded willingly and Dick felt the powerful body working beneath him, smooth and tireless like a perfect machine.

He passed nobody on the road. People hugged their fires on such a cold night, and he rode hour after hour without interruption. It was nearly midnight when he stopped on a high hill, free of forest, and looked down upon Pendleton. The wonderful clearness of the winter night helped him. All the stars known to man were out, and helped to illuminate the world with a clear but cold radiance.

Although a long distance away Dick could see Pendleton clearly. There was no foliage on the trees now, and nearly every house was visible. The great pulse in his throat throbbed hard as he looked. He saw the steeples of the churches, the white pillars of the court house, and off to one side the academy in which he and Harry Kenton had gone to school together. He saw further away Colonel Kenton's own house on another hill. It, too, had porticos, supported by white pillars which gleamed in the moonlight.

Then his eyes traveled again around the half circle before him. The place for which he was looking could not be seen. But he knew that it would be so. It was a low house, and the evergreens about it, the pines and cedars would hide it at any time. But he knew the exact spot, and he wanted his eyes to linger there a little before he rode straight for it.

Now the great pulse in his throat leaped, and something like a sob came from him. But it was not a sob of unhappiness. He clucked to his horse and turned from the main road into a narrower one that led by the low house among the evergreens. Yet he was a boy of powerful will, and despite his eagerness, he restrained his horse and advanced very slowly. Sometimes he turned the animal upon the dead turf by the side of the road in order that his footsteps might make no sound.

He drew slowly nearer, and when he saw the roof and eaves of the low house among the evergreens the great pulse in his throat leaped so hard that it was almost unbearable. He reached the edge of the lawn that came down to the road, and hidden by the clipped cone of a pine he saw a faint light shining.

He dismounted, opened the gate softly, and led his horse upon the lawn, hitching him between two pines that grew close together, concealing him perfectly.

"Be quiet, old fellow," he whispered, stroking the great intelligent head. "Nobody will find you here and I'll come back for you."

The horse rubbed his nose against his arm but made no other movement. Then Dick walked softly toward the house, pulses beating hard and paused just at the edge of a portico, where he stood in the shadow of a pillar. He saw the light clearly now. It shone from a window of the low second story. It came from her window and her room. Doubtless she was thinking at that very moment of him. His throat ached and tears came into his eyes. The light, clear and red, shone steadily from the window and made a band across the lawn.

He picked a handful of sand from the walk that led to the front door and threw it against the window. He knew that she was brave and would respond, but waiting only a moment or two he threw a second handful fully and fairly against the glass.

The lower half of the window was thrown open and a head appeared, where the moonlight fell clearly upon it. It was the head of a beautiful woman, framed in thick, silken yellow hair, the eyes deep blue, and the skin of the wonderful fairness so often found in that state. The face was that of a woman about thirty-seven or eight years of age, and without a wrinkle or flaw.

"Mother!" called Dick in a low voice as he stepped from the shadow of the pillar.

There was a cry and the face disappeared like a flash from the window. But he had only a few moments to wait. Her swift feet brought her from the room, down the stairway, and along the hall to the door, which she threw open. The next instant Mrs. Mason had her son in her arms.

"Oh, Dick, Dicky, boy, how did you come!" she exclaimed. "You were here under my window, and I did not even know that you were alive!"

Her tears of joy fell upon his face and he was moved profoundly. Dick loved his beautiful young mother devoutly, and her widowhood had bound them all the more closely together.

"I've come a long distance, and I've come in many ways, mother," he replied, "by train, by horseback, and I have even walked."

"You have come here on foot?"

"No, mother. I rode directly over your own smooth lawn on one of the biggest horses you ever saw, and he's tied now between two of the pine trees. Come, we must go in the house. It's too cold for you out here. Do you know that the mercury is about ten degrees below zero."

"What a man you have grown! Why, you must be two inches taller than you were, when you went away, and how sunburned and weather-beaten you are, too! Oh, Dicky, this terrible, terrible war! Not a word from you in months has got through to me!"

"Nor a word from you to me, mother, but I have not suffered so much so far. I was at Bull Run, where we lost, and I was at Mill Spring, where we won, but I was unhurt."

"Perhaps you have come back to stay," she said hopefully.

"No, mother, not to stay. I took a chance in coming by here to see you, but I couldn't go on without a few minutes. Inside now, mother, your hands are growing cold."

They went in at the door, and closed it behind them. But there was another faithful soul on guard that night. In the dusky hall loomed a gigantic black figure in a blue checked dress, blue turban on head.

"Marse Dick?" she said.

"Juliana!" he exclaimed. "How did you know that I was here?"

"Ain't I done heard Miss Em'ly cry out, me always sleepin' so light, an' I hears her run down the hail. An' then I dresses an' comes an' sees you two through the crack o' the do', an' then I waits till you come in."

Dick gave her a most affectionate greeting, knowing that she was as true as steel. She rejoiced in her flowery name, as many other colored women rejoiced in theirs, but her heart inhabited exactly the right spot in her huge anatomy. She drew mother and son into the sitting-room, where low coals still burned on the hearth. Then she went up to Mrs. Mason's bedroom and put out the light, after which she came back to the sitting-room, and, standing by a window in silence, watched over the two over whom she had watched so long.

"Why is it that you can stay such a little while?" asked Mrs. Mason.

"Mother," replied Dick in a low tone, "General Thomas, who won the battle at Mill Spring, has trusted me. I bear a dispatch of great importance. It is to go to General Buell, and it has to do with the gathering of the Union troops in the western and southern parts of our state, and in Tennessee. I must get through with it, and in war, mother, time counts almost as much as battles. I can stop only a few minutes even for you."

"I suppose it is so. But oh, Dicky, won't this terrible war be over soon?"

"I don't think so, mother. It's scarcely begun yet."

Mrs. Mason said nothing, but stared into the coals. The great negress, Juliana, standing at the window, did not move.

"I suppose you are right, Dick," she said at last with a sigh, "but it is awful that our people should be arrayed so against one another. There is your cousin, Harry Kenton, a good boy, too, on the other side."

"Yes, mother, I caught a glimpse of him at Bull Run. We came almost face to face in the smoke. But it was only for an instant. Then the smoke rushed in between. I don't think anything serious has happened to him."

Mrs. Mason shuddered.

"I should mourn him next to you," she said, "and my brother-in-law, Colonel Kenton, has been very good. He left orders with his people to watch over us here. Pendleton is strongly Southern as you know, but nobody would do us any harm, unless it was the rough people from the hills."

Colonel Kenton's wife had been Mrs. Mason's elder sister, and Dick, as he also sat staring into the coals, wondered why people who were united so closely should yet be divided so much.

"Mother," he said, "when I came through the mountains with my friends we stopped at a house in which lived an old, old woman. She must have been nearly a hundred. She knew your ancestor and mine, the famous and learned Paul Cotter, from whom you and I are descended, and she also knew his friend and comrade, the mighty scout and hunter, Henry Ware, who became the great governor of Kentucky."

"How strange!"

"But the strangest is yet to be told. Harry Kenton, when he went east to join Beauregard before Bull Run, stopped at the same house, and when she first saw him she only looked into the far past. She thought it was Henry Ware himself, and she saluted him as the governor. What do you think of that, mother?"

"It's a startling coincidence."

"But may it not be an omen? I'm not superstitious, mother, but when things come together in such a queer fashion it's bound to make you think. When Harry's paths and mine cross in such a manner maybe it means that we shall all come together again, and be united as we were."

"Maybe."

"At any rate," said Dick with a little laugh, "we'll hope that it does."

While the boy was not noticing his mother had made a sign to Juliana, who had crept out of the room. Now she returned, bearing food upon a tray, and Dick, although he was not hungry, ate to please his mother.

"You will stay until morning?" she said.

"No, mother. I can't afford to be seen here. I must leave in the dark."

"Then until it is nearly morning."

"Nor that either, mother. My time is about up already. I could never betray the trust that General Thomas has put in me. My dispatches not only tell of the gathering of our own troops, but they contain invaluable information concerning the Confederate concentration which General Thomas learned from his scouts and spies. Mother, I think a great battle is coming here in the west."

She shuddered, but she did not seek again to delay him in his duty.

"I am proud," she said, "that you have won the confidence of your general, and that you ride upon such an important errand. I should have been glad if you had stayed at home, Dick, but since you have chosen to be a soldier, I am rejoiced that you have risen in the esteem of your officers. Write to me as often as you can. Maybe none of your letters will reach me, but at least start them. I shall start mine, too."

"Of course, mother," said Dick, "and now it's time for me to ride hard."

"Why, you have been here only a half hour!"

"Nearer an hour, mother, and on this journey of mine time means a lot. I must say good-bye now to you and Juliana."

The two women followed him down the lawn to the point where his horse was hitched between the two big pines. Mrs. Mason patted the horse's great head and murmured to him to carry her son well.

"Did you ever see a finer horse, mother?" said Dick proudly. "He's the very pick of the army."

He threw his arms around her neck, kissed her more than once, sprang into the saddle and rode away in the darkness.

The two women, the black and the white, sisters in grief, and yet happy that he had come, went slowly back into the house to wait, while the boy, a man's soul in him, strode on to war.

Dick was far from Pendleton when the dawn broke, and now he had full need of caution. His horse was bearing him fast into debatable ground, where every man suspected his neighbor, and it remained for force alone to tell to which side the region belonged. But the extreme delicacy of the tension came to Dick's aid. People hesitated to ask questions, lest questions equally difficult be asked of them in return. It was a great time to mind one's own business.

He rode on, fortune with him for the present, and his course was still west slightly by north. He slept under roofs, and he learned that in the country into which he had now come the Union sympathizers were more numerous than the Confederate. The majority of the Kentuckians, whatever their personal feelings, were not willing to shatter the republic.

He heard definitely that here in the west the North was gathering armies greater than any that he had supposed. Besides the troops from the three states just across the Ohio River the hardy lumbermen and pioneers were pouring down from Michigan, Wisconsin, and Minnesota. Hunters in deerskin suits and buffalo moccasins had already come from the far Nebraska Territory.

The power of the west and the northwest was converging upon his state, which gave eighty thousand of its men to the Northern cause, while half as many more went away to the Southern armies,

94

particularly to the one under the brilliant and daring Albert Sidney Johnston, which hung a sinister menace before the Northern front. One hundred and twenty thousand troops sent to the two armies by a state that contained but little more than a million people! It was said at the time that as Kentucky went, so would go the fortunes of the Union and in the end it was so.

But these facts and reckonings were not much in Dick's mind just then. He was thinking of Buell's camp and of the message that he bore. Again and again he felt of that little inside pocket of his vest to see that it was there, although he knew that by no chance could he have lost it.

When he was within fifteen miles of Buell's camp a heavy snow began to fall. But he did not mind it. The powerful horse that had borne him so well carried him safely on to his destination, and before the sundown of that day the young messenger was standing before General Don Carlos Buell, one of the most puzzling characters whom he was to meet in the whole course of the war. He had found Thomas a silent man, but he found Buell even more so. He received Dick in an ordinary tent, thanked him as he saluted and handed him the dispatch, and then read General Thomas' message.

Dick saw before him a shortish, thickset man, grim of feature, who did not ask him a word until he had finished the dispatch.

"You know what this contains?" he said, when he came to the end.

"Yes, General Thomas made me memorize it, that I might destroy it if I were too hard pressed."

"He tells us that Johnston is preparing for some great blow and he gives the numbers and present location of the hostile forces. Valuable information for us, if it is used. You have done well, Mr. Mason. To what force were you attached?"

"A small division of Pennsylvania troops under Major Hertford. They were to be sent by General Thomas to General Grant at Cairo, Illinois."

"And you would like to join them."

"If you please, sir."

"In view of your services your wish is granted. It is likely that General Grant will need all the men whom he can get. A detachment leaves here early in the morning for Elizabethtown, where it takes the train for Louisville, proceeding thence by water to Cairo. You shall go with these men. They are commanded by Colonel Winchester. You may go now, Mr. Mason."

He turned back to his papers and Dick, thinking his manner somewhat curt, left his tent. But he was pleased to hear that the detail was commanded by Colonel Winchester. Arthur Winchester was a man of forty-one or two who lived about thirty miles north of Pendleton. He was a great landowner, of high character and pleasant manners. Dick had met him frequently in his childhood, and the Colonel received him with much warmth.

"I'm glad to know, Dick," he said familiarly, "that you're going with us. I'm fond of Pendleton, and I like to have one of the Pendleton boys in my command. If all that we hear of this man Grant is true, we'll see action, action hot and continuous."

They rode to Elizabethtown, where Dick was compelled to leave his great horse for Buell's men, and went by train to Louisville, going thence by steamer down the Ohio River to Cairo, at its junction with the Mississippi, where they stood at last in the presence of that general whose name was beginning to be known in the west.

# CHAPTER IX

## TAKING A FORT

Dick was with Colonel Winchester when he was admitted to the presence of the general who had already done much to strengthen the Union cause in the west, and he found him the plainest and simplest of men, under forty, short in stature, and careless in attire. He thanked Colonel Winchester for the reinforcement that he had brought him, and then turned with some curiosity to Dick.

"So you were at the battle of Mill Spring," he said. "It was hot, was it not?"

"Hot enough for me," replied Dick frankly.

Grant laughed.

"They caught a Tartar in George Thomas," he said, "and I fancy that others who try to catch him will be glad enough to let him go."

"He is a great man, sir," said Dick with conviction.

Then Grant asked him more questions about the troops and the situation in Eastern Kentucky, and Dick noticed that all were sharp and penetrating.

"Your former immediate commander, Major Hertford, and some of his men are due here today," said Grant. "General Thomas, knowing that his own campaign was over, sent them north to Cincinnati and they have come down the river to Cairo. When they reach here they will be attached to the regiment of Colonel Winchester."

Dick was overjoyed. He had formed a strong liking for Major Hertford and he was quite sure that Warner and Sergeant Whitley would be with him. Once more they would be reunited, reunited for battle. He could not doubt that they would go to speedy action as the little town at the junction of the mighty rivers resounded with preparation.

When Colonel Winchester and the boy had saluted and retired from General Grant's tent they saw the smoke pouring from the funnels of numerous steamers in the Mississippi, and they saw thousands of troops encamped in tents along the shores of both the Ohio and Mississippi. Heavy cannon were drawn up on the wharves, and ammunition and supplies were being transferred from hundreds of wagons to the steamers. It was evident to any one that this expedition, whatever it might be, was to proceed by water. It was a land of mighty rivers, close together, and a steamer might go anywhere.

As Dick and Colonel Winchester, on whose staff he would now be, were watching this active scene, a small steamer, coming down the Ohio, drew in to a wharf, and a number of soldiers in faded blue disembarked. The boy uttered a shout of joy.

"What is it, Dick?" asked Colonel Winchester.

"Why, sir, there's my former commander, Colonel Newcomb, and just behind him is my comrade, Lieutenant George Warner of Vermont, and not far away is Sergeant Whitley, late of the regular army, one of the best soldiers in the world. Can I greet them, colonel?"

"Of course."

Dick rushed forward and saluted Colonel Newcomb, who grasped him warmly by the hand.

"So you got safely through, my lad," he said. "Major Hertford, who came down the Kentucky with his detachment and joined us at Carrollton at the mouth of that river, told us of your mission. The major is bringing up the rear of our column, but here are other friends of yours."

Dick the next moment was wringing the hand of the Vermont boy and was receiving an equally powerful grip in return.

"I believed that we would meet you here," said Warner, "I calculated that with your courage, skill and knowledge of the country the chances were at least eighty per cent in favor of your getting through to Buell. And if you did get through to Buell I knew that at least ninety per cent of the circumstances would represent your desire and effort to come here. That was a net percentage of seventy-two in favor of meeting you here in Cairo, and the seventy-two per cent has prevailed, as it usually does."

"Nothing is so bad that it can't be worse," said Sergeant Whitley, as he too gave Dick's hand an iron grasp, "and I knew that when we lost you we'd be pretty glad to see you again. Here you are safe an' sound, an' here we are safe an' sound, a most satisfactory condition in war."

"But not likely to remain so long, judging from what we see here," said Warner. "We hear that this man Grant is a restless sort of a person who thinks that the way to beat the enemy is just to go in and beat him."

Major Hertford came up at that moment, and he, too, gave Dick a welcome that warmed his heart. But the boy did not get to remain long with his old comrades. The Pennsylvania regiment had been much cut down through the necessity of leaving detachments as guards at various places along the river, but it was yet enough to make a skeleton and its entity was preserved, forming a little eastern band among so many westerners.

Dick, at General Grant's order, was transferred permanently to the staff of Colonel Winchester, and he and the other officers slept that night in a small building in the outskirts of Cairo. He knew that a great movement was at hand, but he was becoming so thoroughly inured to danger and hardship that he slept soundly all through the night.

They heard early the next morning the sound of many trumpets and Colonel Winchester's regiment formed for embarkation. All the puffing steamers were now in the Ohio, and Dick saw with them many other vessels which were not used for carrying soldiers. He saw broad, low boats, with flat bottoms, their sides sheathed in iron plates. They were floating batteries moved by powerful engines beneath. Then there were eight huge mortars, a foot across the muzzle, every one mounted separately upon a strong barge and towed. Some of the steamers were sheathed in iron also.

Dick's heart throbbed hard when he saw the great equipment. The fighting ships were under the command of Commodore Foote, an able man, but General Grant and his lieutenants, General McClernand and General Smith, commanded the army aboard the transports. On the transport next to them Dick saw the Pennsylvanians and he waved his hand to his friends who stood on the deck. They waved back, and Dick felt powerfully the sense of comradeship. It warmed his heart for them all to be together again, and it was a source of strength, too.

The steamer that bore his regiment was named the River Queen, and many of her cabins had been torn away to make more room for the troops who would sleep in rows on her decks, as thick as buffaloes in a herd. The soldiers, like all the others whom he saw, were mostly boys. The average could not be over twenty, and some were not over sixteen. But they had the adaptability of youth. They had scattered themselves about in easy positions. One was playing an accordion, and another a fiddle. The officers did not interrupt them.

As Dick looked over the side at the yellow torrent some one said beside him:

"This is a whopping big river. You don't see them as deep as this where I come from."

Dick glanced at the speaker, and saw a lad of about his own age, of medium height, but powerfully built, with shoulders uncommonly thick. His face was tanned brown, but his eyes were blue and his natural complexion was fair. He was clad completely in deerskin, mocassins on his feet and a raccoon skin cap on his head.

Dick had noticed the Nebraska hunters in such garb, but he was surprised to see this boy dressed in similar fashion among the Kentuckians.

The youth smiled when he saw Dick's glance of surprise.

"I know I look odd among you," he said, "and you take me for one of the Nebraska hunters. So I am, but I'm a Kentuckian, too, and I've a right to a place with you fellows. My name is Frank Pennington. I was born about forty miles north of Pendleton, but when I was six months old my parents went out on the plains, where I've hunted buffalo, and where I've fought Indians, too. But I'm a Kentuckian by right of birth just as you are, and I asked to be assigned to the regiment raised in the region from which we came."

"And mighty welcome you are, too," said Dick, offering his hand. "You belong with us, and we'll stick together on this campaign."

The two youths, one officer and one private, became fast friends in a moment. Events move swiftly in war. Both now felt the great engines throbbing faster beneath them, and the flotilla, well into the mouth of the Ohio, was leaving the Mississippi behind them. But the Ohio here for a distance is apparently the mightier stream, and they gazed with interest and a certain awe at the vast yellow sheet enclosed by shores, somber in the gray garb of winter. It was the beginning of February, and cold winds swept down from the Illinois prairies. Cairo had been left behind and there was no sign of human habitation. Some wild fowl, careless of winter, flew over the stream, dipped toward the water, and then flew away again.

As far as the eye was concerned the wilderness circled about them and enclosed them. The air was cold and flakes of snow dropped upon the decks and the river, but were gone in an instant. The skies were an unbroken sheet of gray. The scene so lonely and desolate contained a majesty that impressed them all, heightened for these youths by the knowledge that many of them were going on a campaign from which they would never return.

"Looks as wild as the great plains on which I've hunted with my father," said Pennington.

"But we hunt bigger game than buffalo," said Dick.

"Game that is likely to turn and hunt us."

"Yes."

"Do you know where we're going?"

"Not exactly, but I can make a good guess. I know that we've taken on Tennessee River pilots, and I'm sure that we'll turn into the mouth of that river at Paducah. I infer that we're to attack Fort Henry, which the Confederates have erected some distance up the Tennessee to guard that river."

100

"Looks likely. Do you know much about the fort?"

"I've heard of it only since I came to Cairo. I know that it stands on low, marshy ground facing the Tennessee, and that it contains seventeen big guns. I haven't heard anything about the size of its garrison."

"But we'll have a fight, that's sure," said young Pennington. "I've been in battle only once—at Columbus—but the Johnny Rebs don't give up forts in a hurry."

"There's another fort, a much bigger one, named Donelson, on the Cumberland," said Dick. "Both the forts are in Tennessee, but as the two rivers run parallel here in the western parts of the two states, Fort Donelson and Fort Henry are not far apart. I risk a guess that we attack both."

"You don't risk much. I tell you, Dick, that man Grant is a holy terror. He isn't much to look at, but he's a marcher and a fighter. We fellows in the ranks soon learn what kind of a man is over us. I suppose it's like the horse feeling through the bit the temper of his rider. President Lincoln has stationed General Halleck at St. Louis with general command here in the West. General Halleck thinks that General Grant is a meek subordinate without ambition, and will always be sending back to him for instructions, which is just what General Halleck likes, but we in the ranks have learned to know our Grant better."

Dick's eyes glistened.

"So you think, then," he said, "that General Grant will push this campaign home, and that he'll soon be where he can't get instructions from General Halleck?"

"Looks that way to a man up a tree," said Pennington slowly, and solemnly winking his left eye.

They were officer and private, but they were only lads together, and they talked freely with each other. Dick, after a while, returned to his commanding officer, Colonel Winchester, but there was little to do, and he sat on the deck with him, looking out over the fleet, the transports, the floating batteries, the mortar boats, and the iron-clads. He saw that the North, besides being vastly superior in numbers and resources, was the supreme master on the water through her equipment and the mechanical skill of her people. The South had no advantage save the defensive, and the mighty generals of genius who appeared chiefly on her Virginia line.

Dick had inherited a thoughtful temperament from his famous ancestor, Paul Cotter, whose learning had appeared almost superhuman to the people of his time, and he was extremely sensitive to impressions. His mind would register them with instant truth. As he looked now upon this floating army he felt that the

Union cause must win. On land the Confederates might be invincible or almost so, but the waters of the rivers and the sea upheld the Union cause.

The fleet steamed on at an even pace. Foote, the commodore who had daringly reconnoitered Fort Henry from a single gunboat in the Tennessee, managed everything with alertness and skill. The transports were in the center of the stream. The armed and armored vessels kept on the flanks.

The river, a vast yellow sheet, sometimes turning gray under the gray, wintry skies, seemed alone save for themselves. Not a single canoe or skiff disturbed its surface. Toward evening the flakes of snow came again, and the bitter wind blew once more from the Illinois prairies. All the troops who were not under shelter were wrapped in blankets or overcoats. Dick and the colonel, with the heavy coats over their uniforms, did not suffer. Instead, they enjoyed the cold, crisp air, which filled their lungs and seemed to increase their power.

"When shall we reach the Tennessee?" asked Dick.

"You will probably wake up in the morning to find yourself some distance up that stream."

"I've never seen the Tennessee."

"Though not the equal of the Ohio, it would be called a giant river in many countries. The whole fleet, if it wanted to do it, could go up it hundreds of miles. Why, Dick, these boats can go clear down into Alabama, into the very heart of the Confederacy, into the very state at the capital of which Jefferson Davis was inaugurated President of the seceding states."

"I was thinking of that some time ago," said Dick. "The water is with us."

"Yes, the water is with us, and will stay with us."

They were silent a little while longer and watched the coming of the early winter twilight over the waters and the lonely land. The sky was so heavy with clouds that the gray seemed to melt into the brown. The low banks slipped back into the dark. They saw only the near surface of the river, the dark hulls of the fleet, occasional showers of sparks from smoke stacks, and an immense black cloud made by the smoke of the fleet, trailing behind them far down the river.

"Dick," said Colonel Winchester suddenly, "as you came across Kentucky from Mill Spring, and passed so near Pendleton it must have been a great temptation to you to stop and see your mother."

"It was. It was so great that I yielded to it. I was at our home about midnight for nearly an hour. I hope I did nothing wrong, colonel."

"No, Dick, my boy. Some martinets might find fault with you, but I should blame you had you not stopped for those few moments. A noble woman, your mother, Dick. I hope that she is watched over well."

Dick glanced at the colonel, but he could not see his face in the deepening twilight.

"My uncle, Colonel Kenton, has directed his people to give her help in case of need," he replied, "but that means physical help against raiders and guerillas. Otherwise she has sufficient for her support."

"That is well. War is terrible on women. And now, Dick, my lad, we'll get our supper. This nipping air makes me hungry, and the Northern troops do not suffer for lack of food."

The officers ate in one of the cabins, and when the supper was finished deep night had come over the river, but Dick, standing on the deck, heard the heavy throb of many engines, and he knew that a great army was still around him, driven on by the will of one man, deep into the country of the foe.

The decks, every foot of plank it seemed, were already covered with the sleeping boys, wrapped in their blankets and overcoats. He saw his friend, the young hunter from Nebraska, lying with his head on his arm, sound asleep, a smile on his face.

Dick watched until the first darkness thinned somewhat, and the stars came out. Then he retired to one of the cabins, which he shared with three or four others, and slept soundly until he was aroused for breakfast. He had not undressed, and, bathing his face, he went out at once on the deck. Many of the soldiers were up, there was a hum of talk, and all were looking curiously at the river up which they were steaming.

They were in the Tennessee, having passed in the night the little town of Paducah—now an important city—at its mouth. It was not so broad as the Ohio, but it was broad, nevertheless, and it had the aspect of great depth. But here, as on the Ohio, they seemed to be steaming through the wilderness. The banks were densely wooded, and the few houses that may have been near were hidden by the trees. No human beings appeared upon the banks.

Dick knew why the men did not come forth to see the ships. The southwestern part of the state, the old Jackson's Purchase, and the region immediately adjacent, was almost solidly for the South. They would not find here that division of sentiment, with the majority inclined to the North, that prevailed in the higher regions of Kentucky. The country itself was different. It was low and the waters that came into the Tennessee flowed more sluggishly.

But Dick was sure that keen eyes were watching the fleet from the undergrowth, and he had no doubt that every vessel had long since been counted and that every detail of the fleet had been carried to the Southern garrisons in the fort.

The cold was as sharp as on the day before, and Dick, like the others, rejoiced in the hot and abundant breakfast. The boats, an hour or two later, stopped at a little landing, and many of the lads would gladly have gone ashore for a few moments, risking possible sharpshooters in the woods, but not one was allowed to leave the vessels. But Dick's steamer lay so close to the one carrying the Pennsylvanians that he could talk across the few intervening feet of water with Warner and Whitley. He also took the opportunity to introduce his new friend Pennington, of Nebraska.

"Are you the son of John Pennington, who lived for a little while at Fort Omaha?" asked the sergeant.

"Right you are," replied the young hunter, "I'm his third son."

"Then you're the third son of a brave man. I was in the regular army and often we helped the pioneers against the Indians. I remember being in one fight with him against the Sioux on the Platte, and in another against the Northern Cheyennes in the Jumping Sand Hills."

"Hurrah!" cried Pennington. "I'm sorry I can't jump over a section of the Tennessee River and shake hands with you."

"We'll have our chance later," said the sergeant. At that moment the fleet started again, and the boats swung apart. Through Dick's earnest solicitation young Pennington was taken out of the ranks and attached to the staff of Colonel Winchester as an orderly. He was well educated, already a fine campaigner, and beyond a doubt he would prove extremely useful.

They steamed the entire day without interruption. Now and then the river narrowed and they ran between high banks. The scenery became romantic and beautiful, but always wild. The river, deep at any time, was now swollen fifteen feet more by floods on its upper courses, and the water always lapped at the base of the forest.

Dick and Pennington, standing side by side, saw the second sun set over their voyage, and it was as wild and lonely as the first. There was a yellow river again, and hills covered with a bare forest. Heavy gray clouds trooped across the sky, and the sun was lost among them before it sank behind the hills in the west.

Dick and Pennington, wrapped in their blankets and overcoats, slept upon the deck that night, with scores of others strewed about them. They were awakened after eleven o'clock by a sputter of rifle shots. Dick sat up in a daze and heard a bullet hum by his ear. Then he heard a powerful voice shouting: "Down! Down, all of you! It's only some skirmishers in the woods!" Then a cannon on one of the armor clads thundered, and a shell ripped its way through the underbrush on the west bank. Many exclamations were uttered by the half-awakened lads.

"What is it? Has an army attacked us?"

"Are we before the fort and under fire?"

"Take your foot off me, you big buffalo!"

It was Colonel Winchester who had commanded them to keep down, but Dick, a staff officer, knew that it did not apply to him. Instead he sprang erect and assisted the senior officers in compelling the others to lie flat upon the decks. He saw several flashes of fire in the undergrowth, but he had logic enough to know that it could only be a small Southern band. Three or four more shells raked the woods, and then there was no reply.

The boats steamed steadily on. Only one or two of the young soldiers had been hurt and they but lightly. All rolled themselves again in their blankets and coats and went back to sleep.

The second awakening was about half way between midnight and dawn. Something cold was continually dropping on Dick's face and he awoke to find hundreds of sheeted and silent white forms lying motionless upon the deck. Snow was falling swiftly out of a dark sky, and the fleet was moving slowly. In the darkness and stillness the engines throbbed powerfully, and the night was lighted fitfully by the showers of sparks that gushed now and then from the smoke stacks.

Dick thought of rising and brushing the snow from his blankets, but he was so warm inside them that he yawned once or twice and went to sleep again. When he awoke it was morning again, the snow had ceased and the men were brushing it from themselves and the decks.

The young soldiers, as they ate breakfast, spoke of the rifle shots that had been fired at them the night before and, since little damage had been done, they appreciated the small spice of danger. The wildness and mystery of their situation appealed to them, too. They were like explorers, penetrating new regions.

"To most of us it's something like the great plains," said Pennington to Dick. "There you seldom know what you're coming to; maybe a blizzard, maybe a buffalo herd, and maybe a band of Indians, and you take a pleasure in the uncertainty. But I suppose it's not the same to you, this being your state."

"I don't know much about Western Kentucky," said Dick, "my part lies to the center and east, but anyway, our work is to be done in Tennessee. Those two forts, which I'm sure we're after, lie in that state."

"And when do you think we'll reach 'em?"

"Tomorrow, I suppose."

The day passed without any interruption to the advance of the fleet, although there was occasional firing, but not of a serious nature. Now and then small bands of Confederate skirmishers sent rifle shots from high points along the bank toward the fleet, but they did no damage and the ships steamed steadily on.

The third night out came, and again the young soldiers slept soundly, but the next morning, soon after breakfast, the whole fleet stopped in the middle of the river. A thrill of excitement ran through the army when the news filtered from ship to ship that they were now in Tennessee, and that Fort Henry, which they were to attack, was just ahead.

Nevertheless, they seemed to be yet in the wilderness. The Tennessee, in flood, spread its yellow waters through forest and undergrowth, and the chill gray sky still gave a uniform somber, gray tint to everything. Bugles blew in the boats, and every soldier began to put himself and his weapons in order. The command to make a landing had been given, and Commodore Foote was feeling about for a place.

Dick now realized the enormous advantage of supremacy upon the water. Had the Confederates possessed armored ships to meet them, the landing of a great army under fire would be impossible, but now they chose their own time and went about it unvexed.

A place was found at last, a rude wharf was constructed hastily, and the fleet disgorged the army, boat by boat. Vast quantities of stores and heavy cannon were also brought ashore. Despite the cold, Dick and his comrades perspired all the morning over their labors and were covered with mud when the camp was finally constructed at some distance back of the Tennessee, on the high ground beyond the overflow. The transports remained at anchor, but the fighting boats were to drop down the stream and attack the fort at noon the next day from the front, while the army assailed it at the same time from the rear.

The detachment of Pennsylvanians was by the side of Colonel Winchester's Kentucky regiment, and Colonel Newcomb and his staff messed with Colonel Winchester and his officers. There was water everywhere, and before they ate they washed the mud off themselves as best they could.

"I suppose," said Warner, "that seventy per cent of our work henceforth will be marching through the mud, and thirty per cent of it will be fighting the rebels in Fort Henry. I hear that we're not to attack until tomorrow, so I mean to sleep on top of a cannon tonight, lest I sink out of sight in the mud while I'm asleep."

"There's some pleasure," said Pennington, "in knowing that we won't die of thirst. You could hardly call this a parched and burning desert."

But as they worked all the remainder of the day on the construction of the camp, they did not care where they slept. When their work was over they simply dropped where they stood and slumbered soundly until morning.

The day opened with a mixture of rain, snow, and fiercely cold winds. Grant's army moved out of its camp to make the attack, but it was hampered by the terrible weather and the vast swamp through which its course must lead. Colonel Winchester, who knew the country better than any other high officer, was sent ahead on horseback with a small detachment to examine the way. He naturally took Dick and Pennington, who were on his staff, and by request, Colonel Newcomb, Major Hertford, Warner and Sergeant Whitley went also. The whole party numbered about a hundred men.

Dick and the other lads rejoiced over their mission. It was better to ride ahead than to remain with an army that was pulling itself along slowly through the mud. The fort itself was only about three miles away, and as it stood upon low, marshy ground, the backwater from the flooded Tennessee had almost surrounded it.

Despite their horses, Winchester's men found their own advance slow. They had to make many a twist and turn to avoid marshes and deep water before they came within the sight of the fort, and then Dick's watch told him that it was nearly noon, the time for the concerted attacks of army and fleet. But it was certain now that the army could not get up until several hours later, and he wondered what would happen.

They saw the fort very clearly from their position on a low hill, and they saw that the main Confederate force was gathered on a height outside, connected with the fort, and as well as he could judge, the mass seemed to number three or four thousand men.

"What does that mean?" he asked Colonel Winchester.

"I surmise," replied the colonel, "that Tilghman, the Confederate commander, is afraid his men may be caught in a trap. We know his troops are merely raw militia, and he has put them where they can retreat in case of defeat. He, himself, with his trained cannoneers, is inside the fort."

"There can be no attack until tomorrow," said Colonel

Newcomb. "It will be impossible for General Grant's army to get here in time."

"You are certainly right about the army, but I'm not so sure that you're right about the attack. Look what's coming up the river."

"The fleet!" exclaimed Newcomb in excitement. "As sure as I'm here it's the fleet, advancing to make the attack alone. Foote is a daring and energetic man, and the failure of the army to co-operate will not keep him back."

"Daring and energy, seventy per cent, at least," Dick heard Warner murmur, but he paid no more attention to his comrades because all his interest was absorbed in the thrilling spectacle that was about to be unfolded before them.

The fleet, the armor clads, the floating batteries, and the mortar boats, were coming straight toward the fort. Colonel Winchester lent Dick his glasses for a moment, and the boy plainly saw the great, yawning mouths of the mortars. Then he passed the glasses back to the colonel, but he was able to see well what followed with the naked eye. The fleet came on, steady, but yet silent.

There was a sudden roar, a flash of fire and a shell was discharged from one of the seventeen great guns in the fort. But it passed over the boat at which it was aimed, and a fountain of water spurted up where it struck. The other guns replied rapidly, and the fleet, with a terrific roar, replied. It seemed to Dick that the whole earth shook with the confusion. Through the smoke and flame he saw the water gushing up in fountains, and he also saw earth and masonry flying from the fort.

"It's a fine fight," said Colonel Winchester, suppressed excitement showing in his tone. "By George, the fleet is coming closer. Not a boat has been sunk! What a tremendous roar those mortars make. Look! One of their shells has burst directly on the fort!"

The fleet, single handed, was certainly making a determined and powerful attack upon the fort, which standing upon low, marshy ground, was not much above the level of the boats, and offered a fair target to their great guns. Both fort and fleet were now enveloped in a great cloud of smoke, but it was repeatedly rent asunder by the flashing of the great guns, and, rapt by the spectacle from which he could not take his eyes, Dick saw that all the vessels of the fleet were still afloat and were crowding closer and closer.

The artillery kept up a steady crash now, punctuated by the hollow boom of the great mortars, which threw huge, curving shells. The smoke floated far up and down the river, and the Southern troops on the height adjoining the fort moved back and forth uneasily, uncertain what to do. Finally they broke and retreated into the forest.

But General Tilghman, the Confederate commander, and the heroic gunners inside the fort, only sixty in number, made the most heroic resistance. The armor clad boats were only six hundred yards away now, and were pouring upon them a perfect storm of fire.

Their intrenchments, placed too low, gave them no advantage over the vessels. Shells and solid shot rained upon them. Some of the guns were exploded and others dismounted by this terrible shower, but they did not yet give up. As fast as they could load and fire the little band sent back their own fire at the black hulks that showed through the smoke.

"The fleet will win," Dick heard Colonel Winchester murmur. "Look how magnificently it is handled, and it converges closer and closer. A fortification located as this one is cannot stand forever a fire like that."

But the fleet was not escaping unharmed. A shell burst the boiler of the Essex, killing and wounding twenty-nine men. Nevertheless, the fire of the boats increased rather than diminished, and Dick saw that Colonel Winchester's words were bound to come true.

Inside the fort there was only depression. It had been raked through by shells and solid shot. Most of the devoted band were wounded and scarcely a gun could be worked. Tilghman, standing amid his dead and wounded, saw that hope was no longer left, and gave the signal.

Dick and his comrades uttered a great shout as they saw the white flag go up over Fort Henry, and then the cannonade ceased, like a mighty crash of thunder that had rolled suddenly across the sky.

# CHAPTER X

## BEFORE DONELSON

Dick was the first in Colonel Winchester's troop to see the white flag floating over Fort Henry and he uttered a shout of joy.

"Look! look!" he cried, "the fleet has taken the fort!"

"So it has," said Colonel Winchester, "and the army is not here. Now I wonder what General Grant will say when he learns that Foote has done the work before he could come."

But Dick believed that General Grant would find no fault, that he would approve instead. The feeling was already spreading among the soldiers that this man, whose name was recently so new among them, cared only for results. He was not one to fight over precedence and to feel petty jealousies.

The smoke of battle was beginning to clear away. Officers were landing from the boats to receive the surrender of the fort, and Colonel Winchester and his troops galloped rapidly back toward the army, which they soon met, toiling through swamps and even through shallow overflow toward the Tennessee. The men had been hearing for more than an hour the steady booming of the cannon, and every face was eager.

Colonel Winchester rode straight toward a short, thickset figure on a stout bay horse near the head of one of the columns. This man, like all the others, was plastered with mud, but Colonel Winchester gave him a salute of deep respect.

"What does the cessation of firing mean, Colonel?" asked General Grant.

"It means that Fort Henry has surrendered to the fleet. The Southern force, which was drawn up outside, retreated southward, but the fort, its guns and immediate defenders, are ours."

Dick saw the faintest smile of satisfaction pass over the face of the General, who said:

"Commodore Foote has done well. Ride back and tell him that the army is coming up as fast as the nature of the ground will allow."

In a short time the army was in the fort which had been taken so gallantly by the navy, and Grant, his generals, and Commodore Foote, were in anxious consultation. Most of the troops were soon camped on the height, where the Southern force had stood, and there was great exultation, but Dick, who had now seen so much, knew that the high officers considered this only a beginning.

Across the narrow stretch of land on the parallel river, the Cumberland, stood the great fort of Donelson. Henry was a small affair compared with it. It was likely that men who had been stationed at Henry had retreated there, and other formidable forces were marching to the same place. The Confederate commander, Johnston, after the destruction of his eastern wing at Mill Spring by Thomas, was drawing in his forces and concentrating. The news of the loss of Fort Henry would cause him to hasten his operations. He was rapidly falling back from his position at Bowling Green in Kentucky. Buckner, with his division, was about to march from that place to join the garrison in Donelson, and Floyd, with another division, would soon be on the way to the same point. Floyd had been the United States Secretary of War before secession, and the Union men hated him. It was said that the great partisan leader, Forrest, with his cavalry, was also at the fort.

Much of this news was brought in by farmers, Union sympathizers, and Dick and his comrades, as they sat before the fires at the close of the short winter day, understood the situation almost as well as the generals.

"Donelson is ninety per cent and Henry only ten per cent," said Warner. "So long as the Johnnies hold Donelson on the Cumberland, they can build another fort anywhere they please along the Tennessee, and stop our fleet. This general of ours has a good notion of the value of time and a swift blow, and, although I'm neither a prophet nor the son of a prophet, I predict that he will attack Donelson at once by both land and water."

"How can he attack it by water?" asked Pennington. "The distance between them is not great, but our ships can't steam overland from the Tennessee to the Cumberland."

"No, but they can steam back up the Tennessee into the Ohio, thence to the mouth of the Cumberland, and down the Cumberland to Donelson. It would require only four or five days, and it will take that long for the army to invade from the land side."

Dick had his doubts about the ability of the army and the fleet to co-operate. Accustomed to the energy of the Southern commanders in the east he did not believe that Grant would be allowed to arrange things as he chose. But several days passed and they heard nothing from the Confederates, although Donelson was only about twenty miles away. Johnston himself, brilliant and sagacious, was not there, nor was his lieutenant, Beauregard, who had won such a great reputation by his victory at the first Bull Run.

111

Dick was just beginning to suspect a truth that later on was to be confirmed fully in his mind. Fortune had placed the great generals of the Confederacy, with the exception of Albert Sidney Johnston, in the east, but it had been the good luck of the North to open in the west with its best men.

Now he saw the energy of Grant, the short man of rather insignificant appearance. Boats were sent down the Tennessee to meet any reinforcements that might be coming, take them back to the Ohio, and thence into the Cumberland. Fresh supplies of ammunition and food were brought up, and it became obvious to Dick that the daring commander meant to attack Donelson, even should its garrison outnumber his own besieging force.

Along a long line from Western Tennessee to Eastern Kentucky there was a mighty stir. Johnston had perceived the energy and courage of his opponent. He had shared the deep disappointment of all the Southern leaders when Kentucky failed to secede, but instead furnished so many thousands of fine troops to the Union army.

Johnston, too, had noticed with alarm the tremendous outpouring of rugged men from the states beyond the Ohio and from the far northwest. The lumbermen who came down in scores of thousands from Michigan, Wisconsin and Minnesota, were a stalwart crowd. War, save for the bullets and shell, offered to them no hardships to which they were not used. They had often worked for days at a time up to their waists in icy water. They had endured thirty degrees below zero without a murmur, they had breasted blizzard and cyclone, they could live on anything, and they could sleep either in forest or on prairie, under the open sky.

It was such men as these, including men of his own state, and men of the Tennessee mountains, whom Johnston, who had all the qualities of a great commander, had to face. The forces against him were greatly superior in number. The eastern end of his line had been crushed already at Mill Spring, the extreme western end had suffered a severe blow at Fort Henry, but Jefferson Davis and the Government at Richmond expected everything of him. And he manfully strove to do everything.

There was a mighty marching of men, some news of which came through to Dick and his comrades with Grant. Johnston with his main army, the very flower of the western South, fell back from Bowling Green, in Kentucky, toward Nashville, the capital of Tennessee. But Buckner, with his division, was sent from Bowling Green to help defend Donelson against the threatened attack by

Grant, and he arrived there six days after the fall of Henry. On the way were the troops of Floyd, defeated in West Virginia, but afterwards sent westward. Floyd was at the head of them. Forrest, the great cavalry leader, was also there with his horsemen. The fort was crowded with defenders, but the slack Pillow did not yet send forward anybody to see what Grant was doing, although he was only twenty miles away.

All eyes were now turned upon the west. The center of action had suddenly shifted from Kentucky to Tennessee. The telegraph was young yet, but it was busy. It carried many varying reports to the cities North and South. The name of this new man, Grant, spelled trouble. People were beginning to talk much about him, and already some suspected that there was more in the back of his head than in those of far better known and far more pretentious northern generals in the east. None at least could dispute the fact that he was now the one whom everybody was watching.

But the Southern people, few of whom knew the disparity of numbers, had the fullest confidence in the brilliant Johnston. He was more than twenty years older than his antagonist, but his years had brought only experience and many triumphs, not weakness of either mind or body. At his right hand was the swarthy and confident Beauregard, great with the prestige of Bull Run, and Hardee, Bragg, Breckinridge and Polk. And there were many brilliant colonels, too, foremost among whom was George Kenton.

A tremor passed through the North when it was learned that Grant intended to plunge into the winter forest, cross the Cumberland, and lay siege to Donelson. He was going beyond the plans of his superior, Halleck, at St. Louis. He was too daring, he would lose his army, away down there in the Confederacy. But others remembered his successes, particularly at Belmont and Fort Henry. They said that nothing could be won in war without risk, and they spoke of his daring and decision. They recalled, too, that he was master upon the waters, that there was no Southern fleet to face his, as it sailed up the Southern rivers. The telegraph was already announcing that the gunboats, which had been handled with such skill and courage, would be in the Cumberland ready to co-operate with Grant when he should move on Donelson.

Buell was moving also to form another link in the steel chain that was intended to bind the Confederacy in the west. Here again the mastery of the rivers was of supreme value to the North. Buell embarked his army on boats on Green River in the very heart of Kentucky, descended that river to the Ohio, passing down the latter to Smithland, where the Cumberland, coming up from the south, entered it, and met another convoy destined for the huge invasion.

But the first convoy had come, also by boat, from another direction, and from points far distant. There were fresh regiments of farmers and pioneers from Iowa, Nebraska, and Minnesota. They were all eager, full of enthusiasm, anxious to be led against the enemy, and confident of triumph.

Grant and his army, meanwhile, lying in the bleak forest beside the Tennessee, knew little of what was being said of them in the great world without. All their thoughts were of Donelson, across there on the other river, and the men asked to be led against it. Inured to the hardships of border life, there was little sickness among them, despite the winter and the overflow of the flooded streams. They gathered the dead wood that littered the forest, built numerous fires, and waited as patiently as they could for the word to march.

The Pennsylvanians were still camped with the Kentucky regiment to which Dick now belonged, and the fifth evening after the capture of Henry he and his friends sat by one of the big fires.

"We'll advance either tomorrow or the next day," said Warner. "The chances are at least ninety per cent in favor of my statement. What do you say, sergeant?"

"I'd raise the ninety per cent to one hundred," replied Whitley. "We are all ready an' as you've observed, gentlemen, General Grant is a man who acts."

"The Johnnies evidently expect us," said Pennington. "Our scouts have seen their cavalry in the woods watching us, but only in the last day or two. It's strange that they didn't begin it earlier."

"They say that General Pillow, who commands them, isn't of much force," said Dick.

"Well, it looks like it," said Warner, "but from what we hear he'll have quite an army at Donelson. General Grant will have his work cut out for him. The Johnnies, besides having their fort, can go into battle with just about as many men as we have, unless he waits for reinforcements, which I am quite certain he isn't going to do."

That evening several bags of mail were brought to the camp on a small steamer, which had come on three rivers, the Green, the Ohio, and the Tennessee, and Dick, to his great surprise and delight, received a letter from his mother. He had written several letters himself, but he had no way of knowing until now that any of them had reached her. Only one had succeeded in getting through, and that had been written from Cairo.

"My dearest son," she wrote, "I am full of joy to know that you have reached Cairo in safety and in health, though I dread the great expedition upon which you say you are going. I hear in Pendleton many reports about General Grant. They say that he does not spare his men. The Southern sympathizers here say that he is pitiless and cares not how many thousands of his own soldiers he may sacrifice, if he only gains his aim. But of that I know not. I know it is a characteristic of our poor human nature to absolve one's own side and to accuse those on the other side.

"I was in Pendleton this morning, and the reports are thick; thick from both Northerners and Southerners, that the armies are moving forward to a great battle. They have all marched south of us, and I do not know either whether these reports are true or false, though I fear that they are true. Your uncle, Colonel Kenton, is with General Johnston, and I hear is one of his most trusted officers. Colonel Kenton is a good man, and it would be one of the terrible tragedies of war if you and he were to meet on the field in this great battle, which so many hear is coming.

"I am very glad that you are now in the regiment of Colonel Winchester, and that you are an aide on his staff. It is best to be with one's own people. I have known Colonel Winchester a long time, and he has all the qualities that make a man, brave and gentle. I hope that you and he will become the best of friends."

There was much more in the letter, but it was only the little details that concern mother and son. Dick was sitting by the fire when he read it. Then he read it a second time and a third time, folded it very carefully and put it in the pocket in which he had carried the dispatch from General Thomas.

Colonel Winchester was sitting near him, and Dick noticed again what a fine, trim man he was. Although a little over forty, his figure was still slender, and he had an abundant head of thick, vital hair. His whole effect was that of youth. His glance met Dick's and he smiled.

"A letter from home?" he said.

"Yes, sir, from mother. She writes to me that she is glad I am in your command. She speaks very highly of you, sir, and my mother is a woman of uncommon penetration."

A faint red tinted the tanned cheeks of the colonel. Dick thought it was merely the reflection of the fire.

"Would you care for me to read what she says about you?" asked Dick.

"If you don't mind."

Dick drew out the letter again and read the paragraph.

"Your mother is a very fine woman," said Colonel Winchester.

"You're right, sir," said Dick with enthusiasm.

Colonel Winchester said no more, but rose presently and went to the tent of General Grant, where a conference of officers was to be held. Dick remained by the fire, where Warner and Pennington soon joined him.

"Our scouts have exchanged some shots with the enemy," said Pennington, "and they have taken one or two prisoners, bold fellows who say they're going to lick the spots off us. They say they have a big army at Donelson, and they're afraid of nothing except that Grant won't come on. Between ourselves, the Johnny Rebs are getting ready for us."

It was Dick's opinion, too, that the Southern troops were making great preparations to meet them, but, like the others, he was feeling the strong hand on the reins. He did not notice here the doubt and uncertainty that had reigned at Washington before the advance on Bull Run; in Grant's army were order and precision, and with perfect confidence in his commander he rolled himself in his blankets that night and went to sleep.

The order to advance did not come the next morning, and Dick, for a few moments, thought it might not come at all. The reports from Donelson were of a formidable nature, and Grant's own army was not provided for a winter campaign. It had few wagons for food and ammunition, and some of the regiments from the northwest, cherishing the delusion that winter in Tennessee was not cold, were not provided with warm clothing and sufficient blankets.

But Warner abated his confidence not one jot.

"The chance of our moving against Donelson is one hundred per cent," he said. "I passed the General today and his lips were shut tight together, which means a resolve to do at all costs what one has intended to do. I still admit that the prophets and the sons of prophets live no more, but I predict with absolute certainty that we will move in the morning."

The Vermonter's faith was justified. The army, being put in thorough trim, started at dawn upon its momentous march. Wintry fogs were rising from the great river and the submerged lowlands, and the air was full of raw, penetrating chill. An abundant breakfast was served to everybody, and then with warmth and courage the lads of the west and northwest marched forward with eagerness to an undertaking which they knew would be far greater than the capture of Fort Henry.

Dick and Pennington, as staff officers, were mounted, although the horses that had been furnished to them were not much more than ponies. Warner rode with Colonel Newcomb and Major Hertford, who led the slender Pennsylvania detachment beside the Kentucky regiment. Thus the army emerged from its camp and began the march toward the Cumberland. It was now about fifteen thousand strong, but it expected reinforcements, and its fleet held the command of the rivers.

As they entered the leafless forest Dick saw ahead of them, perhaps a quarter of a mile away, a numerous band of horsemen wearing faded Confederate gray. They were the cavalry of Forrest, but they were too few to stay the Union advances. There was a scattered firing of rifles, but the heavy brigades of Grant moved steadily on, and pushed them out of the way. Forrest could do no more than gallop back to the fort with his men and report that the enemy was coming at last.

"Those fellows ride well," said Pennington, as the last of Forrest's cavalrymen passed out of sight, "and if we were not in such strong force I fancy they would sting us pretty hard."

"We'll see more of 'em," said Dick. "This is the enemy's country, and we needn't think that we're going to march as easy as you please from one victory to another."

"Maybe not," said Pennington, "but I'll be glad when we get Donelson. I've been hearing so much about that place that I'm growing real curious."

Their march across the woods suffered no further interruption. Sometimes they saw Confederate cavalrymen at a distance in front, but they did not try to impede Grant's advance. When the sun was well down in the west, the vanguard of the army came within sight of the fortress that stood by the Cumberland. At that very moment the troops under Floyd, just arrived, were crossing the river to join the garrison in the fortress.

Dick looked upon extensive fortifications, a large fort, a redoubt upon slightly higher ground, other batteries at the water's edge, powerful batteries upon a semi-circular hill which could command the river for a long distance, and around all of these extensive works, several miles in length, including a deep creek on the north. Inside the works was the little town of Dover, and they were defended by fifteen thousand men, as many as Grant had without.

When Dick beheld this formidable position bristling with cannon, rifles and bayonets, his heart sank within him. How could one army defeat another, as numerous as itself, inside powerful intrenchments, and in its own country? Nor could they prevent Southern reinforcements from reaching the other side of the river and crossing to the fort under the shelter of its numerous great guns. He was yet to learn the truth, or at least the partial truth, of Napoleon's famous saying, that in war an army is nothing, a man is everything. The army to which he belonged was led by a man of clear vision and undaunted resolution. The chief commander inside the fort had neither, and his men were shaken already by the news of Fort Henry, exaggerated in the telling.

But after the first sinking of the heart Dick felt an extraordinary thrill. Sensitive and imaginative, he was conscious even at the moment that he looked in the face of mighty events. The things of the minute did not always appeal to him with the greatest force. He had, instead, the foreseeing mind, and the meaning of that vast panorama of fortress, hills, river and forest did not escape him.

"Well, Dick, what do you think of it?" asked Pennington.

"We've got our work cut out for us, and if I didn't know General Grant I'd say that we're engaged in a mighty rash undertaking."

"Just what I'd say, also. And we need that fleet bad, too, Dick. I'd like to see the smoke of its funnels as the boats come steaming up the Cumberland."

Dick knew that the fleet was needed, not alone for encouragement and fighting help, but to supply an even greater want. Grant's army was short of both food and ammunition. The afternoon had turned warm, and many of the northwestern lads, still clinging to their illusions about the climate of the lower Mississippi Valley, had dropped their blankets. Now, with the setting sun, the raw, penetrating chill was coming back, and they shivered in every bone.

But the Union army, in spite of everything, gradually spread out and enfolded the whole fortress, save on the northern side where Hickman Creek flowed, deep and impassable. The general's own headquarters were due west of Fort Donelson, and Colonel Winchester's Kentucky regiment was stationed close by.

Low campfires burned along the long line of the Northern army, and Dick and others who sat beside him saw many lights inside the great enclosure held by the South. An occasional report was heard, but it was only the pickets exchanging shots at long range and without hurt. Dick and Pennington wrapped their blankets about them and sat with their backs against a log, ready for any command from Colonel Winchester. Now and then they were sent with orders, because there was much moving to and fro, the placing of men in position and the bringing up of cannon.

Thus the night moved slowly on, raw, cold and dark. Mists and fogs rose from the Cumberland as they had risen from the Tennessee. This, too, was a great river. Dick was glad when the last of his errands was done, and he could come back to the fire, and rest his back once more against the log. The fire was only a bed of coals now, but they gave out much grateful heat.

Dick could see General Grant's tent from where he sat. Officers of high rank were still entering it or leaving it, and he was quite sure that they were planning an attack on the morrow.

But the idea of an assault did not greatly move him now. He was too tired and sleepy to have more than a vague impression of anything. He saw the coals glowing before him, and then he did not see them. He had gone sound asleep in an instant.

The next morning was gray and troubled, with heavy clouds, rolling across the sky. The rising sun was blurred by them, and as the men ate their breakfasts some of the great guns from the fort began to fire at the presumptuous besieger. The heavy reports rolled sullenly over the desolate forests, but the Northern cannon did not yet reply. The Southern fire was doing no damage. It was merely a threat, a menace to those who should dare the assault.

Colonel Winchester signalled to Dick and Pennington, and mounting their horses they rode with him to the crest of the highest adjacent hill. Presently General Grant came and with him were the generals, McClernand and Smith. Colonel Newcomb also arrived, attended by Warner. The high officers examined the fort a long time through their glasses, but Dick noticed that at times they watched the river. He knew they were looking there for the black plumes of smoke which should mark the coming of the steamers out of the Ohio.

But nothing showed on the surface of the Cumberland. The river, dark gray under lowering clouds, flowed placidly on, washing the base of Fort Donelson. At intervals of a minute or two there was a flash of fire from the fort, and the menacing boom of the cannon rolled through the desolate forest. Now and then, a gun from one of the Northern batteries replied. But it was as yet a desultory battle, with much noise and little danger, merely a threat of what was to come.

After a while Colonel Winchester wrote something on a slip of paper:

"Take this to our lieutenant-colonel," he said. "It is an order for the regiment to hold itself in complete readiness, although no action may come for some time. Then return here at once."

Dick rode back swiftly, but on his way he suddenly bent over his saddle bow. A shell from the fort screamed over his head in such a menacing fashion that it seemed to be only a few inches from him. But it passed on, leaving him unharmed, and burst three hundred yards away.

Dick instantly straightened up in the saddle, looked around, breathed a sigh of relief when he saw that no one had noticed his sudden bow, and galloped on with the order. The lieutenant-colonel read it and nodded. Then Dick rode back to the hill where the generals were yet watching in vain for those black plumes of smoke on the Cumberland.

They left the hill at last and the generals went to their brigades. General Grant was smoking a cigar and his face was impassive.

"We're to open soon with the artillery," said Colonel Winchester to Dick. "General Grant means to push things."

The desultory firing, those warning guns, ceased entirely, and for a while both armies stood in almost complete silence. Then a Northern battery on the right opened with a tremendous crash and the battle for Donelson had begun. A Southern battery replied at once and the firing spread along the whole vast curve. Shells and solid shot whistled through the air, but the troops back of the guns crouched in hasty entrenchments, and waited.

The great artillery combat went on for some time. To many of the lads on either side it seemed for hours. Then the guns on the Northern side ceased suddenly, bugles sounded, and the regiments, drawn up in line, rushed at the outer fortifications.

Colonel Winchester and his staff had dismounted, but Dick and Pennington, keeping by the colonel's side, drew their swords and rushed on shouting. The Southerners inside the fort fired their cannon as fast as they could now, and at closer range opened with the rifles. Dick heard once again that terrible shrieking of metal so close to his ears, and then he heard, too, cries of pain. Many of the young soldiers behind him were falling.

The fire now grew so hot and deadly that the Union regiments were forced to give ground. It was evident that they could not carry the formidable earthworks, but on the right, where Dick's regiment charged, and just above the little town of Dover, they pressed in far enough to secure some hills that protected them from the fire of the enemy, and from which Southern cannon and rifles could not drive them. Then, at the order of Grant, his troops withdrew elsewhere and the battle of the day ceased. But on the low hills above Dover, which they had taken, the Union regiments held their ground, and from their position the Northern cannon could threaten the interior of the Southern lines.

Dick's regiment stood here, and beside them were the few companies of Pennsylvanians so far from their native state. Neither Dick nor Pennington was wounded. Warner had a bandaged arm, but the wound was so slight that it would not incapacitate him. The officers were unhurt.

"They've driven our army back," said Pennington, "and it was not so hard for them to do it either. How can we ever defeat an army as large as our own inside powerful works?"

But Dick was learning fast and he had a keen eye.

"We have not failed utterly," he said. "Don't you see that we have here a projection into the enemy's lines, and if those reinforcements come it will be thrust further and further? I tell you that general of ours is a bull dog. He will never let go."

Yet there was little but gloom in the Union camp. The short winter day, somber and heavy with clouds, was drawing to a close. The field upon which the assault had taken place was within the sweep of the Southern guns. Some of the Northern wounded had crawled away or had been carried to their own camp, but others and the numerous dead still lay upon the ground.

The cold increased. The Southern winter is subject to violent changes. The clouds which had floated up without ceasing were massing heavily. Now the young troops regretted bitterly the blankets that they had dropped on the way or left at Fort Henry. Detachments were sent back to regain as many as possible, but long before they could return a sharp wind with an edge of ice sprang up, the clouds opened and great flakes poured down, driven into the eyes of the soldiers by the wind.

The situation was enough to cause the stoutest heart to weaken, but the unflinching Grant held on. The Confederate army within the works was sheltered at least in part, but his own, outside, and with the desolate forest rimming it around, lay exposed fully to the storm. Dick, at intervals, saw the short, thickset figure of the commander passing among the men, and giving them orders or encouragement. Once he saw his face clearly. The lips were pressed tightly together, and the whole countenance expressed the grimmest determination. Dick was confirmed anew in his belief that the chief would never turn back.

The spectacle, nevertheless, was appalling. The snow drove harder and harder. It was not merely a passing shower of flakes. It was a storm. The snow soon lay upon the ground an inch deep, then three inches, then four and still it gained. Through the darkness and the storm the Southern cannon crashed at intervals, sending shells at random into the Union camp or over it. There was full need then for the indomitable spirit of Grant and those around him to encourage anew the thousands of boys who had so lately left the farms or the lumber yards.

Dick and his comrades, careless of the risk, searched over the battlefield for the wounded who were yet there. They carried lanterns, but the darkness was so great and the snow drove so hard and lay so deep that they knew many would never be found.

Back beyond the range of the fort's cannon men were building fires with what wood they could secure from the forest. All the tents they had were set up, and the men tried to cook food and make coffee, in order that some degree of warmth and cheer might be provided for the army beset so sorely.

The snow, after a while, slackening somewhat, was succeeded by cold much greater than ever. The shivering men bent over the fires and lamented anew the discarded blankets. Dick did not sleep an instant that terrible night. He could not. He, Pennington, and Warner, relieved from staff service, worked all through the cold and darkness, helping the wounded and seeking wood for the fires. And with them always was the wise Sergeant Whitley, to whom, although inferior in rank, they turned often and willingly for guidance and advice.

"It's an awful situation," said Pennington; "I knew that war would furnish horrors, but I didn't expect anything like this."

"But General Grant will never retreat," said Dick. "I feel it in every bone of me. I've seen his face tonight."

"No, he won't," said the experienced sergeant, "because he's making every preparation to stay. An' remember, Mr. Pennington, that while this is pretty bad, worse can happen. Remember, too, that while we can stand this, we can also stand whatever worse may come. It's goin' to be a fight to a finish."

Far in the night the occasional guns from the Southern fortress ceased. The snow was falling no longer, but it lay very deep on the ground, and the cold was at its height. Along a line of miles the fires burned and the men crowded about them. But Dick, who had been working on the snowy plain that was the battlefield, and who had heard many moans there, now heard none. All who lay in that space were sleeping the common sleep of death, their bodies frozen stiff and hard under the snow.

Dick, sitting by one of the fires, saw the cold dawn come, and in those chill hours of nervous exhaustion he lost hope for a moment or two. How could anybody, no matter how resolute, maintain a siege without ammunition and without food. But he spoke cheerfully to Pennington and Warner, who had slept a little and who were just awakening.

The pale and wintry sun showed the defiant Stars and Bars floating over Donelson, and Dick from his hill could see men moving inside the earthworks. Certainly the Southern flags had a right to wave defiance at the besieging army, which was now slowly and painfully rising from the snow, and lighting the fires anew.

"Well, what's the program today, Dick?" asked Pennington.

"I don't know, but it's quite certain that we won't attempt another assault. It's hopeless."

"That's true," said Warner, who was standing by, "but we—hark, what was that?"

The boom of a cannon echoed over the fort and forest, and then another and another. To the northward they saw thin black spires of smoke under the horizon.

"It's the fleet! It's the fleet!" cried Warner joyously, "coming up the Cumberland to our help! Oh, you men of Donelson, we're around you now, and you'll never shake us off!"

Again came the crash of great guns from the fleet, and the crash of the Southern water batteries replying.

# CHAPTER XI

# THE SOUTHERN ATTACK

The excitement in the Union army was intense and joyous. The cheers rolled like volleys among these farmer lads of the West. Dick, Warner and Pennington stood up and shouted with the rest.

"I should judge that our chances of success have increased at least fifty, yes sixty, per cent," said Warner. "As we have remarked before, this control of the water is a mighty thing. We fight the Johnnie Rebs for the land, but we have the water already. Look at those gunboats, will you? Aren't they the sauciest little things you ever saw?"

Once more the navy was showing, as it has always shown throughout its career, its daring and brilliant qualities. Foote, the commodore, although he had had no time to repair his four small fighting boats after the encounter with Fort Henry, steamed straight up the river and engaged the concentric fire from the great guns of the Southern batteries, which opened upon him with a tremendous crash. The boys watched the duel with amazement. They did not believe that small vessels could live under such fire, but live they did. Great columns of smoke floated over them and hid them at times from the watchers, but when the smoke lifted a little or was split apart by the shattering fire of the guns the black hulls of the gunboats always reappeared, and now they were not more than three or four hundred yards from Donelson.

"I take it that this is a coverin' fire," said Sergeant Whitley, who stood by. "Four little vessels could not expect to reduce such a powerful fortress as Donelson. It's not Fort Henry that they're fightin' now."

"The chances are at least ninety-five per cent in favor of your supposition," said Warner.

The sergeant's theory, in fact, was absolutely correct. Further down the river the transports were unloading regiment after regiment of fresh troops, and vast supplies of ammunition and provisions. Soon five thousand men were formed in line and marched to Grant's relief, while long lines of wagons brought up the stores so badly needed. Now the stern and silent general was able to make the investment complete, but the fiery little fleet did not cease to push the attack.

There was a time when it seemed that the gunboats would be able to pass the fortress and rake it from a point up the river. Many of the guns in the water batteries had been silenced, but the final achievement was too great for so small a force. The rudder of one of Foote's gunboats was shot away, the wheel of another soon went the same way, and both drifted helplessly down the stream. The other two then retreated, and the fire of both fort and fleet ceased.

But there was joy in the Union camp. The soldiers had an abundance of food now, and soon the long ring of fires showed that they were preparing it. Their forces had been increased a third, and there was a fresh outburst of courage and vigor. But Grant ordered no more attacks at present. After the men had eaten and rested a little, picks and spades were swung along a line miles in length. He was fortifying his own position, and it was evident to his men that he meant to stay there until he won or was destroyed.

Dick was conscious once more of a sanguine thrill. Like the others, he felt the strong hand over him, and the certainty that they were led with judgment and decision made him believe that all things were possible. Yet the work of fortifying continued but a little while. The men were exhausted by cold and fatigue, and were compelled to lay down their tools. The fires were built anew, and they hovered about them for shelter and rest.

The wan twilight showed the close of the wintry day, and with the increasing chill a part of Dick's sanguine feeling departed. The gallant little fleet, although it had brought fresh men and supplies and had protected their landing, had been driven back. The investment of the fort was complete only on one side of the river, and steamers coming up the Cumberland from Nashville might yet take off the garrison in safety. Then the work of the silent general, all their hardship and fighting would be at least in part a failure. The Vermont youth, who seemed to be always of the same temper, neither very high nor very low, noticed his change of expression.

"Don't let your hopes decrease, Dick," he said. "Remember that at least twenty per cent of the decline is due to the darkness and inaction. In the morning, when the light comes once more, and we're up and doing again, you'll get back all the twenty per cent you're losing now."

"It's not to be all inaction with you boys tonight, even," said Colonel Winchester, who overheard his closing words. "I want you three to go with me on a tour of inspection or rather scouting duty. It may please you to know that it is the special wish of General Grant. Aware that I had some knowledge of the country, he has detailed me for the duty, and I choose you as my assistants. I'm sure that the skill and danger such a task requires will make you all the more eager for it."

The three youths responded quickly and with zeal, and Sergeant Whitley, when he was chosen, too, nodded in silent gratitude. The night was dark, overcast with clouds, and in an hour Colonel Winchester with his four departed upon his perilous mission. He was to secure information in regard to the Southern army, and to do that they were to go very near the Southern lines, if not actually inside them. Such an attempt would be hazardous in the extreme in the face of a vigilant watch; but on the other hand they would be aided by the fact that both North and South were of like blood and language. Even more, many of those in the opposing camps came from the same localities, and often were of kin.

Dick's regiment had been stationed at the southern end of the line, near the little town of Dover, but they now advanced northward and westward, marching for a long time along their inner line. It was Colonel Winchester's intention to reach Hickman Creek, which formed their northern barrier, creep in the fringe of bushes on its banks, and then approach the fort.

When they reached the desired point the night was well advanced, and yet dark with the somber clouds hanging over river and fort and field of battle. The wind blew out of the northwest, sharp and intensely cold. The snow crunched under their feet. But the four had wrapped themselves in heavy overcoats, and they were so engrossed in their mission that neither wind nor snow was anything to them.

They passed along the bank of the creek, keeping well within the shadow of the bushes, leaving behind them the last outpost of the Union army, and then slowly drew near to the fort. They saw before them many lights burning in the darkness, and at last they discerned dim figures walking back and forth. Dick knew that these were the Southern sentinels. The four went a little nearer, and then crouched down in the snow among some low bushes.

Now they saw the Southern sentinels more distinctly. Some, in fact, were silhouetted sharply as they passed before the Southern fires. Northern sharpshooters could have crept up and picked off many of them, as the Southern sharpshooters in turn might have served many of the Northern watchers, but in this mighty war there was little of such useless and merciless enterprise. The men soon ceased to have personal animosity, and, in the nights between the great battles, when the armies yet lay face to face, the hostile pickets would often exchange gossip and tobacco. Even in a conflict waged so long and with such desperation the essential kindliness of human nature would assert itself.

The four, as they skirted the Southern line, noticed no signs of further preparations by the Confederates. No men were throwing up earthworks or digging trenches. As well as they could surmise, the garrison, like the besieging army, was seeking shelter and rest, and from this fact the keen mind of Colonel Arthur Winchester divined that the defense was confused and headless.

Colonel Winchester knew most of the leaders within Donelson. He knew that Pillow was not of a strong and decided nature. Nor was Floyd, who would rank first, of great military capacity. Buckner had talent and he had served gallantly in the Mexican War, but he could not prevail over the others. The fame of Forrest, the Tennessee mountaineer, was already spreading, but a cavalryman could do little for the defense of a fort besieged by twenty thousand well equipped men, led by a general of unexcelled resolution.

All that Colonel Winchester surmised was true. Inside the fort confusion and doubt reigned. The fleeing garrison from Fort Henry had brought exaggerated reports of Grant's army. Very few of the thousands of young troops had ever been in battle before. They, too, suffered though in a less degree from cold and fatigue, but many were wounded. Pillow and Floyd, who had just arrived with his troops, talked of one thing and then another. Floyd, who might have sent word to his valiant and able chief, Johnston, did not take the trouble or forgot to inform him of his position. Buckner wanted to attack Grant the next morning with the full Southern strength, and a comrade of his on old battlefields, Colonel George Kenton, seconded him ably. The black-bearded Forrest strode back and forth, striking the tops of his riding boots with a small riding whip, and saying ungrammatically, but tersely and emphatically:

"We mustn't stay here like hogs in a pen. We must git at 'em with all our men afore they can git at us."

The illiterate mountaineer and stock driver had evolved exactly the same principle of war that Napoleon used.

But Colonel Winchester and his comrades could only guess at what was going on in Donelson, and a guess always remains to be proved. So they must continue their perilous quest. Once they were hailed by a Southern sentinel, but Colonel Winchester replied promptly that they belonged to Buckner's Kentuckians and had been sent out to examine the Union camp. He passed it off with such boldness and decision that they were gone before the picket had time to express a doubt.

But as they came toward the center of the line, and drew nearer to the fort itself, they met another picket, who was either more watchful or more acute. He hailed them at a range of forty or fifty yards, and when Colonel Winchester made the same reply he ordered them to halt and give the countersign. When no answer came he fired instantly at the tall figure of Colonel Winchester and uttered a loud cry of, "Yankees!"

Luckily the dim light was tricky and his bullet merely clipped the colonel's hair. But there was nothing for the four to do now save to run with all their undignified might for their own camp.

"Come on, lads!" shouted Colonel Winchester. "Our scouting is over for the time!"

The region behind them contained patches of scrub oaks and bushes, and with their aid and that of the darkness, it was not difficult to escape; but Dick, while running just behind the others, stepped in a hole and fell. The snow and the dead leaves hid the sound of his fall and the others did not notice it. As he looked up he saw their dim forms disappearing among the bushes. He rose to his own feet, but uttered a little cry as a ligament in his ankle sent a warning throb of pain through his body.

It was not a wrench, only a bruise, and as he stretched his ankle a few times the soreness went away. But the last sound made by the retreating footsteps of his comrades had died, and their place had been taken by those of his pursuers, who were now drawing very near.

Dick had no intention of being captured, and, turning off at a right angle, he dropped into a gully which he encountered among some bushes. The gully was about four feet deep and half full of snow. Dick threw himself full length on his side, and sank down in the snow until he was nearly covered. There he lay panting hard for a few moments, but quite sure that he was safe from discovery. Only a long and most minute search would be likely to reveal the dark line in the snow beneath the overhanging bushes.

Dick's heart presently resumed its normal beat, and then he heard the sound of voices and footsteps. Some one said:

"They went this way, sir, but they were running pretty fast."

"They'd good cause to run," said a brusque voice. "You'd a done it, too, if you'd expected to have the bullets of a whole army barkin' at your heels."

The footsteps came nearer, crunching on the snow, which lay

deep there among the bushes. They could not be more than a dozen feet away, but Dick quivered only a little. Buried as he was and with the hanging bushes over him he was still confident that no one could see him. He raised himself the least bit, and looking through the boughs, saw a tanned and dark face under the broad brim of a Confederate hat. Just then some one said:

"We might have trailed 'em, general, but the snow an' the earth have already been tramped all up by the army."

"They're not wuth huntin' long anyway," said the same brusque voice. "A few Yankees prowlin' about in the night can't do us much harm. It's hard fightin' that'll settle our quarrel."

General Forrest came a little closer and Dick, from his concealment in the snow, surmising his identity, saw him clearly, although himself unseen. He was fascinated by the stern, dark countenance. The face of the unlettered mountaineer was cut sharp and clear, and he had the look of one who knew and commanded. In war he was a natural leader of men, and he had already assumed the position.

"Don't you agree with me, colonel?" he said over his shoulder to some one.

"I think you're right as usual, General Forrest," replied a voice with a cultivated intonation, and Dick started violently in his bed of snow, because he instantly recognized the voice as that of his uncle, Colonel George Kenton, Harry's father. A moment later Colonel Kenton himself stood where the moonlight fell upon his face. Dick saw that he was worn and thin, but his face had the strong and resolute look characteristic of those descended from Henry Ware, the great borderer.

"You know, general, that I endorse all your views," continued Colonel Kenton. "We are unfortunate here in having a division of counsels, while the Yankees have a single and strong head. We have underrated this man Grant. Look how he surprised us and took Henry! Look how he hangs on here! We've beaten him on land and we've driven back his fleet, but he hangs on. To my mind he has no notion of retreating. He'll keep on pounding us as long as we are here."

"That's his way, an' it ought to be the way of every general," growled Forrest. "You cut down a tree by keepin' on cuttin' out chips with an axe, an' you smash up an army by hittin' an' hittin' an' keepin' on hittin'. We ought to charge right out of our works an' jump on the Yankees with all our stren'th."

The two walked on, followed by the soldiers who had come

with them, and Dick heard no more. But he was too cautious to stir for a long while. He lay there until the cold began to make its way through his boots and heavy overcoat. Then he rose carefully, brushed off the snow, and began his retreat toward the Union lines. Four or five hundred yards further on and he met Colonel Winchester and his own comrades come back to search for him. They welcomed him joyfully.

"We did not miss you until we were nearly to our own pickets," said the colonel. "Then we concluded that you had fallen and had been taken by the enemy, but we intended to see if we could find you. We've been hovering about here for some time."

Dick told what he had seen and heard, and the colonel considered it of much importance.

"I judge from what you heard that they will attack us," he said. "Buckner and Forrest will be strongly for it, and they're likely to have their way. We must report at once to General Grant."

The Southern attack had been planned for the next morning, but it did not come then. Pillow, for reasons unknown, decided to delay another day, and his fiery subordinates could do nothing but chafe and wait. Dick spent most of the day carrying orders for his chief, and the continuous action steadied his nerves.

As he passed from point to point he saw that the Union army itself was far from ready. It was a difficult task to get twenty thousand raw farmer youths in proper position. They moved about often without cohesion and sometimes without understanding their orders. Great gaps remained in the line, and a daring and skilful foe might cut the besieging force asunder.

But Grant had put his heavy guns in place, and throughout the day he maintained a slow but steady fire upon the fort. Great shells and solid shot curved and fell upon Donelson. Grant did not know what damage they were doing, but he shrewdly calculated that they would unsteady the nerves of the raw troops within. These farmer boys, as they heard the unceasing menace of the big guns, would double the numbers of their foe, and attribute to him an unrelaxing energy.

Thus another gray day of winter wore away, and the two forces drew a little nearer to each other. Far away the rival Presidents at Washington and Richmond were wondering what was happening to their armies in the dark wilderness of Western Tennessee.

The night was more quiet than the one that had just gone before. The booming of the cannon as regular as the tolling of funeral bells had ceased with the darkness, but in its place the fierce winter wind had begun to blow again. Dick, relaxed and weary after his day's work, hovered over one of the fires and was grateful for the warmth. He had trodden miles through slush and snow and frozen earth, and he was plastered to the waist with frozen mud, which now began to soften and fall off before the coals.

Warner, who had been on active duty, too, also sank to rest with a sigh of relief.

"It's battle tomorrow, Dick," he said, "and I don't care. As it didn't come off today the chances are at least eighty per cent that it will happen the next day. You say that when you were lying in the snow last night, Dick, you saw your uncle and that he's a colonel in the rebel army. It's queer."

"You're wrong, George, it isn't queer. We're on opposite sides, serving at the same place, and it's natural that we should meet some time or other. Oh, I tell you, you fellows from the New England and the other Northern States don't appreciate the sacrifices that we of the border states make for the Union. Up there you are safe from invasion. Your houses are not on the battlefields. You are all on one side. You don't have to fight against your own kind, the people you hold most dear. And when the war is over, whether we win or lose, you'll go back to unravaged regions."

"You wrong me there, Dick. I have thought of it. It's the people of the border, whether North or South, who pay the biggest price. We risk our lives, but you risk your lives also, and everything else, too."

Dick wrapped himself in a heavy blanket, pillowed his head on a log before one of the fires and dozed a while. His nerves had been tried too hard to permit of easy sleep. He awoke now and then and over a wide area saw the sinking fires and the moving forms of men. He felt that a sense of uneasiness pervaded the officers. He knew that many of them considered their forces inadequate for the siege of a fortress defended by a large army, but he felt with the sincerity of conviction also, that Grant would never withdraw.

He heard from Colonel Winchester about midnight in one of his wakeful intervals that General Grant was going down the river to see Commodore Foote. The brave leader of the fleet had been wounded severely in the last fight with the fort, and the general wished to confer with him about the plan of operations. But Dick heard only vaguely. The statement made no impression upon him at that time. Yet he was conscious that the feeling of uneasiness still pervaded the officers. He noticed it in Colonel Winchester's tone, and he noticed it, too, in the voices of Colonel Newcomb and Major Hertford, who came presently to confer with Winchester.

But the boy fell into his doze again, while they were talking. Warner and Pennington, who had done less arduous duties, were sound asleep near him, the low flames now and then throwing a red light on their tanned faces. It seemed to him that it was about half way between midnight and morning, and the hum and murmur had sunk to a mere minor note. But his sleepy eyes still saw the dim forms of men passing about, and then he fell into his uneasy doze again.

When he awoke once more it was misty and dark, but he felt that the dawn was near. In the east a faint tint of silver showed through the clouds and vapors. Heavy banks of fog were rising from the Cumberland and the flooded marshes. The earth began to soften as if unlocking from the hard frost of the night.

Colonel Winchester stood near him and his position showed that he was intensely awake. He was bent slightly forward, and every nerve and muscle was strained as if he were eager to see and hear something which he knew was there, but which he could not yet either see or hear.

Dick threw off his blanket and sprang to his feet. At the same moment Colonel Winchester motioned him to awaken Warner and Pennington, which he did at once in speed and silence. That tint of silver, the lining of the fogs and vapors, shone more clearly through, and spread across the East. Dick knew now that the dawn was at hand.

The loud but mellow notes of a trumpet came from a distant point toward Donelson, and then others to right and left joined and sang the same mellow song. But it lasted only for a minute. Then it was lost in the rapid crackle of rifles, which spread like a running fire along a front of miles. The sun in the east swung clear of the earth, its beams shooting a way through fogs and vapors. The dawn had come and the attack had come with it.

The Southerners, ready at last, were rushing from their fort and works, and, with all the valor and fire that distinguished them upon countless occasions, they were hurling themselves upon their enemy. The fortress poured out regiment after regiment. Chafing so long upon the defense Southern youth was now at its best. Attacking, not attacked, the farmer lads felt the spirit of battle blaze high in their breasts. The long, terrible rebel yell, destined to be heard upon so many a desperate field, fierce upon its lower note, fierce upon its higher note, as fierce as ever upon its dying note, and coming back in echoes still as fierce, swelled over forest and fort, marsh and river.

The crackling fire of the pickets ceased. They had been driven back in a few moments upon the army, but the whole regiment of Colonel Winchester was now up, rifle in hand, and on either side of it, other regiments steadied themselves also to receive the living torrent.

The little band of Pennsylvanians were on the left of the Kentuckians and were practically a part of them. Colonel Newcomb and Major Hertford stood amid their men, encouraging them to receive the shock. But Dick had time for only a glance at these old comrades of his. The Southern wave, crested with fire and steel, was rolling swiftly upon them, and as the Southern troops rushed on they began to fire as fast as they could pull the trigger, fire and pull again.

Bullets in sheets struck in the Union ranks. Hundreds of men went down. Dick heard the thud of lead and steel on flesh, and the sudden cries of those who were struck. It needs no small courage to hold fast against more than ten thousand men rushing forward at full speed and bent upon victory or death.

Dick felt all the pulses in his temples beating hard, and he had a horrible impulse to break and run, but pride kept him firm. As an officer, he had a small sword, and snatching it out he waved it, while at the same time he shouted to the men to meet the charge.

The Union troops returned the fire. Thousands of bullets were sent against the ranks of the rushing enemy. The gunners sprang to their guns and the deep roar of the cannon rose above the crash of the small arms. But the Southern troops, the rebel yell still rolling through the woods, came on at full speed and struck the Union front.

It seemed to Dick that he was conscious of an actual physical shock. Tanned faces and gleaming eyes were almost against his own. He looked into the muzzles of rifles, and he saw the morning sun flashing along the edges of bayonets. But the regiment, although torn by bullets, did not give ground. The charge shivered against them, and the Southern troops fell back. Yet it was only for a moment. They came again to be driven back as before, and then once more they charged, while their resolute foe swung forward to meet them rank to rank.

Dick was not conscious of much except that he shouted continuously to the men to stand firm, and wondered now and then why he had not been hit. The Union men and their enemy were reeling back and forth, neither winning, neither losing, while the thunder of battle along a long and curving front beat heavily on the drums of every ear. The smoke, low down, was scattered by the cannon and rifles, but above it gathered in a great cloud that seemed to be shot with fire.

The two colonels, Winchester and Newcomb, were able and valiant men. Despite their swelling losses they always filled up the ranks and held fast to the ground upon which they had stood when they were attacked. But for the present they had no knowledge how the battle was going elsewhere. The enemy just before them allowed no idle moments.

Yet Grant, as happened later on at Shiloh, was taken by surprise. When the first roar of the battle broke with the dawn he was away conferring with the wounded naval commander, Foote. His right, under McClernand, had been caught napping, and eight thousand Southern troops striking it with a tremendous impact just as the men snatched up their arms, drove it back in heavy loss and confusion. Its disaster was increased when a Southern general, Baldwin, led a strong column down a deep ravine near the river and suddenly hurled it upon the wavering Union flank.

Whole regiments retreated now, and guns were lost. The Southern officers, their faces glowing, shouted to each other that the battle was won. And still the combat raged without the Union commander, Grant, although he was coming now as fast as he could with the increasing roar of conflict to draw him on. The battle was lost to the North. But it might be won back again by a general who would not quit. Only the bulldog in Grant, the tenacious death grip, could save him now.

Dick and his friends suddenly became conscious that both on their right and left the thunder of battle was moving back upon the Union camp. They realized now that they were only the segment of a circle extending forward practically within the Union lines, and that the combat was going against them. The word was given to retreat, lest they be surrounded, and they fell back slowly disputing with desperation every foot of ground that they gave up. Yet they left many fallen behind. A fourth of the regiment had been killed or wounded already, and there were tears in the eyes of Colonel Winchester as he looked over the torn ranks of his gallant men.

Now the Southerners, meaning to drive victory home, were bringing up their reserves and pouring fresh troops upon the shattered Union front. They would have swept everything away, but in the nick of time a fresh Union brigade arrived also, supported the yielding forces and threw itself upon the enemy.

But Grant had not yet come. It seemed that in the beginning fortune played against this man of destiny, throwing all her tricks in favor of his opponents. The single time that he was away the attack bad been made, and if he would win back a lost battle there was great need to hurry.

The Southern troops, exultant and full of fire and spirit, continually rolled back their adversaries. They wheeled more guns from the fort into position and opened heavily on the yielding foe. If they were beaten back at any time they always came on again, a restless wave, crested with fire and steel.

Dick's regiment continued to give ground slowly. It had no choice but to do so or be destroyed. It seemed to him now that he beheld the wreck of all things. Was this to be Bull Run over again? His throat and eyes burned from the smoke and powder, and his face was black with grime. His lips were like fire to the touch of each other. He staggered in the smoke against some one and saw that it was Warner.

"Have we lost?" he cried. "Have we lost after doing so much?"

The lips of the Vermonter parted in a kind of savage grin.

"I won't say we've lost," he shouted in reply, "but I can't see anything we've won."

Then he lost Warner in the smoke and the regiment retreated yet further. It was impossible to preserve cohesion or keep a line formed. The Southerners never ceased to press upon them with overwhelming weight. Pillow, now decisive in action, continually accumulated new forces upon the Northern right. Every position that McClernand had held at the opening of the battle was now taken, and the Confederate general was planning to surround and destroy the whole Union army. Already he was sending messengers to the telegraph with news for Johnston of his complete victory.

But the last straw had not yet been laid upon the camel's back. McClernand was beaten, but the hardy men of Kentucky, East Tennessee and the northwest still offered desperate resistance. Conspicuous among the defenders was the regiment of young pioneers from Nebraska, hunters, Indian fighters, boys of twenty or less, who had suffered already every form of hardship. They stood undaunted amid the showers of bullets and shells and cried to the others to stand with them.

Yet the condition of the Union army steadily grew worse. Dick himself, in all the smoke and shouting and confusion, could see it. The regiments that formed the core of resistance were being pared down continually. There was a steady dribble of fugitives to the rear, and those who fought felt themselves going back always, like one who slips on ice.

The sun, far up the heavens, now poured down beams upon the vast cloud of smoke and vapor in which the two armies fought. The few people left in Dover, red hot for the South, cheered madly as they saw their enemy driven further and further away.

Grant, the man of destiny, ill clad and insignificant in appearance, now came upon the field and saw his beaten army. But the bulldog in him shut down its teeth and resolved to replace defeat with victory. His greatest qualities, strength and courage in the face of disaster, were now about to shine forth. His countenance showed no alarm. He rode among the men cheering them to renewed efforts. He strengthened the weak places in the line that his keen eyes saw. He infused a new spirit into the army. His own iron temper took possession of the troops, and that core of resistance, desperate when he came, suddenly hardened and enlarged.

Dick felt the change. It was of the mind, but it was like a cool breath upon the face. It was as if the winds had begun to blow courage. A great shout rolled along the Northern line.

"Grant has come!" exclaimed Pennington, who was bleeding from a slight wound in the shoulder, but who was unconscious of it. "And we've quit retreating!"

The Nebraska youth had divined the truth. Just when a complete Southern victory seemed to be certain the reversal of fortune came. The coolness, the courage, and the comprehensive eye of Grant restored the battle for the North. The Southern reserves had not charged with the fire and spirit expected, and, met with a shattering fire by the Indiana troops, they fell back. Grant saw the opportunity, and massing every available regiment, he hurled it upon Pillow and the Southern center.

Dick felt the wild thrill of exultation as they went forward instead of going back, as they had done for so many hours. Just in front of him was Colonel Winchester, waving aloft a sword, the blade of which had been broken in two by a bullet, and calling to his men to come on. Warner and Pennington, grimed with smoke and mud and stained here and there with blood, were near also, shouting wildly.

The smoke split asunder for a moment, and Dick saw the long line of charging troops. It seemed to be a new army now, infused with fresh spirit and courage, and every pulse in the boy's body began to beat heavily with the hope of victory. The smoke closed in again and then came the shock.

Exhausted by their long efforts which had brought victory so near the Southern troops gave way. Their whole center was driven in, and they lost foot by foot the ground that they had gained with so much courage and blood. Grant saw his success and he pressed more troops upon his weakening enemy. The batteries were pushed forward and raked the shattered Southern lines.

Pillow, who had led the attack instead of Floyd, seeing his fortunes pass so suddenly from the zenith to the nadir, gathered his retreating army upon a hill in front of their intrenchments, but he was not permitted to rest there. A fresh Northern brigade, a reserve, had just arrived upon the field. Joining it to the forces of Lew Wallace, afterwards famous as a novelist, Grant hurled the entire division upon Pillow's weakened and discouraged army.

Winchester's regiment joined in the attack. Dick felt himself swept along as if by a torrent. His courage and the courage of those around him was all the greater now, because hope, sanguine hope, had suddenly shot up from the very depths of despair. Their ranks had been thinned terribly, but they forgot it for the time and rushed upon their enemy.

The battle had rolled back and forth for hours. Noon had come and passed. The troops of Pillow had been fighting without ceasing for six hours, and they could not withstand the new attack made with such tremendous spirit and energy. They fought with desperation, but they were compelled at last to yield the field and retreat within their works. Their right and left suffered the same fate. The whole Confederate attack was repulsed. Bull Run was indeed reversed. There the South snatched victory from defeat and here the North came back with a like triumph.

# CHAPTER XII

## GRANT'S GREAT VICTORY

The night, early and wintry, put an end to the conflict, the fiercest and greatest yet seen in the West. Thousands of dead and wounded lay upon the field and the hearts of the Southern leaders were full of bitterness. They had seen the victory, won by courage and daring, taken from them at the very last moment. The farmer lads whom they led had fought with splendid courage and tenacity. Defeat was no fault of theirs. It belonged rather to the generals, among whom had been a want of understanding and concert, fatal on the field of action. They saw, too, that they had lost more than the battle. The Union army had not only regained all its lost positions, but on the right it had carried the Southern intrenchments, and from that point Grant's great guns could dominate Donelson. They foresaw with dismay the effect of these facts upon their young troops.

When the night fell, and the battle ceased, save for the fitful boom of cannon along the lines, Dick sank against an earthwork, exhausted. He panted for breath and was without the power to move. He regarded vaguely the moving lights that had begun to show in the darkness, and he heard without comprehension the voices of men and the fitful fire of the cannon.

"Steady, Dick! Steady!" said a cheerful voice. "Now is the time to rejoice! We've won a victory, and nothing can break General Grant's death grip on Donelson!"

Colonel Winchester was speaking, and he put a firm and friendly hand on the boy's shoulder. Dick came back to life, and, looking into his colonel's face, he grinned. Colonel Winchester could have been recognized only at close range. His face was black with burned gunpowder. His colonel's hat was gone and his brown hair flew in every direction. He still clenched in his hand the hilt of his sword, of which a broken blade not more than a foot long was left. His clothing had been torn by at least a dozen bullets, and one had made a red streak across the back of his left hand, from which the blood fell slowly, drop by drop.

"You don't mind my telling you, colonel, that you're no beauty," said Dick, who felt a sort of hysterical wish to laugh. "You look as if the whole Southern army had tried to shoot you up, but had merely clipped you all around the borders."

"Laugh if it does you good," replied Colonel Winchester, a little gravely, "but, young sir, you must give me the same privilege. This battle, while it has not wounded you, has covered you with its grime. Come, the fighting is over for this day at least, and the regiment is going to take a rest—what there is left of it."

He spoke the last words sadly. He knew the terrible cost at which they had driven the Southern army back into the fort, and he feared that the full price was yet far from being paid. But he preserved a cheerful manner before the brave lads of his who had fought so well.

Dick found that Warner and Pennington both had wounds, although they were too slight to incapacitate them. Sergeant Whitley, grave and unhurt, rejoined them also.

The winter night and their heavy losses could not discourage the Northern troops. They shared the courage and tenacity of their commander. They began to believe now that Donelson, despite its strength and its formidable garrison, would be taken. They built the fires high, and ate heartily. They talked in sanguine tones of what they would do in the morrow. Excited comment ran among them. They had passed from the pit of despair in the morning to the apex of hope at night. Exhausted, all save the pickets fell asleep after a while, dreaming of fresh triumphs on the morrow.

Had Dick's eyes been able to penetrate Donelson he would have beheld a very different scene. Gloom, even more, despair, reigned there. Their great effort had failed. Bravery had availed nothing. Their frightful losses had been suffered in vain. The generals blamed one another. Floyd favored the surrender of the army, but fancying that the Union troops hated him with special vindictiveness, and that he would not be safe as a prisoner, decided to escape.

Pillow declared that Grant could yet be beaten, but after a while changed to the view of Floyd. They yet had two small steamers in the Cumberland which could carry them up the river. They left the command to Buckner, the third in rank, and told him he could make the surrender. The black-bearded Forrest said grimly: "I ain't goin' to surrender my cavalry, not to nobody," and by devious paths he led them away through the darkness and to liberty. Colonel George Kenton rode with him.

The rumor that a surrender was impending spread to the soldiers. Not yet firm in the bonds of discipline confusion ensued, and the high officers were too busy escaping by the river to restore it. All through the night the two little steamers worked, but a vast majority of the troops were left behind.

But Dick could know nothing of this at the time. He was sleeping too heavily. He had merely taken a moment to snatch a bit of food, and then, at the suggestion of his commanding officer, he had rolled himself in his blankets. Sleep came instantly, and it was not interrupted until Warner's hand fell upon his shoulder at dawn, and Warner's voice said in his ear:

"Wake up, Dick, and look at the white flag fluttering over Donelson."

Dick sprang to his feet, sleep gone in an instant, and gazed toward Donelson. Warner had spoken the truth. White flags waved from the walls and earthworks.

"So they're going to surrender!" said Dick. "What a triumph!"

"They haven't surrendered yet," said Colonel Winchester, who stood near. "Those white flags merely indicate a desire to talk it over with us, but such a desire is nearly always a sure indication of yielding, and our lads take it so. Hark to their cheering."

The whole Union army was on its feet now, joyously welcoming the sight of the white flags. They threw fresh fuel on their fires which blazed along a circling rim of miles, and ate a breakfast sweetened with the savor of triumph.

"Take this big tin cup of coffee, Dick," said Warner. "It'll warm you through and through, and we're entitled to a long, brown drink for our victory. I say victory because the chances are ninety-nine per cent out of a hundred that it is so. Let x equal our army, let y equal victory, and consequently x plus y equals our position at the present time."

"And I never thought that we could do it," said young Pennington, who sat with them. "I suppose it all comes of having a general who won't give up. I reckon the old saying is true, an' that Hold Fast is the best dog of them all."

Now came a period of waiting. Colonel Winchester disappeared in the direction of General Grant's headquarters, but returned after a while and called his favorite aide, young Richard Mason.

"Dick," he said, "we have summoned the Southerners to surrender, and I want you to go with me to a conference of their generals. You may be needed to carry dispatches."

Dick went gladly with the group of Union officers, who approached Fort Donelson under the white flag, and who met a group of Confederate officers under a like white flag. He noticed in the very center of the Southern group the figure of General Buckner, a tall, well-built man in his early prime, his face usually ruddy, now pale with fatigue and anxiety. Dick, with his uncle, Colonel Kenton, and his young cousin, Harry Kenton, had once dined at his house.

Nearly all the officers, Northern and Southern, knew one another well. Many of them had been together at West Point. Colonel Winchester and General Buckner were well acquainted and they saluted, each smiling a little grimly.

"I bring General Grant's demand for the surrender of Fort Donelson, and all its garrison, arms, ammunition, and other supplies," said Colonel Winchester. "Can I see your chief, General Floyd?"

The lips of Buckner pressed close together in a smile touched with irony.

"No, you cannot see General Floyd," he said, "because he is now far up the Cumberland."

"Since he has abdicated the command I wish then to communicate with General Pillow."

"I regret that you cannot speak to him either. He is as far up the Cumberland as General Floyd. Both departed in the night, and I am left in command of the Southern army at Fort Donelson. You can state your demands to me, Colonel Winchester."

Dick saw that the brave Kentuckian was struggling to hide his chagrin, and he had much sympathy for him. It was in truth a hard task that Floyd and Pillow had left for Buckner. They had allowed themselves to be trapped and they had thrown upon him the burden of surrendering. But Buckner proceeded with the negotiations. Presently he noticed Dick.

"Good morning, Richard," he said. "It seems that in this case, at least, you have chosen the side of the victors."

"Fortune has happened to be on our side, general," said Dick respectfully. "Could you tell me, sir, if my uncle, Colonel Kenton, is unhurt?"

"He was, when he was last with us," replied General Buckner, kindly. "Colonel Kenton went out last night with Forrest's cavalry. He will not be a prisoner."

"I am glad of that," said the boy.

And he was truly glad. He knew that it would hurt Colonel Kenton's pride terribly to become a prisoner, and although they were now on opposite sides, he loved and respected his uncle.

The negotiations were completed and before night the garrison of Donelson, all except three thousand who had escaped in the night with Floyd and Pillow and Forrest, laid down their arms. The answer to Bull Run was complete. Fifteen thousand men, sixty-five cannon, and seventeen thousand rifles and muskets were surrendered to General Grant. The bulldog in the silent westerner had triumphed. With only a last chance left to him he had turned defeat into complete victory, and had dealt a stunning blow to the Southern Confederacy, which was never able like the North to fill up its depleted ranks with fresh men.

Time alone could reveal to many the deadly nature of this blow, but Dick, who had foresight and imagination, understood it now at least in part. As he saw the hungry Southern boys sharing the food of their late enemies his mind traveled over the long Southern line. Thomas had beaten it in Eastern Kentucky, Grant had dealt it a far more crushing blow here in Western Kentucky, but Albert Sidney Johnston, the most formidable foe of all, yet remained in the center. He was a veteran general with a great reputation. Nay, more, it was said by the officers who knew him that he was a man of genius. Dick surmised that Johnston, after the stunning blow of Donelson, would be compelled to fall back from Tennessee, but he did not doubt that he would return again.

Dick soon saw that all his surmises were correct. The news of Donelson produced for a little while a sort of paralysis at Richmond, and when it reached Nashville, where the army of Johnston was gathering, it was at first unbelievable. It produced so much excitement and confusion that a small brigade sent to the relief of Donelson was not called back, and marched blindly into the little town of Dover, where it found itself surrounded by the whole triumphant Union army, and was compelled to surrender without a fight.

Panic swept through Nashville. Everybody knew that Johnston would be compelled to fall back from the Cumberland River, upon the banks of which the capital of Tennessee stood. Foote and his gunboats would come steaming up the stream into the very heart of the city. Rumor magnified the number and size of his boats. Again the Southern leaders felt that the rivers were always a hostile coil girdling them about, and lamented their own lack of a naval arm.

Floyd had drawn off in the night from Donelson his own special command of Virginians and when he arrived at Nashville with full news of the defeat at the fortress, and the agreement to surrender, the panic increased. Many had striven to believe that the reports were untrue, but now there could be no doubt.

And the panic gained a second impetus when the generals set fire to the suspension bridge over the river and the docks along its banks. The inhabitants saw the signal of doom in the sheets of flame that rolled up, and all those who had taken a leading part in the Southern cause prepared in haste to leave with Johnston's army. The roads were choked with vehicles and fleeing people. The State Legislature, which was then in session, departed bodily with all the records and archives.

But Dick, after the first hours of triumph, felt relaxed and depressed. After all, the victory was over their own people, and five thousand of the farmer lads, North and South, had been killed or wounded. But this feeling did not last long, as on the very evening of victory he was summoned to action. Action, with him, always made the blood leap and hope rise. It was his own regimental chief, Arthur Winchester, who called him, and who told him to make ready for an instant departure from Donelson.

"You are to be a cavalryman for a while, Dick," said Colonel Winchester. "So much has happened recently that we scarcely know how we stand. Above all, we do not know how the remaining Southern forces are disposed, and I have been chosen to lead a troop toward Nashville and see. You, Warner, Pennington, that very capable sergeant, Whitley, and others whom you know are to go with me. My force will number about three hundred and the horses are already waiting on the other side."

They were carried over the river on one of the boats, and the little company, mounting, prepared to ride into the dark woods. But before they disappeared, Dick looked back and saw many lights gleaming in captured Donelson. Once more the magnitude of Grant's victory impressed him. Certainly he had struck a paralyzing blow at the Southern army in the west.

But the ride in the dark over a wild and thinly-settled country soon occupied Dick's whole attention. He was on one side of Colonel Winchester and Warner was on the other. Then the others came four abreast. At first there was some disposition to talk, but it was checked sharply by the leader, and after a while the disposition itself was lacking.

Colonel Winchester was a daring horseman, and Dick soon realized that it would be no light task to follow where he led. Evidently he knew the country, as he rode with certainty over the worst roads that Dick had ever seen. They were deep in mud which froze at night, but not solidly enough to keep the feet of the horses from crushing through, making a crackle as they went down and a loud, sticky sigh as they came out. All were spattered with mud, which froze upon them, but they were so much inured to hardship now that they paid no attention to it.

But this rough riding soon showed so much effect upon the horses that Colonel Winchester led aside into the woods and fields, keeping parallel with the road. Now and then they stopped to pull down fences, but they still made good speed. Twice they saw at some distance cabins with the smoke yet rising from the chimneys, but the colonel did not stop to ask any questions. Those he thought could be asked better further on.

Twice they crossed creeks. One the horses could wade, but the other was so deep that they were compelled to swim. On the further bank of the second they stopped a while to rest the horses and to count the men to see that no straggler had dropped away in the darkness. Then they sprang into the saddle again and rode on as before through a country that seemed to be abandoned.

There was a certain thrill and exhilaration in their daring ride. The smoke and odors of the battle about Donelson were blown away. The dead and the wounded, the grewsome price even of victory, no longer lay before their eyes, and the cold air rushing past freshened their blood and gave it a new sparkle. Every one in the little column knew that danger was plentiful about them, but there was pleasure in action in the open.

Their general direction was Nashville, and now they came into a country, richer, better cultivated, and peopled more thickly. Toward night they saw on a gentle hill in a great lawn and surrounded by fine trees a large red brick house, with green shutters and portico supported by white pillars. Smoke rose from two chimneys. Colonel Winchester halted his troop and examined the house from a distance for a little while.

"This is the home of wealthy people," he said at last to Dick, "and we may obtain some information here. At least we should try it."

Dick had his doubts, but he said nothing.

"You, Mr. Pennington, Mr. Warner and Sergeant Whitley, dismount with me," continued the colonel, "and we'll try the house."

He bade his troop remain in the road under the command of the officer next in rank, and he, with those whom he had chosen, opened the lawn gate. A brick walk led to the portico and they strolled along it, their spurs jingling. Although the smoke still rose from the chimneys no door opened to them as they stepped into the portico. All the green shutters were closed tightly.

"I think they saw us in the road," said Dick, "and this is a house of staunch Southern sympathizers. That is why they don't open to us."

"Beat on the door with the hilt of your sword, sergeant," said the colonel to Whitley. "They're bound to answer in time."

The sergeant beat steadily and insistently. Yet he was forced to continue it five or six minutes before it was thrown open. Then a tall old woman with a dignified, stern face and white hair, drawn back from high brows, stood before them. But Dick's quick eyes saw in the dusk of the room behind her a girl of seventeen or eighteen.

"What do you want?" asked the woman in a tone of ice. "I see that you are Yankee soldiers, and if you intend to rob the house there is no one here to oppose you. Its sole occupants are myself, my granddaughter, and two colored women, our servants. But I tell you, before you begin, that all our silver has been shipped to Nashville."

Colonel Winchester flushed a deep crimson, and bit his lips savagely.

"Madame," he said, "we are not robbers and plunderers. These are regular soldiers belonging to General Grant's army."

"Does it make any difference? Your armies come to ravage and destroy the South."

Colonel Winchester flushed again but, remembering his self-control, he said politely:

"Madame, I hope that our actions will prove to you that we have been maligned. We have not come here to rob you or disturb you in any manner. We merely wished to inquire of you if you had seen any other Southern armed forces in this vicinity."

"And do you think, sir," she replied in the same uncompromising tones, "if I had seen them that I would tell you anything about it?"

"No, Madame," replied the Colonel bowing, "whatever I may have thought before I entered your portico I do not think so now."

"Then it gives me pleasure to bid you good evening, sir," she said, and shut the door in his face.

Colonel Winchester laughed rather sorely.

"She had rather the better of me," he said, "but we can't make war on women. Come on, lads, we'll ride ahead, and camp under the trees. It's easy to obtain plenty of fuel for fires."

"The darkness is coming fast," said Dick, "and it is going to be very cold, as usual."

In a half hour the day was fully gone, and, as he had foretold, the night was sharp with chill, setting every man to shivering. They turned aside into an oak grove and pitched their camp. It was never hard to obtain fuel, as the whole area of the great civil war was largely in forest, and the soldiers dragged up fallen brushwood in

145

abundance. Then the fires sprang up and created a wide circle of light and cheerfulness.

Dick joined zealously in the task of finding firewood and his search took him somewhat further than the others. He passed all the way through the belt of forest, and noticed fields beyond. He was about to turn back when he heard a faint, but regular sound. Experience told him that it was the beat of a horse's hoofs and he knew that some distance away a road must lead between the fields.

He walked a hundred yards further, and climbing upon a fence waited. From his perch he could see the road about two hundred yards beyond him, and the hoof beats were rapidly growing louder. Some one was riding hard and fast.

In a minute the horseman or rather horsewoman, came into view. There was enough light for Dick to see the slender figure of a young girl mounted on a great bay horse. She was wrapped in a heavy cloak, but her head was bare, and her long dark hair streamed almost straight out behind her, so great was the speed at which she rode.

She struck the horse occasionally with a small riding whip, but he was already going like a racer. Dick remembered the slim figure of a girl, and it occurred to him suddenly that this was she whom he had seen in the dusk of the room behind her grandmother. He wondered why she was riding so fast, alone and in the winter night, and then he admitted with a thrill of admiration that he had never seen any one ride better. The hoof beats rose, died away and then horse and girl were gone in the darkness. Dick climbed down from the fence and shook himself. Was it real or merely fancy, the product of a brain excited by so much siege and battle?

He picked up a big dead bough in the wood, dragged it back to the camp and threw it on one of the fires.

"What are you looking so grave about, Dick?" asked Warner.

"When I went across that stretch of woods I saw something that I didn't expect to see."

"What was it?"

"A girl on a big horse. They came and they went so fast that I just got a glimpse of them."

"A girl alone, galloping on a horse on a wintry night like this through a region infested by hostile armies! Why Dick, you're seeing shadows! Better sit down and have a cup of this good hot coffee."

But Dick shook his head. He knew now that he had seen reality, and he reported it to Colonel Winchester.

"Are you sure it was the girl you saw at the big house?" asked

Colonel Winchester. "It might have been some farmer's wife galloping home from an errand late in the evening."

"It was the girl. I am sure of it," said Dick confidently.

Just at that moment Sergeant Whitley came up and saluted.

"What is it, sergeant?" asked the Colonel.

"I have been up the road some distance, sir, and I came to another road that crossed it. The second road has been cut by hoofs of eight or nine hundred horses, and I am sure, sir, that the tracks are not a day old."

Colonel Winchester looked grave. He knew that he was deep in the country of the enemy and he began to put together what Dick had seen and what the sergeant had seen. But the thought of withdrawing did not occur to his brave soul. He had been sent on an errand by General Grant and he meant to do it. But he changed his plans for the night. He had intended to keep only one man in ten on watch. Instead, he kept half, and Sergeant Whitley, veteran of Indian wars, murmured words of approval under his breath.

Whitley and Pennington were in the early watch. Dick and Warner were to come on later. The colonel spoke as if he would keep watch all night. All the horses were tethered carefully inside the ring of pickets.

"It doesn't need any mathematical calculation," said Warner, "to tell that the colonel expects trouble of some kind tonight. What its nature is, I don't know, but I mean to go to sleep, nevertheless. I have already seen so much of hardship and war that the mere thought of danger does not trouble me. I took a fort on the Tennessee, I took a much larger one on the Cumberland, first defeating the enemy's army in a big battle, and now I am preparing to march on Nashville. Hence, I will not have my slumbers disturbed by a mere belief that danger may come."

"It's a good resolution, George," said Dick, "but unlike you, I am subject to impulses, emotions, thrills and anxieties."

"Better cure yourself," said the Vermonter, as he rolled himself in the blankets and put his head on his arm. In two minutes he was asleep, but Dick, despite his weariness, had disturbed nerves which refused to let him sleep for a long time. He closed his eyes repeatedly, and then opened them again, merely to see the tethered horses, and beyond them the circle of sentinels, a clear moonlight falling on their rifle barrels. But it was very warm and cosy in the blankets, and he would soon fall asleep again.

He was awakened about an hour after midnight to take his turn at the watch, and he noticed that Colonel Winchester was still standing beside one of the fires, but looking very anxious. Dick felt himself on good enough terms, despite his youth, to urge him to take rest.

"I should like to do so," replied Colonel Winchester, "but Dick I tell you, although you must keep it to yourself, that I think we are in some danger. Your glimpse of the flying horsewoman, and the undoubted fact that hundreds of horsemen have crossed the road ahead of us, have made me put two and two together. Ah, what is it, sergeant?"

"I think I hear noises to the east of us, sir," replied the veteran.

"What kind of noises, sergeant?"

"I should say, sir, that they're made by the hoofs of horses. There, I hear them again, sir. I'm quite sure of it, and they're growing louder!"

"And so do I!" exclaimed Colonel Winchester, now all life and activity. "The sounds are made by a large body of men advancing upon us! Seize that bugle, Dick, and blow the alarm with all your might!"

Dick snatched up the bugle and blew upon it a long shrill blast that pierced far into the forest. He blew and blew again, and every man in the little force sprang to his feet in alarm. Nor were they a moment too soon. From the woods to the east came the answering notes of a bugle and then a great voice cried:

"Forward men an' wipe 'em off the face of the earth!"

It seemed to Dick that he had heard that voice before, but he had no time to think about it, as the next instant came the rush of the wild horsemen, a thousand strong, leaning low over their saddles, their faces dark with the passion of anger and revenge, pistols, rifles, and carbines flashing as they pulled the trigger, giving way when empty to sabres, which gleamed in the moonlight as they were swung by powerful hands.

Colonel Winchester's whole force would have been ridden down in the twinkling of an eye if it had not been for the minute's warning. His men, leaping to their feet, snatched up their own rifles and fired a volley at short range. It did more execution among the horses than among the horsemen, and the Southern rough riders were compelled to waver for a moment. Many of their horses went down, others uttered the terrible shrieking neigh of the wounded, and, despite the efforts of those who rode them, strove to turn and flee from those flaming muzzles. It was only a moment, but it gave the Union troop, save those who were already slain, time to spring upon their horses and draw back, at the colonel's shouted command, to the cover of the wood. But they were driven hard. The Confederate cavalry came on again, impetuous and fierce as ever, and urged continually by the great partisan leader, Forrest, now in the very dawn of his fame.

"It was no phantom you saw, that girl on the horse!" shouted Warner in Dick's ear, and Dick nodded in return. They had no time for other words, as Forrest's horsemen, far outnumbering them, now pressed them harder than ever. A continuous fire came from their ranks and at close range they rode in with the sabre.

Dick experienced the full terror and surprise of a night battle. The opposing forces were so close together that it was often difficult to tell friend from enemy. But Forrest's men had every advantage of surprise, superior numbers and perfect knowledge of the country. Dick groaned aloud as he saw that the best they could do was to save as many as possible. Why had he not taken a shot at the horse of that flying girl?

"We must keep together, Dick!" shouted Warner. "Here are Pennington and Sergeant Whitley, and there's Colonel Winchester. I fancy that if we can get off with a part of our men we'll be doing well."

Pennington's horse, shot through the head, dropped like a stone to the ground, but the deft youth, used to riding the wild mustangs of the prairie, leaped clear, seized another which was galloping about riderless, and at one bound sprang into the saddle.

"Good boy!" shouted Dick with admiration, but the next moment the horsemen of Forrest were rushing upon them anew. More men were killed, many were taken, and Colonel Winchester, seeing the futility of further resistance, gathered together those who were left and took flight through the forest.

Tears of mortification came to Dick's eyes, but Sergeant Whitley, who rode on his right hand, said:

"It's the only thing to do. Remember that however bad your position may be it can always be worse. It's better for some of us to escape than for all of us to be down or be taken."

Dick knew that his logic was good, but the mortification nevertheless remained a long time. There was some consolation, however, in the fact that his own particular friends had neither fallen nor been taken.

They still heard the shouts of pursuing horsemen, and shots rattled about them, but now the covering darkness was their friend. They drew slowly away from all pursuit. The shouts and the sounds of trampling hoofs died behind them, and after two hours of hard riding Colonel Winchester drew rein and ordered a halt.

It was a disordered and downcast company of about fifty who were left. A few of these were wounded, but not badly enough to be disabled. Colonel Winchester's own head had been grazed, but he had bound a handkerchief about it, and sat very quiet in his saddle.

"My lads," he said, and his tone was sharp with the note of defiance. "We have been surprised by a force greatly superior to our own, and scarcely a sixth of us are left. But it was my fault. I take the blame. For the present, at least, we are safe from the enemy, and I intend to continue with our errand. We were to scout the country all the way to Nashville. It is also possible that we will meet the division of General Buell advancing to that city. Now, lads, I hope that you all will be willing to go on with me. Are you?"

"We are!" roared fifty together, and a smile passed over the wan face of the colonel. But he said no more then. Instead he turned his head toward the capital city of the state, and rode until dawn, his men following close behind him. The boys were weary. In truth, all of them were, but no one spoke of halting or complained in any manner.

At sunrise they stopped in dense forest at the banks of a creek, and watered their horses. They cooked what food they had left, and after eating rested for several hours on the ground, most of them going to sleep, while a few men kept a vigilant watch.

When Dick awoke it was nearly noon, and he still felt sore from his exertions. An hour later they all mounted and rode again toward Nashville. Near night they boldly entered a small village and bought food. The inhabitants were all strongly Southern, but villagers love to talk, and they learned there in a manner admitting of no doubt, that the Confederate army was retreating southward from the line of the Cumberland, that the state capital had been abandoned, and that to the eastward of them the Union army, under Buell, was advancing swiftly on Nashville.

"At least we accomplished our mission," said Colonel Winchester with some return of cheerfulness. "We have discovered the retreat of General Johnston's whole army, and the abandonment of Nashville, invaluable information to General Grant. But we'll press on toward Nashville nevertheless."

They camped the next night in a forest and kept a most vigilant watch. If those terrible raiders led by Forrest should strike them again they could make but little defense.

They came the next morning upon a good road and followed it

without interruption until nearly noon, when they saw the glint of arms across a wide field. Colonel Winchester drew his little troop back into the edge of the woods, and put his field glasses to his eyes.

"There are many men, riding along a road parallel to ours," he said. "They look like an entire regiment, and by all that's lucky, they're in the uniforms of our own troops. Yes, they're our own men. There can be no mistake. It is probably the advance guard of Buell's army."

They still had a trumpet, and at the colonel's order it was blown long and loud. An answering call came from the men on the parallel road, and they halted. Then Colonel Winchester's little troop galloped forward and they were soon shaking hands with the men of a mounted regiment from Ohio. They had been sent ahead by Buell to watch Johnston's army, but hearing of the abandonment of Nashville, they were now riding straight for the city. Colonel Winchester and his troop joined them gladly and the colonel rode by the side of the Ohio colonel, Mitchel.

Dick and his young comrades felt great relief. He realized the terrible activity of Forrest, but that cavalry leader, even if he had not now gone south, would hesitate about attacking the powerful regiment with which Dick now rode. Warner and Pennington shared his feelings.

"The chances are ninety per cent in our favor," said the Vermonter, "that we'll ride into Nashville without a fight. I've never been in Tennessee before, and I'm a long way from home, but I'm curious to see this city. I'd like to sleep in a house once more."

They rode into Nashville the next morning amid frowning looks, but the half deserted city offered no resistance.

# CHAPTER XIII

# IN THE FOREST

Dick spent a week or more in Nashville and he saw the arrival of one of General Grant's divisions on the fleet under Commodore Foote. Once more he appreciated the immense value of the rivers and the fleet to the North.

He and the two lads who were now knitted to him by sympathy, and hardships and dangers shared, enjoyed their stay in Nashville. It was pleasant to sleep once more in houses and to be sheltered from rain and frost and snow. It was pleasant, too, for these youths, who were devoted to the Union, to think that their armies had made such progress in the west. The silent and inflexible Grant had struck the first great blow for the North. The immense Confederate line in the west was driven far southward, and the capital of one of the most vigorous of the secessionist states was now held by the Union.

But a little later, news not so pleasant came to them. The energy and success of Grant had aroused jealousy. Halleck, his superior, the general of books and maps at St. Louis, said that he had transcended the limits of his command. He was infringing upon territory of other Northern generals. Halleck had not found him to be the yielding subordinate who would win successes and let others have the credit.

Grant was practically relieved of his command, and when Dick heard it he felt a throb of rage. Boy as he was, he knew that what had been won must be held. Johnston had stopped at Murfreesborough, thirty or forty miles away. His troops had recovered from their panic, caused by the fall of Donelson. Fresh regiments and brigades were joining him. His army was rising to forty thousand men, and officers like Colonel Winchester began to feel apprehensive.

Now came a period of waiting. The Northern leaders, as happened so often in this war, were uncertain of their authority, and were at cross-purposes. They seldom had the power of initiative that was permitted to the Southern generals, and of which they made such good use. Dick saw that the impression made by Donelson was fading. The North was reaping no harvest, and the South was lifting up its head again.

While he was in Nashville he received a letter from his mother in reply to one of his that he had written to her just after Donelson.

She was very thankful that her son had gone safely through the battle, and since he must fight in war, which was terrible in any aspect, she was glad that he had borne himself bravely. She was glad that Colonel Kenton had escaped capture. Her brother-in-law was always good to her and was a good man. She had also received a letter from his son, her nephew, written from Richmond, She loved Harry Kenton, too, and sympathized with him, but she could not see how both sides could prevail.

Dick read the letter over and over again and there was a warm glow about his heart. What a brave woman his mother was! She said nothing about his coming back home, or leaving the war. He wrote a long reply, and he told her only of the lighter and more cheerful events that they had encountered. He described Warner, Pennington, and the sergeant, and said that he had the best comrades in the world. He told, too, of his gallant and high-minded commander, Colonel Arthur Winchester.

He was sure that the letter would reach her promptly, as it passed all the way through territory now controlled by the North. The next day after sending it he heard with joy that Grant was restored to his command, and two days later Colonel Winchester and his men were ordered to join him at Pittsburg Landing, on the Tennessee River. They heard also that Buell, with his whole division, was soon to march to the same place, and they saw in it an omen of speedy and concentrated action.

"I imagine," said Warner, "that we'll soon go down in Mississippi hunting Johnston. We must outnumber the Johnny Rebs at least two to one. I'm not a general, though any one can see that I ought to be, and if we were to follow Johnston's army and crush it the war would soon be ended in the west."

"You've got a mighty big 'if'," said Dick. "If we march into Mississippi we get pretty far from our base. We'll have to send a long distance through hostile country for fresh supplies and fresh troops, while the Southerners will be nearer to their own. Besides, it's not so certain that we can destroy Johnston when we find him."

"Your talk sounds logical, and that being the case, I'll leave our future movements to General Grant. Anyway, it's a good thing not to have so much responsibility on your shoulders."

They came in a few days to the great camp on the Tennessee. Spring was now breaking through the crust of winter. Touches of green were appearing on the forests and in the fields. Now and then the wonderful pungent odor of the wilderness came to them and life seemed to have taken on new zest. They were but boys in years, and the terrible scenes of Donelson could not linger with them long.

They found Colonel Newcomb and the little detachment of

Pennsylvanians with Grant, and Colonel Winchester, resuming command of his regiment, camped by their side, delighted to be with old friends again. Colonel Winchester had lost a portion of his regiment, but there were excuses. It had happened in a country well known to the enemy and but little known to him, and he had been attacked in overwhelming force by the rough-riding Forrest, who was long to be a terror to the Union divisions. But he had achieved the task on which he had been sent, and he was thanked by his commander.

Dick, as he went on many errands or walked about in the course of his leisure hours with his friends, watched with interest the growth of a great army. There were more men here upon the banks of the Tennessee than he had seen at Bull Run. They were gathered full forty thousand strong, and General Buell's army also, he learned, had been put under command of General Grant and was advancing from Nashville to join him.

Dick also observed with extreme interest the ground upon which they were encamped and the country surrounding it. There was the deep Tennessee, still swollen by spring rains, upon the left bank of which they lay, with the stream protecting one flank. In the river were some of the gunboats which had been of such value to Grant. All about them was rough, hilly country, almost wholly covered with brushwood and tall forest. There were three deep creeks, given significant names by the pioneers. Lick Creek flowed to the south of them into the Tennessee, and Owl Creek to the north sought the same destination. A third, Snake Creek, was lined with deep and impassable swamps to its very junction with the river.

Some roads of the usual frontier type ran through this region, and at a point within the Northern lines stood a little primitive log church that they called Shiloh. It was of the kind that the pioneers built everywhere as they moved from the Atlantic to the Pacific. Shiloh belonged to a little body of Methodists. Dick went into it more than once. There was no pastor and no congregation now, but the little church was not molested. He sat more than once on an uncompromising wooden bench, and looked out through a window, from which the shutter was gone, at the forest and the army.

Sitting here in this primitive house of worship, he would feel a certain sadness. It seemed strange that a great army, whose purpose was to destroy other armies, should be encamped around a building erected in the cause of the Prince of Peace. The mighty and terrible nature of the war was borne in upon him more fully than ever.

But optimism was supreme among the soldiers. They had achieved the great victory of Donelson in the face of odds that had seemed impossible. They could defeat all the Southern forces that lay between them and the Gulf. The generals shared their confidence. They did not fortify their camp. They had not come that far South to fight defensive battles. It was their place to attack and that of the men in gray to defend. They had advanced in triumph almost to the Mississippi line, and they would soon be pursuing their disorganized foe into that Gulf State.

Several new generals came to serve under Grant. Among them was one named Sherman, to whom Dick bore messages several times, and who impressed him with his dry manner and curt remarks which were yet so full of sense.

It was Sherman's division, in fact, that was encamped around the little church, and Dick soon learned his opinions. He did not believe that they would so easily conquer the South. He did not look for any triumphal parade to the Gulf. In the beginning of the war he had brought great enmity and criticism upon himself by saying that 200,000 men at least would be needed at once to crush the Confederacy in the west alone. And yet it was to take more than ten times that number four bitter years to achieve the task in both west and east.

But optimism continued to reign in the Union army. Buell would arrive soon with his division and then seventy thousand strong they would resume their march southward, crushing everything. Meanwhile it was pleasant while they waited. They had an abundance of food. They were well sheltered from the rains. The cold days were passing, nature was bursting into its spring bloom, and the crisp fresh winds that blew from the west and south were full of life and strength. It was a joy merely to breathe.

One rainy day the three boys, who had met by chance, went into the little church for shelter from a sudden spring rain. From the shutterless window Dick saw Sergeant Whitley scurrying in search of a refuge, and they called to him. He came gladly and took a seat in one of the rough wooden pews of the little church of Shiloh. The three boys had the greatest respect for the character and judgment of the sergeant, and Dick asked him when he thought the army would march.

"They don't tell these things to sergeants," said Whitley.

"But you see and you know a lot about war."

"Well, you've noticed that the army ain't gettin' ready to march. When General Buell gets here we'll have nigh onto seventy thousand men, and seventy thousand men can't lift themselves up by their bootstraps an' leave, all in a mornin'."

"But we don't have to hurry," said Pennington. "There's no Southern army west of the Alleghanies that could stand before our seventy thousand men for an hour."

"General Buell ain't here yet."

"But he's coming."

"But he ain't here yet," persisted the sergeant, "an' he can't be here for several days, 'cause the roads are mighty deep in the spring mud. Don't say any man is here until he is here. An' I tell you that General Johnston, with whom we've got to deal, is a great man. I wasn't with him when he made that great march through the blizzards an' across the plains to Salt Lake City to make the Mormons behave, but I've served with them that was. An' I've never yet found one of them who didn't say General Johnston was a mighty big man. Soldiers know when the right kind of a man is holdin' the reins an' drivin' 'em. Didn't we all feel that we was bein' driv right when General Grant took hold?"

"We all felt it," said the three in chorus.

"Of course you did," said the sergeant, "an' now I've got a kind of uneasy feelin' over General Johnston. Why don't we hear somethin' from him? Why don't we know what he's doin'? We haven't sent out any scoutin' parties. On the plains, no matter how strong we was, we was always on the lookout for hostile Indians, while here we know there is a big Confederate army somewhere within fifty miles of us, but don't take the trouble to look it up."

"That's so," said Warner. "Caution represents less than five per cent of our effectiveness. But I suppose we can whip the Johnnies anyway."

"Of course we can," said Pennington, who was always of a most buoyant temperament.

Sergeant Whitley went to the shutterless window, and looked out at the forest and the long array of tents.

"The rain is about over," he said. "It was just a passin' shower. But it looks as if it had already added a fresh shade of green to the leaves and grass. Cur'us how quick a rain can do it in spring, when everything is just waitin' a chance to grow, and bust into bloom. I've rid on the plains when everything was brown an' looked dead. 'Long come a big rain an' the next day everything was green as far as the eye could reach an' you'd see little flowers bloomin' down under the shelter of the grass."

"I didn't know you had a poetical streak in you, sergeant," said Dick, who marked his abrupt change from the discussion of the war to a far different topic.

"I think some of it is in every man," replied Sergeant Whitley gravely. "I remember once that when we had finished a long chase after some Northern Cheyennes through mighty rough and dry country we came to a little valley, a kind of a pocket in the hills, fed by a fine creek, runnin' out of the mountains on one side, into the

156

mountains on the other. The pocket was mebbe two miles long an' mebbe a mile across, an' it was chock full of green trees an' green grass, an' wild flowers. We enjoyed its comforts, but do you think that was all? Every man among us, an' there was at least a dozen who couldn't read, admired its beauties, an' begun to talk softer an' more gentle than they did when they was out on the dry plains. An' you feel them things more in war than you do at any other time."

"I suppose you do," said Dick. "The spring is coming out now in Kentucky where I live, and I'd like to see the new grass rippling before the wind, and the young leaves on the trees rustling softly together."

"Stop sentimentalizing," said Warner. "If you don't it won't be a minute before Pennington will begin to talk about his Nebraska plains, and how he'd like to see the buffalo herds ten million strong, rocking the earth as they go galloping by."

Pennington smiled.

"I won't see the buffalo herds," he said, "but look at the wild fowl going north."

They left the window as the rain had ceased, and went outside. All this region was still primitive and thinly settled, and now they saw flocks of wild ducks and wild geese winging northward. The next day the heavens themselves were darkened by an immense flight of wild pigeons. The country cut up by so many rivers, creeks and brooks swarmed with wild fowl, and more than once the soldiers roused up deer from the thickets.

The second day after the talk of the four in the little church Dick, who was now regarded as a most efficient and trusty young staff officer, was sent with a dispatch to General Buell requesting him to press forward with as much speed as he could to the junction with General Grant. Several other aides were sent by different routes, in order to make sure that at least one would arrive, but Dick, through his former ride with Colonel Winchester to Nashville, had the most knowledge of the country, and hence was likely to reach Buell first.

As the boy rode from the camp and crossed the river into the forest he looked back, and he could not fail to notice to what an extent it was yet a citizen army, and not one of trained soldiers. The veteran sergeant had already called his attention to what he deemed grave omissions. In the three weeks that they had been lying there they had thrown up no earthworks. Not a spade had touched the earth. Nor was there any other defense of any kind. The high forest circled close about them, dense now with foliage and underbrush, hiding even at a distance of a few hundred yards anything that might lie within. The cavalry in these three weeks had made one scouting expedition, but it was slight and superficial, resulting in nothing. The generals of divisions posted their own pickets separately, leaving numerous wide breaks in the line, and the farmer lads, at the change of guard, invariably fired their rifles in the air, to signify the joy of living, and because it was good to hear the sound.

Now that he was riding away from them, these things impressed Dick more than when he was among them. Sergeant Whitley's warning and pessimistic words came back to him with new force, but, as he rode into the depths of the forest, he shook off all depression. Those words, "Seventy thousand strong!" continually recurred to him. Yes, they would be seventy thousand strong when Buell came up, and the boys were right. Certainly there was no Confederate force in the west that could resist seventy thousand troops, splendidly armed, flushed with victory and led by a man like Grant.

Seventy thousand strong! Dick's heart beat high at the unuttered words. Why should Grant fortify? It was for the enemy, not for him, to do such a thing. Nor was it possible that Johnston even behind defenses could resist the impact of the seventy thousand who had been passing from one victory to another, and who were now in the very heart of the enemy's country.

His heart continued to beat high and fast as he rode through the green forest. Its strong, sweet odors gave a fillip to his blood, and he pressed his horse to new speed. He rode without interruption night and day, save a few hours now and then for sleep, and reached the army of Buell which deep in mud was toiling slowly forward.

Buell was not as near to Shiloh as Dick had supposed, but his march had suffered great hindrances. Halleck, in an office far away in St. Louis, had undertaken to manage the campaign. His orders to Buell and his command to Grant had been delayed. Buell, who had moved to the town of Columbia, therefore had started late through no fault of his.

Duck River, which Buell was compelled to cross, was swollen like all the other streams of the region, by the great rains and was forty feet deep. The railway bridge across it had been wrecked by the retreating Confederates and he was compelled to wait there two weeks until his engineers could reconstruct it.

War plays singular chances. Halleck in St. Louis, secure in his plan of campaign, had sent an order after Dick left Shiloh, for Buell to turn to the north, leaving Grant to himself, and occupy a town that he named. Through some chance the order never reached Buell. Had it done so the whole course of American history might have been changed. Grant himself, after the departure of the earlier messengers, changed his mind and sent messengers to Nelson, who led Buell's vanguard, telling him not to hurry. This army was to come to Pittsburg Landing or Shiloh partly by the Tennessee, and Grant stated that the vessels for him would not be ready until some days later. It was the early stage of the war when generals behaved with great independence, and Nelson, a rough, stubborn man, after reading the order marched on faster than ever. It seemed afterward that the very stars were for Grant, when one order was lost, and another disobeyed.

But Dick was not to know of these things until later. He delivered in person his dispatch to General Buell, who remembered him and gave him a friendly nod, but who was as chary of speech as ever. He wrote a brief reply to the dispatch and gave it sealed to Dick.

"The letter I hand you," he said, "merely notifies General Grant that I have received his orders and will hurry forward as much as possible. If on your return journey you should deem yourself in danger of falling into the hands of the enemy destroy it at once."

Dick promised to do so, saluted, and retired. He spent only two hours in General Buell's camp, securing some fresh provisions to carry in his saddle bags and allowing his horse a little rest. Then he mounted and took as straight a course as he could for General Grant's camp at Pittsburg Landing.

The boy felt satisfied with himself. He had done his mission quickly and exactly, and he would have a pleasant ride back. On his strong, swift horse, and with a good knowledge of the road, he could go several times faster than Buell's army. He anticipated a pleasant ride. The forest seemed to him to be fairly drenched in spring. Little birds flaming in color darted among the boughs and others more modest in garb poured forth a full volume of song. Dick, sensitive to sights and sounds, hummed a tune himself. It was the thundering song of the sea that he had heard Samuel Jarvis sing in the Kentucky Mountains:

> They bore him away when the day had fled,
> And the storm was rolling high,
> And they laid him down in his lonely bed
> By the light of an angry sky.
> The lightning flashed and the wild sea lashed
> The shore with its foaming wave,
> And the thunder passed on the rushing blast,
> As it howled o'er the rover's grave.

He pressed on, hour after hour, through the deep woods, meeting no one, but content. At noon his horse suddenly showed signs of great weariness, and Dick, remembering how much he had ridden him over muddy roads, gave him a long rest. Besides, there was no need to hurry. The Southern army was at Corinth, in Mississippi, three or four days' journey away, and there had been no scouts or skirmishers in the woods between.

After a stop of an hour he remounted and rode on again, but the horse was still feeling his great strain, and he did not push him beyond a walk. He calculated that nevertheless he would reach headquarters not long after nightfall, and he went along gaily, still singing to himself. He crossed the river at a point above the army, where the Union troops had made a ferry, and then turned toward the camp.

About sunset he reached a hill from which he could look over the forest and see under the horizon faint lights that were made by Grant's campfires at Pittsburg Landing. It was a welcome sight. He would soon be with his friends again, and he urged his horse forward a little faster.

"Halt!" cried a sharp voice from the thicket.

Dick faced about in amazement, and saw four horsemen in gray riding from the bushes. The shock was as great as if he had been struck by a bullet, but he leaned forward on his horse's neck, kicked him violently with his heels and shouted to him. The horse plunged forward at a gallop. The boy, remembering General Buell's instructions, slipped the letter from his pocket, and in the shelter of the horse's body dropped it to the ground, where he knew it would be lost among the bushes and in the twilight.

"Halt!" was repeated more loudly and sharply than ever. Then a bullet whizzed by Dick's ear, and a second pierced the heart of his good horse. He tried to leap clear of the falling animal, and succeeded, but he fell so hard among the bushes that he was stunned for a few moments. When he revived and stood up he saw the four horsemen in gray looking curiously at him.

"'Twould have been cheaper for you to have stopped when we told you to do it," said one in a whimsical tone.

Dick noticed that the tone was not unkind—it was not the custom to treat prisoners ill in this great war. He rubbed his left shoulder on which he had fallen and which still pained him a little.

"I didn't stop," he said, "because I didn't know that you would be able to hit either me or my horse in the dusk."

"I s'pose from your way of lookin' at it you was right to take the chance, but you've learned now that we Southern men are tol'able good sharpshooters."

160

"I knew it long ago, but what are you doing here, right in the jaws of our army? They might close on you any minute with a snap. You ought to be with your own army at Corinth."

Dick noticed that the men looked at one another, and there was silence for a moment or two.

"Young fellow," resumed the spokesman, "you was comin' from the direction of Columbia, an' your hoss, which I am sorry we had to kill, looked as if he was cleaned tuckered out. I judge that you was bearin' a message from Buell's army to Grant's."

"You mustn't hold me responsible for your judgment, good or bad."

"No, I reckon not, but say, young fellow, do you happen to have a chaw of terbacker in your clothes?"

"If I had any I'd offer it to you, but I never chew."

The man sighed.

"Well, mebbe it's a bad habit," he said, "but it's powerful grippin'. I'd give a heap for a good twist of old Kentucky. Now we're goin' to search you an' it ain't wuth while to resist, 'cause we've got you where we want you, as the dog said to the 'coon when he took him by the throat. We're lookin' for letters an' dispatches, 'cause we're shore you come from Buell, but if we should run across any terbacker we'll have to he'p ourselves to it. We ain't no robbers, 'cause in times like these it ain't no robbery to take terbacker."

Dick noticed that while they talked one of the men never ceased to cover him with a rifle. They were good-humored and kindly, but he knew they would not relax an inch from their duty.

"All right," he said, "go ahead. I'll give you a good legal title to everything you may find."

He knew that the letter was lying in the bushes within ten feet of them and he had a strong temptation to look in that direction and see if it were as securely hidden as he had thought, but he resisted the impulse.

Two of the men searched him rapidly and dexterously, and much to their disappointment found no dispatch.

"You ain't got any writin' on you, that's shore," said the spokesman. "I'd expected to find a paper, an' I had a lingerin' hope, too, that we might find a little terbacker on you 'spite of what you said."

"You don't think I'd lie about the tobacco, would you?"

"Sonny, it ain't no lyin' in a big war to say you ain't got no terbacker, when them that's achin' for it are standin' by, ready to grab it. If you had a big diamond hid about you, an' a robber was to ask you if you had it, you'd tell him no, of course."

"I think," said Dick, "that you must be from Kentucky. You've got our accent."

"I shorely am, an' I'm a longer way from it than I like. I noticed from the first that you talked like me, which is powerful flatterin' to you. Ain't you one of my brethren that the evil witches have made take up with the Yankees?"

"I'm from the same state," replied Dick, who saw no reason to conceal his identity. "My name is Richard Mason, and I'm an aide on the staff of Colonel Arthur Winchester, who commands a Kentucky regiment in General Grant's army."

"I've heard of Colonel Winchester. The same that got a part of his regiment cut up so bad by Forrest."

"Yes, we did get cut up. I was there," confessed Dick a little reluctantly.

"Don't feel bad about it. It's likely to happen to any of you when Forrest is around. Now, since you've introduced yourself so nice I'll introduce myself. I'm Sergeant Robertson, in the Orphan Brigade. It's a Kentucky brigade, an' it gets its nickname 'cause it's made up of boys so young that they call me gran'pa, though I'm only forty-four. These other three are Bridge, Perkins, and Connor, just plain privates."

The three "just plain privates" grinned.

"What are you going to do with me?" asked Dick.

"We're goin' to give you a pleasant little ride. We killed your hoss, for which I 'pologize again, but I've got a good one of my own, and you'll jump up behind me."

A sudden spatter of rifle fire came from the direction of the Northern pickets.

"Them sentinels of yours have funny habits," said Robertson grinning. "Just bound to hear their guns go off. They're changin' the guard now."

"How do you know that?" asked Dick.

"Oh, I know a heap. I'm a terrible wise man, but bein' so wise I don't tell all I know or how I happen to know it. Hop up, sonny."

"Don't you think I'll be a lot of trouble to you," said Dick, "riding behind you thirty or forty miles to your camp?"

The four men exchanged glances, and no one answered. The boy felt a sudden chill, and his hair prickled at the roots. He did not know what had caused it, but surely it was a sign of some danger.

The night deepened steadily as they were talking. The twilight had gone long since. The last afterglow had faded. The darkness was heavy with warmth. The thick foliage of spring rustled gently. Dick's sensation that something unusual was happening did not depart.

The four men, after looking at one another, looked fixedly at Dick.

"Sonny," said Robertson, "you ain't got no call to worry 'bout our troubles. As I said, this is a good, strong hoss of mine, an' it will carry us just as far as we go an' no further."

It was an enigmatical reply, and Dick saw that it was useless to ask them questions. Robertson mounted, and Dick, without another word, sprang up behind him. Two of the privates rode up close, one on either side, and the other kept immediately behind. He happened to glance back and he saw that the man held a drawn pistol on his thigh. He wondered at such extreme precautions, and the ominous feeling increased.

"Now, lads," said Robertson to his men, "don't make no more noise than you can help. There ain't much chance that any Yankee scoutin' party will be out, but if there should be one we don't want to run into it. An' as for you, Mr. Mason, you're a nice boy. We all can see that, but just as shore as you let go with a yell or anything like it at any time or under any circumstances, you'll be dead the next second."

A sudden fierce note rang in his voice, and Dick, despite all his courage, shuddered. He felt as if a nameless terror all at once threatened not only him, but others. His lips and mouth were dry.

Robertson spoke softly to his horse, and then rode slowly forward through the deep forest. The others rode with him, never breaking their compact formation, and preserving the utmost silence. Dick did not ask another question. Talk and fellowship were over. Everything before him now was grim and menacing.

The dense woods and the darkness hid them so securely that they could not have been seen twenty yards away, but the men rode on at a sure pace, as if they knew the ground well. The silence was deep and intense, save for the footsteps of the horses and now and then a night bird in the tall trees calling.

Before they had gone far a man stepped from a thicket and held up a rifle.

"Four men from the Orphan Brigade with a prisoner," said Robertson.

"Advance with the prisoner," said the picket, and the four men rode forward. Dick saw to both left and right other pickets, all in the gray uniform of the South, and his heart grew cold within him. The hair on his head prickled again at its roots, and it was a dreadful sensation. What did it mean? Why these Southern pickets within cannon shot of the Northern lines?

The men rode slowly on. They were in the deep forest, but the young prisoner began to see many things under the leafy canopy.

163

On his right the dim, shadowy forms of hundreds of men lay sleeping on the grass. On his left was a massed battery of great guns, eight in number.

Further and further they went, and there were soldiers and cannon everywhere, but not a fire. There was no bed of coals, not a single torch gleamed anywhere. Not all the soldiers were sleeping, but those who were awake never spoke. Silence and darkness brooded over a great army in gray. It was as if they marched among forty thousand phantoms, row on row.

The whole appalling truth burst in an instant upon the boy. The Southern army, which they had supposed was at Corinth, lay in the deep woods within cannon shot of its foe, and not a soul in all Grant's thousands knew of its presence there! And Buell was still far away! It seemed to Dick that for a little space his heart stopped beating. He foresaw it all, the terrible hammer-stroke at dawn, the rush of the fiery South upon her unsuspecting foe, and the cutting down of brigades, before sleep was gone from their eyes.

Not in vain had the South boasted that Johnston was a great general. He had not been daunted by Donelson. While his foe rested on his victory and took his ease, he was here with a new army, ready to strike the unwary. Dick shivered suddenly, and, with a violent impulse, clutched the waist of the man in front of him. It may have been some sort of physical telepathy, but Robertson understood. He turned his head and said in a whisper:

"You're right. The whole Southern army is here in the woods, an' we'd rather lose a brigade tonight than let you escape."

Dick felt a thrill of the most acute agony. If he could only escape! There must be some way! If he could but find one! His single word would save the lives of thousands and prevent irreparable defeat! Again he clutched the waist of the man in front of him and again the man divined.

"It ain't no use," he said, although his tone was gentle, and in a way sympathetic. "After all, it's your own fault. You blundered right in our way, an' we had to take you for fear you'd see us, an' give the alarm. It was your unlucky chance. You'd give a million dollars if you had it to slip out of our hands and tell Ulysses Grant that Albert Sidney Johnston with his whole army is layin' in the woods right alongside of him, ready to jump on his back at dawn, an' he not knowin' it."

"I would," said Dick fervently.

"An' so would I if I was in your place. Just think, Mr. Mason, that of all the hundreds of thousands of men in the Northern armies, of all the twenty or twenty-five million people on the

Northern side, there's just one, that one a boy, and that boy you, who knows that Albert Sidney Johnston is here."

"Held fast as I am, I'm sorry now that I do know it."

"I can't say that I blame you. I said you'd give a million dollars to be able to tell, but if you're to measure such things with money it would be worth a hundred million an' more, yes, it would be cheap at three or four hundred millions for the North to know it. But, after all, you can't measure such things with money. Maybe you think I talk a heap, but I'm stirred some, too."

They rode on a little farther over the hilly ground, covered with thick forest or dense, tall scrub. But there were troops, troops, everywhere, and now and then the batteries. They were mostly boys, like their antagonists of the North, and the sleep of most of them was the sleep of exhaustion, after a forced and rapid march over heavy ground from Corinth. But Dick knew that they would be fresh in the morning when they rose from the forest, and rushed upon their unwarned foe.

# CHAPTER XIV

## THE DARK EVE OF SHILOH

Dick noticed as they went further into the forest how complete was the concealment of a great army, possible only in a country wooded so heavily, and in the presence of a careless enemy. The center was like the front of the Southern force. Not a fire burned, not a torch gleamed. The horses were withdrawn so far that stamp or neigh could not be heard by the Union pickets.

"We'll stop here," said Robertson at length. "As you're a Kentuckian, I thought it would be pleasanter for you to be handed over to Kentuckians. The Orphan Brigade to which I belong is layin' on the ground right in front of us, an' the first regiment is that of Colonel Kenton. I'll hand you over to him, an'—not 'cause I've got anything ag'inst you—I'll be mighty glad to do it, too, 'cause my back is already nigh breakin' with the responsibility."

Dick started violently.

"What's hit you?" asked Robertson.

"Oh, nothing. You see, I'm nervous."

"You ain't tellin' the truth. But I don't blame you an' it don't matter anyway. Here we are. Jump down."

Dick sprang to the ground, and the others followed. While they held the reins they stood in a close circle about him. He had about as much chance of escape as he had of flying.

Robertson walked forward, saluted some one who stood up in the dark, and said a few words in a low tone.

"Bring him forward," said a clear voice, which Dick recognized at once.

The little group of men opened out and Dick, stepping forth, met his uncle face to face. It was now the time of Colonel George Kenton to start violently.

"My God! You, Dick!" he exclaimed. "How did you come here?"

"I didn't come," replied the boy, who was now feeling more at ease. "I was brought here by four scouts of yours, who I must say saw their duty and did it."

Colonel Kenton grasped his hand and shook it. He was very fond of this young nephew of his. The mere fact that he was on the other side did not alter his affection.

"Tell me about it, Dick," he said. "And you, Sergeant Robertson, you and your men are to be thanked for your vigilance

166

and activity. You can go off duty. You are entitled to your rest."

As they withdrew the sergeant, who passed by Dick and who had not missed a word of the conversation between him and his uncle, said to him:

"At least, young sir, I've returned you to your relatives, an' you're a minor, as I can see."

"It's so," said Dick as the sergeant passed on.

"They have not ill treated you?" said Colonel Kenton.

"No, they've been as kind as one enemy could be to another."

"It is strange, most strange, that you and I should meet here at such a time. Nay, Dick, I see in it the hand of Providence. You're to be saved from what will happen to your army tomorrow."

"I'd rather not be saved in this manner."

"I know it, but it is perhaps the only way. As sure as the stars are in Heaven your army will be destroyed in the morning, an' you'd be destroyed with it. I'm fond of you, Dick, and so I'd rather you'd be in our rear, a prisoner, while this is happening."

"General Grant is a hard man to crush."

"Dick! Dick, lad, you don't know what you're talking about! Look at the thing as it stands! We know everything that you're doing. Our spies look into the very heart of your camp. You think that we are fifty miles away, but a cannon shot from the center of our camp would reach the center of yours. Why, while we are here, ready to spring, this Grant, of whom you think so much, is on his way tonight to the little village of Savannah to confer with Buell. In the dawn when we strike and roll his brigades back he will not be here. And that's your great general!"

Dick knew that his uncle was excited. But he had full cause to be. There was everything in the situation to inflame an officer's pride and anticipation. It was not too dark for Dick to see a spark leap from his eyes, and a sudden flush of red appear in either tanned cheek. But for Dick the chill came again, and once more his hair prickled at the roots. The ambush was even more complete than he had supposed, and General Grant would not be there when it was sprung.

"Dick," said Colonel Kenton, "I have talked to you as I would not have talked to anyone else, but even so, I would not have talked to you as I have, were not your escape an impossibility. You are unharmed, but to leave this camp you would have to fly."

"I admit it, sir."

"Come with me. There are men higher in rank than I who would wish to see a prisoner taken as you were."

Dick followed him willingly and without a word. Aware that he was not in the slightest physical danger he was full of curiosity concerning what he was about to see. The words, "men higher in rank than I," whipped his blood.

Colonel Kenton led through the darkness to a deep and broad ravine, into which they descended. The sides and bottom of this ravine were clothed in bushes, and they grew thick on the edges above. It was much darker here, but Dick presently caught ahead of him the flicker of the first light that he had seen in the Southern army.

The boy's heart began to beat fast and hard. All the omens foretold that he was about to witness something that he could never by any possibility forget. They came nearer to the flickering light, and he made out seated figures around it. They were men wrapped in cavalry cloaks, because the night air had now grown somewhat chill, and Dick knew instinctively that these were the Southern generals preparing for the hammer-stroke at dawn.

A sentinel, rifle in hand, met them. Colonel Kenton whispered with him a moment, and he went to the group. He returned in a moment and escorted Dick and his uncle forward. Colonel Kenton saluted and Dick involuntarily did the same.

It was a small fire, casting only a faint and flickering light, but Dick, his eyes now used to the dusk, saw well the faces of the generals. He knew at once which was Johnston, the chief. He seemed older than the rest, sixty at least, but his skin was clear and ruddy, and the firm face and massive jaw showed thought and power. Yet the countenance appeared gloomy, as if overcast with care. Perhaps it was another omen!

By the side of Johnston sat a small but muscular man, swarthy, and in early middle years. His face and gestures when he talked showed clearly that he was of Latin blood. It was Beauregard, the victor of Bull Run, now second in command here, and he made a striking contrast to the stern and motionless Kentuckian who sat beside him and who was his chief. There was no uneasy play of Johnston's hands, no shrugging of the shoulders, no jerking of the head. He sat silent, his features a mask, while he listened to his generals.

On the other side was Braxton Bragg, brother-in-law of Jefferson Davis, who could never forget Bragg's kinship, and the service that he had done fifteen years before at Buena Vista, when he had broken with his guns the last of Santa Anna's squares, deciding the victory. By the side of him was Hardee, the famous tactician, taught in the best schools of both America and Europe. Then there was Polk, who, when a youth, had left the army to enter the church and become a bishop, and who was now a soldier again and a general. Next to the bishop-general sat the man who had been

Vice-President of the United States and who, if the Democracy had held together would now have been in the chair of Lincoln, John C. Breckinridge, called by his people the Magnificent, commonly accounted the most splendid looking man in America.

"Bring the prisoner forward, Colonel Kenton," said General Johnston, a general upon whom the South, with justice, rested great hopes.

Dick stepped forward at once and he held himself firmly, as he felt the eyes of the six generals bent upon him. He was conscious even at the moment that chance had given him a great opportunity. He was there to see, while the military genius of the South planned in the shadow of a dark ravine a blow which the six intended to be crushing.

"Where was the prisoner taken?" said Johnston to Colonel Kenton.

"Sergeant Robertson and three other men of my command seized him as he was about to enter the Northern lines. He was coming from the direction of Buell, where it is likely that he had gone to take a dispatch."

"Did you find any answer upon him."

"My men searched him carefully, sir, but found nothing."

"He is in the uniform of a staff officer. Have you found to what regiment in the Union army he belongs?"

"He is on the staff of Colonel Arthur Winchester, who commands one of the Kentucky regiments. I have also to tell you, sir, that his name is Richard Mason, and that he is my nephew."

"Ah," said General Johnston, "it is one of the misfortunes of civil war that so many of us fight against our own relatives. For those who live in the border states yours is the common lot."

But Dick was conscious that the six generals were gazing at him with renewed interest.

"Your surmise about his having been to Buell is no doubt correct," said Beauregard quickly and nervously. "You left General Buell this morning, did you not, Mr. Mason?"

Dick remained silent.

"It is also true that Buell's army is worn down by his heavy march over muddy roads," continued Beauregard as if he had not noticed Dick's failure to reply.

Dick's teeth were shut firmly, and he compressed his lips. He stood rigidly erect, gazing now at the flickering flames of the little fire.

"I suggest that you try him on some other subject than Buell, General Beauregard," said the bishop-general, a faint twinkle appearing in his eyes. Johnston sat silent, but his blue eyes missed nothing.

"It is true also, is it not," continued Beauregard, "that General Grant has gone or is going tonight to Savannah to meet General Buell, and confer with him about a speedy advance upon our army at Corinth?"

Dick clenched his teeth harder than ever, and a spasm passed over his face. He was conscious that six pairs of eyes, keen and intent, ready to note the slightest change of countenance and to read a meaning into it, were bent upon him. It was only by a supreme effort that he remained master of himself, but after the single spasm his countenance remained unmoved.

"You do not choose to answer," said Bragg, always a stern and ruthless man, "but we can drag what you know from you."

"I am a prisoner of war," replied Dick steadily. "I was taken in full uniform. I am no spy, and you cannot ill treat me."

"I do not mean that we would inflict any physical suffering upon you," said Bragg. "The Confederacy does not, and will never resort to such methods. But you are only a boy. We can question you here, until, through very weakness of spirit, you will be glad to tell us all you know about Buell's or any other Northern force."

"Try me, and see," said Dick proudly.

The blue eye of the silent Johnston flickered for an instant.

"But it is true," said Beauregard, resuming his role of cross-examiner, "that your army, considering itself secure, has not fortified against us? It has dug no trenches, built no earthworks, thrown up no abatis!"

The boy stood silent with folded arms, and Colonel George Kenton, standing on one side, threw his nephew a glance of sympathy, tinged with admiration.

"Still you do not answer," continued Beauregard, and now a strong note of irony appeared in his tone, "but perhaps it is just as well. You do your duty to your own army, and we miss nothing. You cannot tell us anything that we do not know already. Whatever you may know we know more. We know tonight the condition of General Grant's army better than General Grant himself does. We know how General Buell and his army stand better than General Buell himself does. We know the position of your brigades and the missing links between them better than your own brigade commanders do."

The eyes of the Louisianian flashed, his swarthy face swelled and his shoulders twitched. The French blood was strong within him. Just so might some general of Napoleon, some general from the Midi, have shown his emotion on the eve of battle, an emotion which did not detract from courage and resolution. But the Puritan general, Johnston, raised a deprecatory hand.

"It is enough, General Beauregard," he said. "The young prisoner will tell us nothing. That is evident. As he sees his duty he does it, and I wish that our young men when they are taken may behave as well. Mr. Mason, you are excused. You remain in the custody of your uncle, but I warn you that there is none who will guard better against the remotest possibility of your escape."

It was involuntary, but Dick gave his deepest military salute, and said in a tone of mingled admiration and respect:

"General Johnston, I thank you."

The commander-in-chief of the Southern army bowed courteously in return, and Dick, following his uncle, left the ravine.

The six generals returned to their council, and the boy who would not answer was quickly forgotten. Long they debated the morrow. Several have left accounts of what occurred. Johnston, although he had laid the remarkable ambush, and was expecting victory, was grave, even gloomy. But Beauregard, volatile and sanguine, rejoiced. For him the triumph was won already. After their great achievement in placing their army, unseen and unknown, within cannon shot of the Union force, failure was to him impossible.

Breckinridge, like his chief, Johnston, was also grave and did not say much. Hardee, as became one of his severe military training, discussed the details, the placing of the brigades and the time of attack by each. Polk, the bishop-general, and Bragg, also had their part.

As they talked in low tones they moved the men over their chessboard. Now and then an aide was summoned, and soon departed swiftly and in silence to move a battery or a regiment a little closer to the Union lines, but always he carried the injunction that no noise be made. Not a sound that could be heard three hundred yards away came from all that great army, lying there in the deep woods and poised for its spring.

Meanwhile security reigned in the Union camp. The farm lads of the west and northwest had talked much over their fires. They had eaten good suppers, and by and by they fell asleep. But many of the officers still sat by the coals and discussed the march against the Southern army at Corinth, when the men of Buell should join those of Grant. The pickets, although the gaps yet remained between those of the different brigades, walked back and forth and wondered at the gloom and intensity of the woods in front of them, but did not dream of that which lay in the heart of the darkness.

The Southern generals in the ravine lingered yet a little

longer. A diagram had been drawn upon a piece of paper. It showed the position of every Southern brigade, regiment, and battery, and of every Northern division, too. It showed every curve of the Tennessee, the winding lines of the three creeks, Owl, Lick, and Snake, and the hills and marshes.

The last detail of the plan was agreed upon finally, and they made it very simple, lest their brigades and regiments should lose touch and become confused in the great forest. They were to attack continually by the right, press the Union army toward the right always, in order to rush in and separate it from Pittsburg Landing on the Tennessee, and from the fleet and its stores. Then they meant to drive it into the marshes enclosed by the river and Snake Creek and destroy it.

The six generals rose, leaving the little fire to sputter out. General Johnston was very grave, and so were all the others as they started toward their divisions, except Beauregard, who said in sanguine tones:

"Gentlemen, we shall sleep tomorrow night in the enemy's camp."

Word, in the mysterious ways of war, had slid through the camp that the generals were in council, and many soldiers, driven by overwhelming curiosity, had crept through the underbrush to watch the figures by the fire in the ravine. They could not hear, they did not seek to hear, but they were held by a sort of spell. When they saw them separate, every one moving toward his own headquarters, they knew that there was nothing to await now but the dawn, and they stole back toward their own headquarters.

Dick had gone with Colonel Kenton to his own regiment, in the very heart of the Orphan Brigade, and on his way his uncle said:

"Dick, you will sleep among my own lads, and I ask you for your own sake to make no attempt to escape tonight. You would certainly be shot."

"I recognize that fact, sir, and I shall await a better opportunity."

"What to do with you in the morning I don't know, but we shall probably be able to take care of you. Meanwhile, Dick, go to sleep if you can. See, our boys are spread here through the woods. If it were day you'd probably find at least a dozen among them whom you know, and certainly a hundred are of blood kin to you, more or less."

Dick saw the dim forms stretched in hundreds on the ground, and, thanking his uncle for his kindness, he stretched himself upon an unoccupied bit of turf and closed his eyes. But it was impossible for young Richard Mason to sleep. He felt again that terrible thrill of agony, because he, alone, of all the score and more of Northern millions, knew that the Southern trap was about to fall, and he could not tell.

Never was he further from sleep. His nerves quivered with actual physical pain. He opened his eyes again and saw the dim forms lying in row on row as far in the forest as his eye could reach. Then he listened. He might hear the rifle of some picket, more wary or more enterprising than the others, sounding the alarm. But no such sound came to his ears. It had turned warmer again, and he heard only the Southern wind, heavy with the odors of grass and flower, sighing through the tall forest.

An anger against his own surged up in his breast. Why wouldn't they look? How could they escape seeing? Was it possible for one great army to remain unknown within cannon shot of another a whole night? It was incredible, but he had seen it, and he knew it. Fierce and bitter words rose to his lips, but he did not utter them.

Dick lay a long time, with his eyes open, and the night was passing as peacefully as if there would be no red dawn. Occasionally he heard a faint stir near him, as some restless soldier turned on his side in his sleep, and now and then a muttered word from an officer who passed near in the darkness.

Hours never passed more slowly. Colonel Kenton had gone back toward the Northern lines, and the boy surmised that he would be one of the first in the attack at dawn. He began to wonder if dawn would ever really come. Stars and a fair moon were out, and as nearly as he could judge from them it must be about three o'clock in the morning. Yet it seemed to him that he had been lying there at least twelve hours.

He shut his eyes again, but sleep was as far from him as ever. After another long and almost unendurable period he opened them once more, and it seemed to him that there was a faint tint of gray in the east. He sat up, and looking a long time, he was sure of it. The gray was deepening and broadening, and at its center it showed a tint of silver. The dawn was at hand, and every nerve in the boy's body thrilled with excitement and apprehension.

A murmur and a shuffling sound arose all around him. The sleepers were awake, and they stood up, thousands of them. Cold food was given to them, and they ate it hastily. But they fondled their rifles and muskets, and turned their faces toward the point where the Northern army lay, and from which no sound came.

Dick shivered all over. His head burned and his nerves throbbed. Too late now! He had hoped all through the long night that something would happen to carry a warning to that

173

unsuspecting army. Nothing had happened, and in five minutes the attack would begin.

He stood up at his full height and sought to pierce with his eyes the foliage in front of him, but the massed ranks of the Southerners now stood between, and the batteries were wheeling into line.

A great throb and murmur ran through the forest. Dick looked upon faces brown with the sun, and eyes gleaming with the fierce passion of victory and revenge. They were going to avenge Henry and Donelson and all the long and mortifying retreat from Kentucky. Dick saw them straining and looking eagerly at their officers for the word to advance.

As if by a concerted signal the long and mellow peal of many trumpets came from the front, the officers uttered the shout to charge, the wild and terrible rebel yell swelled from forty thousand throats, and the Southern army rushed upon its foe.

The red dawn of Shiloh had come.

# CHAPTER XV

# THE RED DAWN OF SHILOH

Dick stood appalled when he heard that terrible shout in the dawn, and the crash of cannon and rifles rolling down upon the Union lines. It was already a shout of triumph and, as he gazed, he saw through the woods the red line of flame, sweeping on without a halt.

The surprise had been complete. Hardee, leading the Southern advance, struck Peabody's Northern brigade and smashed it up instantly. The men did not have time to seize their rifles. They had no chance to form into ranks, and the officers themselves, as they shouted commands, were struck down. Men killed or wounded were falling everywhere. Almost before they had time to draw a free breath the remnants of the brigade were driven upon those behind it.

Hardee also rushed upon Sherman, but there he found a foe of tough mettle. The man who had foreseen the enormous extent of the war, although taken by surprise, too, did not lose his courage or presence of mind. His men had time to seize their arms, and he formed a hasty line of battle. He also had the forethought to send word to the general in his rear to close up the gap between him and the next general in the line. Then he shifted one of his own brigades until there was a ravine in front of it to protect his men, and he hurried a battery to his flank.

Never was Napoleon's maxim that men are nothing, a man is everything, more justified, and never did the genius of Sherman shine more brilliantly than on that morning. It was he, alone, cool of mind and steady in the face of overwhelming peril, who first faced the Southern rush. He inspired his troops with his own courage, and, though pale of face, they bent forward to meet the red whirlwind that was rushing down upon them.

Like a blaze running through dry grass the battle extended in almost an instant along the whole front, and the deep woods were filled with the roar of eighty thousand men in conflict. And Grant, as at Donelson, was far away.

The thunder and blaze of the battle increased swiftly and to a frightful extent. The Southern generals, eager, alert and full of success, pushed in all their troops. The surprised Northern army was giving away at all points, except where Sherman stood. Hardee, continuing his rush, broke the Northern line asunder, and his brigades, wrapping themselves around Sherman, strove to destroy him.

Although he saw his lines crumbling away before him, Sherman never flinched. The ravine in front of him and rough ground on one side defended him to a certain extent. The men fired their rifles as fast as they could load and reload, and the cannon on their flanks never ceased to pour shot and shell into the ranks of their opponents. The gunners were shot down, but new ones rose at once in their place. The fiercest conflict yet seen on American soil was raging here. North would not yield, South ever rushed anew to the attack, and a vast cloud of mingled flame and smoke enclosed them both.

Dick had stood as if petrified, staring at the billows of flame, while the thunder of great armies in battle stunned his ears. He realized suddenly that he was alone. Colonel Kenton had said the night before that he did not know what to do with him, but that he would find a way in the morning. But he had been forgotten, and he knew it was natural that he should be. His fate was but a trifle in the mighty event that was passing. There was no time for any one in the Southern army to bother about him.

Then he understood too, that he was free. The whole Orphan Brigade had passed on into the red heart of the battle, and had left him there alone. Now his mind leaped out of its paralysis. All his senses became alert. In that vast whirlwind of fire and smoke no one would notice that a single youth was stealing through the forest in an effort to rejoin his own people.

Action followed swift upon thought. He curved about in the woods and then ran rapidly toward the point where the fire seemed thinnest. He did not check his pace until he had gone at least a mile. Then he paused to see if he could tell how the battle was going. Its roar seemed louder than ever in his ears, and in front of him was a vast red line, which extended an unseen distance through the forest. Now and then the wild and thrilling rebel yell rose above the roar of cannon and the crash of rifles.

Dick saw with a sinking of the heart—and yet he had known that it would be so—that the red line of flame had moved deeper into the heart of the Northern camp. It had passed the Northern outposts and, at many points, it had swept over the Northern center. He feared that there was but a huddled and confused mass beyond it.

He saw something lying at his feet. It was a Confederate military cloak which some officer had cast off as he rushed to the charge. He picked it up, threw it about his own shoulders, and then tossed away his cap. If he fell in with Confederate troops they would not know him from one of their own, and it was no time now to hold cross-examinations.

He took a wide curve, and, after another mile, came to a hillock, upon which he stood a little while, panting. Again he was appalled at the sight he beheld. Bull Run and Donelson were small beside this. Here eighty thousand men were locked fast in furious conflict. Raw and undisciplined many of these farmer lads of the west and south were, but in battle they showed a courage and tenacity not surpassed by the best trained troops that ever lived.

The floating smoke reached Dick where he stood and stung his eyes, and a powerful odor of burned gunpowder assailed his nostrils. But neither sight nor odors held him back. Instead, they drew him on with overwhelming force. He must rejoin his own and do his best however little it counted in the whole.

It was now well on into the morning of a brilliant and hot Sunday. He did not know it, but the combat was raging fiercest then around the little church, which should have been sacred. Drawing a deep breath of an air which was shot with fire and smoke, and which was hot to his lungs, Dick began to run again. Almost before he noticed it he was running by the side of a Southern regiment which had been ordered to veer about and attack some new point in the Northern line. Keeping his presence of mind he shouted with them as they rushed on, and presently dropped away from them in the smoke.

He was conscious now of a new danger. Twigs and bits of bark began to rain down upon him, and he heard the unpleasant whistle of bullets over his head. They were the bullets of his own people, seeking to repel the Southern charge. A minute later a huge shell burst near him, covering him with flying earth. At first he thought he had been hit by fragments of the shell, but when he shook himself he found that he was all right.

He took yet a wider curve and before he was aware of the treacherous ground plunged into a swamp bordering one of the creeks. He stood for a few moments in mud and water to his waist, but he knew that he had passed from the range of the Union fire. Twigs and bark no longer fell around him and that most unpleasant whizz of bullets was gone.

He pulled himself out of the mire and ran along the edge of the creek toward the roar of the battle. He knew now that he had passed around the flank of the Southern army and could approach the flank of his own. He ran fast, and then began to hear bullets again. But now they were coming from the Southern army. He threw away the cloak and presently he emerged into a mass of men, who, under the continual urging of their officers, were making a desperate defense, firing, drawing back, reloading and firing again. In front, the woods swarmed with the Southern troops who drove incessantly upon them.

Dick snatched up a rifle—plenty were lying upon the ground, where the owners had fallen with them—and fired into the attacking ranks. Then he reloaded swiftly, and pressed on toward the Union center.

"What troops are these?" he asked of an officer who was knotting a handkerchief about a bleeding wrist.

"From Illinois. Who are you?"

"I'm Lieutenant Richard Mason of Colonel Arthur Winchester's Kentucky regiment. I was taken prisoner by the enemy last night, but I escaped this morning. Do you know where my regiment is?"

"Keep straight on, and you'll strike it or what's left of it, if anything at all is left. It's a black day."

Dick scarcely caught his last words, as he dashed on through bullets, shell and solid shot over slain men and horses, over dismantled guns and gun carriages, and into the very heart of the flame and smoke. The thunder of the battle was at its height now, because he was in the center of it. The roar of the great guns was continuous, but the unbroken crash of rifles by the scores of thousands was fiercer and more deadly.

The officer had pointed toward the Kentucky regiment with his sword, and following the line Dick ran directly into it. The very first face he saw was that of Colonel Winchester.

"Dick, my lad," shouted the Colonel, "where have you come from?"

"From the Southern army. I was taken prisoner last night almost within sight of our own, but when they charged this morning they forgot me and here I am."

Colonel Winchester suddenly seized him by the shoulders and pushed him down. The regiment was behind a small ridge which afforded some protection, and all were lying down except the senior officers.

"Welcome, Dick, to our hot little camp! The chances are about a hundred per cent out of a hundred per cent that this is the hottest place on the earth today!"

The long, thin figure of Warner lay pressed against the ground. A handkerchief, stained red, was bound about his head and his face was pale, but indomitable courage gleamed from his eyes. Just beyond him was Pennington, unhurt.

"Thank God you haven't fallen, and that I've found you!" exclaimed Dick.

"I don't know whether you're so lucky after all," said Warner. "The Johnnies have been mowing us down. They dropped on us so suddenly this morning that they must have been sleeping in the same bed with us last night, and we didn't know it. I hear that we're routed nearly everywhere except here and where Sherman stands. Look out! Here they come again!"

They saw tanned faces and fierce eyes through the smoke, and the bullets swept down on them in showers. Lucky for them that the little ridge was there, and that they had made up their minds to stand to the last. They replied with their own deadly fire, yet many fell, despite the shelter, and to both left and right the battle swelled afresh. Dick felt again that rain of bark and twigs and leaves. Sometimes a tree, cut through at its base by cannon balls, fell with a crash. Along the whole curving line the Southern generals ever urged forward their valiant troops.

Now the courage and skill of Sherman shone supreme. Dick saw him often striding up and down the lines, ordering and begging his men to stand fast, although they were looking almost into the eyes of their enemies.

The conflict became hand to hand, and assailant and assailed reeled to and fro. But Sherman would not give up. The fiercest attacks broke in vain on his iron front. McClernand, with whom he had quarreled the day before as to who should command the army while Grant was away, came up with reinforcements, and seeing what the fearless and resolute general had done, yielded him the place.

The last of the charges broke for the time upon Sherman, and his exhausted regiment uttered a shout of triumph, but on both sides of him the Southern troops drove their enemy back and yet further back. Breckinridge, along Lick Creek, was pushing everything before him. The bishop-general was doing well. Many of the Northern troops had not yet recovered from their surprise. A general and three whole regiments, struck on every side, were captured.

It seemed that nothing could deprive the Southern army of victory, absolute and complete. General Johnston had marshalled his troops with superb skill, and intending to reap the full advantage of the surprise, he continually pushed them forward upon the shattered Northern lines. He led in person and on horseback the attack upon the Federal center. Around and behind him rode his staff, and the wild rebel yell swept again through the forest, when the soldiers saw the stern and lofty features of the chief whom they trusted, leading them on.

But fate in the very moment of triumph that seemed

179

overwhelming and sure was preparing a terrible blow for the South. A bullet struck Johnston in the ankle. His boot filled with blood, and the wound continued to bleed fast. But, despite the urging of his surgeon, who rode with him, he refused to dismount and have the wound bound up. How could he dismount at such a time, when the battle was at its height, and the Union army was being driven into the creeks and swamps! He was wounded again by a piece of shell, and he sank dying from his horse. His officers crowded around him, seeking to hide their irreparable loss from the soldiers, the most costly death, with the exception of Stonewall Jackson's, sustained by the Confederacy in the whole war.

But the troops, borne on by the impetus that success and the spirit of Johnston had given them, drove harder than ever against the Northern line. They crashed through it in many places, seizing prisoners and cannon. Almost the whole Northern camp was now in their possession, and many of the Southern lads, hungry from scanty rations, stopped to seize the plenty that they found there, but enough persisted to give the Northern army no rest, and press it back nearer and nearer to the marshes.

The combat redoubled around Sherman. Johnston was gone, but his generals still shared his resolution. They turned an immense fire upon the point where stood Sherman and McClernand, now united by imminent peril. Their ranks were searched by shot and shell, and the bullets whizzed among them like a continuous swarm of hornets.

Dick was still unwounded, but so much smoke and vapor had drifted about his face that he was compelled at times to rub his eyes that he might see. He felt a certain dizziness, too, and he did not know whether the incessant roaring in his ears came wholly from the cannon and rifle fire or partly from the pounding of his blood.

"I feel that we are shaking," he shouted in the ears of Warner, who lay next to him. "I'm afraid we're going to give ground."

"I feel it, too," Warner shouted back. "We've been here for hours, but we're shot to pieces. Half of our men must be killed or wounded, but how old Sherman fights!"

The Southern leaders brought up fresh troops and hurled them upon Sherman. Again the combat was hand to hand, and to the right and left the supports of the indomitable Northern general were being cut away. Those brigades who had proved their mettle at Donelson, and who had long stood fast, were attacked so violently that they gave way, and the victors hurled themselves upon Sherman's flank.

Dick and his two young comrades perceived through the flame and smoke the new attack. It seemed to Dick that they were being enclosed now by the whole Southern army, and he felt a sense of suffocation. He was dizzy from such a long and terrible strain and so much danger, and he was not really more than half conscious. He was loading and firing his rifle mechanically, but he always aimed at something in the red storm before them, although he never knew whether he hit or missed, and was glad of it.

The division of Sherman had been standing there seven hours, sustaining with undaunted courage the resolute attacks of the Southern army, but the sixth sense warning Dick that it had begun to shake at last was true. The sun had now passed the zenith and was pouring intense and fiery rays upon the field, sometimes piercing the clouds of smoke, and revealing the faces of the men, black with sweat and burned gunpowder.

A cry arose for Grant. Why did not their chief show himself upon the field! Was so great a battle to be fought with him away? And where was Buell? He had a second great army. He was to join them that day. What good would it be for him to come tomorrow? Many of them laughed in bitter derision. And there was Lew Wallace, too! They had heard that he was near the field with a strong division. Then why did he not come upon it and face the enemy? Again they laughed that fierce and bitter laugh deep down in their throats.

The attack upon Sherman never ceased for an instant. Now he was assailed not only from the front, but from both flanks, and some even gaining the rear struck blows upon his division there. One brigade upon his left was compelled to give way, scattered, and lost its guns. The right wing was also driven in, and the center yielded slowly, although retaining its cohesion.

The three lads were on their feet now, and it seemed to them that everything was lost. They could see the battle in front of them only, but rumors came to them that the army was routed elsewhere. But neither Sherman nor McClernand would yield, save for the slow retreat, yielding ground foot by foot only. And there were many unknown heroes around them. Sergeant Whitley blazed with courage and spirit.

"We could be worse off than we are!" he shouted to Dick. "General Buell's army may yet come!"

"Maybe we could be worse off than we are, but I don't see how it's possible!" shouted Dick in return, a certain grim humor possessing him for the moment.

"Look! What I said has come true already!" shouted the sergeant. "Here is shelter that will help us to make a new stand!"

In their slow retreat they reached two low hills, between which a small ravine ran. It was not a strong position, but Sherman used it to the utmost. His men fired from the protecting crests of the hills, and he filled the ravine with riflemen, who poured a deadly fire upon their assailants.

Now Sherman ordered them to stand fast to the last man, because it was by this road that the division of Lew Wallace must come, if it came at all. But Southern brigades followed them and the battle raged anew, as fierce and deadly as ever.

Although their army was routed at many points the Northern officers showed indomitable courage. Driven back in the forest they always strove to form the lines anew, and now their efforts began to show some success. Their resistance on the right hardened, and on the left they held fast to the last chain of hills that covered the wharves and their stores at the river landing. As they took position here two gunboats in the river began to send huge shells over their heads at the attacking Southern columns, maintaining a rapid and heavy fire which shook assailants and strengthened defenders. Again the water had come to the help of the North, and at the most critical moment. The whole Northern line was now showing a firmer front, and Grant, himself, was directing the battle.

Fortune, which had played a game with Grant at Donelson, played a far greater one with him on the far greater field of Shiloh. The red dawn of Shiloh, when Johnston was sweeping his army before him, had found him at Savannah far from the field of battle. The hardy and vigorous Nelson had arrived there in the night with Buell's vanguard, and Grant had ordered it to march at speed the next day to join his own army. But he, himself, did not reach the field of Shiloh until 10 o'clock, when the fiercest battle yet known on the American continent had been raging for several hours.

Grant and his staff, as they rode away from his headquarters, heard the booming of cannon in the direction of Shiloh. Some of them thought it was a mere skirmish, but it came continuously, like rolling thunder, and their trained ears told them that it rose from a line miles in length. One seeks to penetrate the mind of a commanding general at such a time, and see what his feelings were. Again the battle had been joined, and was at its height, and he away!

Those trained ears told him also that the rolling thunder of the cannon was steadily moving toward them. It could mean only that the Northern army had been driven from its camp and that the Southern army was pushing its victory to the utmost. In those moments his agony must have been intense. His great army not only attacked, but beaten, and he not there! He and his staff urged their horses forward, seeking to gain from them new ounces of speed, but the country was difficult. The hills were rough and there were swamps and mire. And, as they listened, the roar of battle steadily came nearer and nearer. There was no break in the Northern retreat. The sweat, not of heat but of mental agony, stood upon their faces. Grant was not the only one who suffered.

Now they met some of those stragglers who flee from every battlefield, no matter what the nation. Their faces were white with fear and they cried out that the Northern army was destroyed. Officers cursed them and struck at them with the flats of their swords, but they dodged the blows and escaped into the bushes. There was no time to pursue them. Grant and his staff never ceased to ride toward the storm of battle which raged far and wide around the little church of Shiloh.

The stream of fugitives increased, and now they saw swarms of men who stood here and there, not running, but huddled and irresolute. Never did Fortune, who brought this, her favorite, from the depths, bring him again in her play so near to the verge of destruction. When he came upon the field, the battle seemed wholly lost, and the whole world would have cried that he was to blame.

But the bulldog in Grant was never of stauncher breed than on that day. His face turned white, and he grew sick at the sight of the awful slaughter. A bullet broke the small sword at his side, but he did not flinch. Preserving the stern calm that always marked him on the field he began to form his lines anew and strengthen the weaker points.

Yet the condition of his army would have appalled a weaker will. It had been driven back three miles. His whole camp had been taken. His second line also had been driven in. Many thousands of men had fallen and other thousands had been taken. Thirty of his cannon were in the hands of the enemy, and although noon had now come and gone there was no sound to betoken the coming of the troops led by Wallace or Nelson. Well might Grant's own stout heart have shrunk appalled from the task before him.

Wallace was held back by confused orders, pardonable at such a time. The eager Nelson was detained at Savannah by Buell, who thought that the sounds of the engagement they heard in the Shiloh woods was a minor affair, and who wanted Nelson to wait for boats to take him there.

It seemed sometimes to Dick long afterward, when the whole of the great Shiloh battle became clear, that Fortune was merely playing a game of chess, with the earth as a board, and the armies as pawns. Grant's army was ambushed with its general absent. The other armies which were almost at hand were delayed for one reason or another. While as for the South, the genius that had planned the attack and that had carried it forward was quenched in death, when victory was at its height.

But for the present the lad had little time for such thoughts as these. The success of Sherman in holding the new position infused new courage into him and those around him. The men in gray, wearied with their immense exertions, and having suffered frightful losses themselves, abated somewhat the energy and fierceness of their attack.

The dissolved Northern regiments had time to reform. Grant seized a new position along a line of hills, in front of which ran a deep ravine filled with brushwood. He and his officers appreciated the advantage and they massed the troops there as fast as they could.

Now Fortune, after having brought Grant to the verge of the pit, was disposed to throw chances in his way. The hills and the ravine were one. Another, and most important it was, was the presence of guns of the heaviest calibre landed some days ago from the fleet, and left there until their disposition could be determined. A quick-witted colonel, Webster by name, gathered up all the gunners who had lost their own guns and who had been driven back in the retreat, and manned this great battery of siege guns, just as the Southern generals were preparing to break down the last stand of the North.

Meanwhile, a terrible rumor had been spreading in the ranks of the Southern troops. The word was passed from soldier to soldier that their commander, Johnston, whom they had believed invincible, had been killed, and they did not trust so much Beauregard, who was left in command, nor those who helped. Their fiery spirit abated somewhat. There was no decrease of courage, but continuous victory did not seem so easy now.

Confusion invaded the triumphant army also. Beauregard had divided the leadership on the field among three of his lieutenants. Hardee now urged on the center, Bragg commanded the right, and Polk, the bishop-general, led the left. It was Bragg's division that was about to charge the great battery of siege guns that the alert Webster had manned so quickly. Five minutes more and Webster would have been too late. Here again were the fortunes of Grant brought to the very verge of the pit. The Northern gunboats at the mouth of Lick Creek moved forward a little, and their guns were ready to support the battery.

The Kentucky regiment was wedged in between the battery and a brigade, and it was gasping for breath. Colonel Winchester, slightly wounded in three places, commanded his men to lie down, and they gladly threw themselves upon the earth.

There was a momentary lull in the battle. Wandering winds caught up the banks of smoke and carried most of them away. Dick, as he rose a little, saw the Southern troops massing in the forest for an attack upon their new position. They seemed to be only a few yards away and he clearly observed the officers walking along the front of the lines. It flashed upon him that they must hold these hills or Grant's army would perish. Where was Buell? Why did he not come? If the Southerners destroyed one Northern army today they would destroy another tomorrow! They would break the two halves of the Union force in the west into pieces, first one and then the other.

"What do you see, Dick?" asked Warner, who was lying almost flat upon his face.

"The Confederate army is getting ready to wipe us off the face of the earth! Up with your rifle, George! They'll be upon us in two minutes!"

They heard a sudden shout behind them. It was a glad shout, and well it might be. Nelson, held back by Buell's orders, had listened long to the booming of the cannon off in the direction of Shiloh. Nothing could convince him that a great battle was not going on, and all through the morning he chafed and raged. And as the sound of the cannon grew louder he believed that Grant's army was losing.

Nelson obtained Buell's leave at last to march for Shiloh, but it was a long road across hills and creeks and through swamps. The cannon sank deep in the mire, and then the ardent Nelson left them behind. Now he knew there was great need for haste. The flashing and thundering in front of them showed to the youngest soldier in his command that a great battle was in progress, and that it was going against the North. His division at last reached Pittsburg Landing and was carried across the river in the steamers. One brigade led by Ammen outstripped the rest, and rushed in behind the great battery and to its support, just as the Southern bugles once more sounded the charge.

Dick shouted with joy, too, when he saw the new troops. The next moment the enemy was upon them, charging directly through a frightful discharge from the great guns. The riddled regiments, which had fought so long, gave way before the bayonets, but the fresh troops took their places and poured a terrible fire into the assaulting columns. And the great guns of the battery hurled a new storm of shell and solid shot. The ranks of the Southern troops, worn by a full day of desperate fighting, were broken. They had crossed the ravine into the very mouths of the Northern guns, but now they were driven back into the ravine and across it. Cannon and rifles rained missiles upon them there, and they withdrew into the woods, while for the first time in all that long day a shout of triumph rose from the Union lines.

Another lull came in the battle.

"What are they doing now, Dick?" asked the Vermonter.

"I can't see very well, but they seem to be gathering in the forest for a fresh attack. Do you know, George, that the sun is almost down?"

"It's certainly time. It's been at least a month since the Johnnies ran out of the forest in the dawn, and jumped on us."

It was true that the day was almost over, although but few had noticed the fact. The east was already darkening, and a rosy glow from the west fell across the torn forest. Here and there a dead tree, set on fire by the shells, burned slowly, little flames creeping along trunk and boughs.

Bragg was preparing to hurl his entire force upon Sherman and the battery. At that moment Beauregard, now his chief, arrived. But a few minutes of daylight were left and the swarthy Louisianian looked at the great losses in his own ranks. He believed that the army of Buell was so far away that it could not arrive that night and he withheld the charge.

The Southern army withdrew a little into the woods, the night rushed down, and Shiloh's terrible first day was over.

# CHAPTER XVI

## THE FIERCE FINISH OF SHILOH

Dick, who had been lying under cover just behind the crest of one of the low ridges, suddenly heard the loud beating of his heart. He did not know, for a moment or two, that the sound came so distinctly because the mighty tumult which had been raging around him all day had ceased, as if by a concerted signal. Those blinding flashes of flame no longer came from the forest before him, the shot and shell quit their horrible screaming, and the air was free from the unpleasant hiss of countless bullets.

He stretched himself a little and stood up. The lads all around him were standing up, and were beginning to talk to each other in the high-pitched, shouting voices that they had been compelled to use all day long, not yet realizing to the full that the tumult of the battle had ceased. The boy felt stiff and sore in every bone and muscle, and, although the cannon and rifles were silent, there was still a hollow roaring in his ears. His eyes were yet dim from the smoke, and his head felt heavy and dull. He gazed vacantly at the forest in front of him, and wondered dimly why the Southern army was not still there, attacking, as it had attacked for so many hours.

But the deep woods were silent and empty. Coils and streamers of smoke floated about among the trees, and suddenly a gray squirrel hopped out on a bough and began to chatter wildly. Dick, despite himsclf, laughed, but the laugh was hysterical. He could appreciate the feelings of the squirrel, which probably had been imprisoned in a hollow of the tree all day long, listening to this tremendous battle, and squirrels were not used to such battles. It was a trifle that made him laugh, but everything was out of proportion now. Life did not go on in the usual way at all. The ordinary occupations were gone, and people spent most of their time trying to kill one another.

He rubbed his hands across his eyes and cleared them of the smoke. The battle was certainly over for the day at least, and neither he nor his comrades had sufficient vitality yet to think of the morrow. The twilight was fast deepening into night. The last rosy glow of the sun faded, and thick darkness enveloped the vast forest, in which twenty thousand men had fallen, and in which most of them yet lay, the wounded with the dead.

There was presently a deep boom from the river, and a shell fired by one of the gunboats curved far over their heads and dropped into the forest, where the Southern army was encamped. All through the night and at short but regular intervals the gunboats maintained this warning fire, heartening the Union soldiers, and telling them at every discharge that however they might have to fight for the land, the water was always theirs.

Dick saw Colonel Winchester going among his men, and pulling himself together he saluted his chief.

"Any orders, sir?" he said.

"No, Dick, my boy, none for the present," replied the colonel, a little sadly. "Half of my poor regiment is killed or wounded, and the rest are so exhausted that they are barely able to move. But they fought magnificently, Dick! They had to, or be crushed! It is only here that we have withstood the rush of the Southern army, and it is probable that we, too, would have gone had not night come to our help."

"Then we have been beaten?"

"Yes, Dick, we have been beaten, and beaten badly. It was the surprise that did it. How on earth we could have let the Southern army creep upon us and strike unaware I don't understand. But Dick, my boy, there will be another battle tomorrow, and it may tell a different tale. Some prisoners whom we have taken say that Johnston has been killed, and Beauregard is no such leader as he."

"Will the army of General Buell reach us tonight?"

"Buell, himself, is here. He has been with Grant for some time, and all his brigades are marching at the double quick. Lew Wallace arrived less than half an hour ago with seven thousand men fresh and eager for battle. Dick! Dick, my boy, we'll have forty thousand new troops on the field at the next dawn, and before God we'll wipe out the disgrace of today! Listen to the big guns from the boats as they speak at intervals! Why, I can understand the very words they speak! They are saying to the Southern army: 'Look out! Look out! We're coming in the morning, and it's we who'll attack now!'"

Dick saw that Colonel Winchester himself was excited. The pupils of his eyes were dilated, and a red spot glowed in either cheek. Like all the other officers he was stung by the surprise and defeat, and he could barely wait for the morning and revenge.

Colonel Winchester walked away to a council that had been called, and Dick turned to Pennington and Warner, who were not hurt, save for slight wounds. Warner had recovered his poise, and was soon as calm and dry as ever.

"Dick," he said, "we're some distance from where we started this morning. There's nothing like being shoved along when you don't want to go. The next time they tell me there's nothing in a thicket I expect to search it and find a rebel army at least a hundred thousand strong right in the middle of it."

"How large do you suppose the Southern army was?" asked Pennington.

"I had a number of looks at it," replied Warner, "and I should say from the way it acted that it numbered at least three million men. I know that at times not less than ten thousand were aiming their rifles at my own poor and unworthy person. What a waste of energy for so many men to shoot at me all at once. I wish the Johnnies would go away and let us alone!"

The last words were high-pitched and excited. His habitual self-control broke down for a moment, and the tremendous excitement and nervous tension of the day found vent in his voice. But in a few seconds he recovered himself and looked rather ashamed.

"Boys," he said, "I apologize."

"You needn't," said Pennington. "There have been times today when I felt brave as a lion, and lots of other times I was scared most to death. It would have helped me a lot then, if I could have opened my mouth and yelled at the top of my voice."

Sergeant Daniel Whitley was leaning against a stump, and while he was calmly lighting a pipe he regarded the three boys with a benevolent gaze.

"None of you need be ashamed of bein' scared," he said. "I've been in a lot of fights myself, though all of them were mere skirmishes when put alongside of this, an' I've been scared a heap today. I've been scared for myself, an' I've been scared for the regiment, an' I've been scared for the whole army, an' I've been scared on general principles, but here we are, alive an' kickin', an' we ought to feel powerful thankful for that."

"We are," said Dick. Then he rubbed his head as if some sudden thought had occurred to him.

"What is it, Dick?" asked Warner.

"I've realized all at once that I'm tremendously hungry. The Confederates broke up our breakfast. We never had time to think of dinner, and now its nothing to eat."

"Me, too," said Pennington. "If you were to hit me in the stomach I'd give back a hollow sound like a drum. Why don't somebody ring the supper bell?"

But fires were soon lighted along their whole front, and provisions were brought up from the rear and from the steamers. The soldiers, feeling their strength returning, ate ravenously. They also talked much of the battle. Many of them were yet under the influence of hysterical excitement. They told extraordinary stories of the things they had seen and done, and they believed all they told were true. They ate fiercely, at first almost like wolves, but after a while they resolved into their true state as amiable young human beings and were ashamed of themselves.

All the while Buell's army of the Ohio was passing over the river and joining Grant's army of the Tennessee. Regiment after regiment and brigade after brigade crossed. The guns that Nelson had been forced to leave behind were also brought up and were taken over with the other batteries. While the shattered remnants of the army of the Tennessee were resting, the fresh army of the Ohio was marching by it in the late hours of the night in order to face the Southern foe in the morning.

The Southern army itself lay deep in the woods from which it had driven its enemy. Always the assailant through the day, its losses had been immense. Many thousands had fallen, and no new troops were coming to take their place. Continual reinforcements came to the North throughout the night, not a soldier came to the South. Beauregard, at dawn, would have to face twice his numbers, at least half of whom were fresh troops.

Another conference was held by the Southern generals in the forest, but now the central figure, the great Johnston, was gone. The others, however, summoned their courage anew, and passed the whole night arranging their forces, cheering the men, and preparing for the morn. Their scouts and skirmishers kept watch on the Northern camp, and the Southerners believed that while they had whipped only one army the day before, they could whip two on the morrow.

Dick and his friends meanwhile were lying on the earth, resting, but not able to sleep. The nerves, drawn so tightly by the day's work, were not yet relaxed wholly. A deep apathy seized them all. Dick, from a high point on which he lay, saw the dark surface of the Tennessee, and the lights on the puffing steamers as they crossed, bearing the Army of the Ohio. His mind did not work actively now, but he felt that they were saved. The deep river, although it was on their flank, seemed to flow as a barrier against the foe, and it was, in fact, a barrier more and more, as without its command the second Union army could never have come to the relief of the first.

Dick, after a while, saw Colonel Winchester, and other officers near him. They were talking of their losses. They gave the names of many generals and colonels who had been killed. Presently they moved away, and he fell into an uneasy sleep, or rather doze, from which he was awakened after a while by a heavy rumbling sound of a distant cannonade.

The boy sprang up, wondering why any one should wish to renew the battle in the middle of the night, and then he saw that it was no battle. The sound was thunder rolling heavily on the southern horizon, and the night had become very dark. Vivid flashes of lightning cut the sky, and a strong wind rushed among the trees. Heavy drops of water struck him in the face and then the rain swept down.

Dick did not seek protection from the storm, nor did any of those near him. The cool drops were grateful to their faces after the heat and strife of the day. Their pulses became stronger, and the blood flowed in a quickened torrent through their veins. They let it pour upon them, merely seeking to keep their ammunition dry.

Ten thousand wounded were yet lying untouched in the forest, but the rain was grateful to them, too. When they could they turned their fevered faces up to it that it might beat upon them and bring grateful coolness.

Deep in the night a council like that of the Southern generals was held in the Northern camp, also. Grant, his face an expressionless mask, presided, and said but little. Buell, Sherman, McClernand, Nelson, Wallace and others, were there, and Buell and Sherman, like their chief, spoke little. The three men upon whom most rested were very taciturn that night, but it is likely that extraordinary thoughts were passing in the minds of every one of the three.

Grant, after a day in which any one of a dozen chances would have wrecked him, must have concluded that in very deed and truth he was the favorite child of Fortune. When one is saved again and again from the very verge he begins to believe that failure is impossible, and in that very belief lies the greatest guard against failure.

It is said of Grant that in the night after his great defeat around the church of Shiloh, he was still confident, that he told his generals they would certainly win on the morrow, and he reminded them that if the Union army had suffered terribly, the Southern army must have suffered almost equally so, and would face them at dawn with numbers far less than their own. He had not displayed the greatest skill, but he had shown the greatest moral courage, and now on the night between battles it was that quality that was needed most.

Dick, not having slept any the night before, and having passed through a day of fierce battle, was overcome after midnight, and sank into a sleep that was mere lethargy. He awoke once before dawn and remembered, but vaguely, all that had happened. Yet he was conscious that there was much movement in the forest. He heard the tread of many feet, the sound of commands, the neigh of horses and the rumbling of cannon wheels. The Army of the Ohio was passing to the exposed flank of the Army of the Tennessee and at dawn it would all be in line. He also caught flitting glimpses of the Tennessee, and of the steamers loaded with troops still crossing, and he heard the boom of the heavy cannon on the gunboats which still, at regular and short intervals, sent huge shells curving into the forest toward the camp of the Southern army. He also saw near him Warner and Pennington sound asleep on the ground, and then he sank back into his own lethargic slumber.

He was awakened by the call of a trumpet, and, as he rose, he saw the whole regiment or rather, what was left of it, rising with him. It was not yet dawn, and a light rain was falling, but smoldering fires disclosed the ground for some distance, and also the river on which the gunboats and transports were now gathered in a fleet.

Colonel Winchester beckoned to him.

"All right this morning, Dick?" he said.

"Yes, sir; I'm ready for my duty."

"And you, too, Warner and Pennington?"

"We are, sir," they replied together.

"Then keep close beside me. I don't know when I may want you for a message. Daybreak will be here in a half hour. The entire Army of the Ohio, led by General Buell in person will be in position then or very shortly afterward, and a new, and, we hope, a very different battle will begin."

Food and coffee were served to the men, and while the rain was still falling they formed in line and awaited the dawn. The desire to retrieve their fortunes was as strong among the farmer lads as it was among the officers who took care to spread among them the statement that Buell's army alone was as numerous as the Southern force, and probably more numerous since their enemy must have sustained terrible losses. Thus they stood patiently, while the rain thinned and the sun at last showed a red edge through floating clouds.

They waited yet a little while longer, and then the boom of a heavy gun in the forest told them that the enemy was advancing to begin the battle afresh. Again it was the Southern army that attacked, although it was no surprise now. Yet Beauregard and his generals were still sanguine of completing the victory. Their scouts and skirmishers had failed to discover that the entire army of Buell also was now in front of them.

Bragg was gathering his division on the left to hurl it like a thunderbolt upon Grant's shattered brigades. Hardee and the bishop-general were in the center, and Breckinridge led the right. But as they moved forward to attack the Union troops came out to meet them. Nelson had occupied the high ground between Lick and Owl Creeks, and his and the Southern troops met in a fierce clash shortly after dawn.

Beauregard, drawn by the firing at that point, and noticing the courage and tenacity with which the Northern troops held their ground, sending in volley after volley, divined at once that these were not the beaten troops of the day before, but new men. This swarthy general, volatile and dramatic, nevertheless had great penetration. He understood on the instant a fact that his soldiers did not comprehend until later. He knew that the whole army of Buell was now before him.

For the moment it was Beauregard and Buell who were the protagonists, instead of Grant and Johnston as on the day before. The Southern leader gathered all his forces and hurled them upon Nelson. Weary though the Southern soldiers were, their attack was made with utmost fire and vigor. A long and furious combat ensued. A Southern division under Cheatham rushed to the help of their fellows. Buell's forces were driven in again and again, and only his heavy batteries enabled him to regain his lost ground.

Buell led splendid troops that he had trained long and rigidly, and they had not been in the conflict the day before. Fresh and with unbroken ranks, not a man wounded or missing, they had entered the battle and both Grant and Buell, as well as their division commanders, expected an easy victory where the Army of the Ohio stood.

Buell, to his amazement, saw himself reduced to the defensive. He and Grant had reckoned that the decimated brigades of the South could not stand at all before him, but just as on the first day they came on with the fierce rebel yell, hurling themselves upon superior numbers, taking the cannon of their enemy, losing them, and retaking them and losing them again, but never yielding.

The great conflict increased in violence. Buell, a man of iron courage, saw that his soldiers must fight to the uttermost, not for victory only, but even to ward off defeat. The dawn was now far advanced. The rain had ceased, and the sun again shot down sheaves of fiery rays upon a vast low cloud of fire and smoke in which thousands of men met in desperate combat.

Nine o'clock came. It had been expected by Grant that Buell long before that time would have swept everything before him. But for three hours Buell had been fighting to keep himself from being swept away. The Southern troops seemed animated by that extraordinary battle fever and absolute contempt of death which distinguished them so often during this war. Buell's army was driven in on both flanks, and only the center held fast. It began to seem possible that the South, despite her reduced ranks might yet defeat both Northern armies. Another battery dashed up to the relief of the men in blue. It was charged at once by the men in gray so fiercely that the gunners were glad to escape with their guns, and once more the wild rebel yell of triumph swelled through the southern forest.

Dick, standing with his comrades on one of the ridges that they had defended so well, listened to the roar of conflict on the wing, ever increasing in volume, and watched the vast clouds of smoke gathering over the forest. He could see from where he stood the flash of rifle fire and the blaze of cannon, and both eye and ear told him that the battle was not moving back upon the South.

"It seems that we do not make headway, sir," he said to Colonel Winchester, who also stood by him, looking and listening.

"Not that I can perceive," replied the colonel, "and yet with the rush of forty thousand fresh troops of ours upon the field I deemed victory quick and easy. How the battle grows! How the South fights!"

Colonel Winchester walked away presently and joined Sherman, who was eagerly watching the mighty conflict, into which he knew that his own worn and shattered troops must sooner or later be drawn. He walked up and down in front of his lines, saying little but seeing everything. His tall form was seen by all his men. He, too, must have felt a singular thrill at that moment. He must have known that his star was rising. He, more than any other, with his valor, penetrating mind and decision had saved the Northern army from complete destruction the first day at Shiloh. He had not been able to avert defeat, but he had prevented utter ruin. His division alone had held together in the face of the Southern attack until night came.

Sherman must have recalled, too, how his statement that the North would need 200,000 troops in the west alone had been sneered at, and he had been called mad. But he neither boasted nor predicted, continuing to watch intently the swelling battle.

"I had enough fighting yesterday to last me a hundred years," said Warner to Dick, "but it seems that I'm to have more today. If the Johnnies had any regard for the rules of war they'd have retreated long ago."

"We'll win yet," said Dick hopefully, "but I don't think we can achieve any big victory. Look, there's General Grant himself."

Grant was passing along his whole line. While leaving the main battle to Buell he retained general command and watched everything. He, too, observed the failure of Buell's army to drive the enemy before them, and he must have felt a sinking of the heart, but he did not show it. Instead he spoke only of victory, when he made any comment at all, and sent the members of his staff to make new arrangements. He must bring into action every gun and man he had or he would yet lose.

It was now 10 o'clock and the new battle had lasted with the utmost fury and desperation for four hours. Dick, after General Grant rode on, felt as if a sudden thrill had run through the whole army. He saw men rising from the earth and tightening their belts. He saw gunners gathering around their guns and making ready with the ammunition. He knew the remains of Grant's army were about to march upon the enemy, helping the Army of the Ohio to achieve the task that had proved so great.

Sherman, McClernand and other generals now passed among their troops, cheering them, telling them that the time had come to win back what they had lost the day before, and that victory was sure. They called upon them for another great effort, and a shout rolled along the line of willing soldiers.

Sherman's whole division now raised itself up and rushed at the enemy, Dick and his comrades in the front of their own regiment. The whole Northern line was now engaged. Grant, true to his resolution, had hurled every man and every gun upon his foe.

The Southern generals felt the immense weight of the numbers that were now driving down upon them. Their decimated ranks could not withstand the charge of two armies. In the center where Buell's men, having stood fast from the first, were now advancing, they were compelled to give way and lost several guns. On the wings the heavy Northern brigades were advancing also, and the whole Southern line was pushed back. So much inferior was the South in numbers that her enemy began to overlap her on the flanks also.

A tremendous shout of exultation swept through the Northern ranks, as they felt themselves advancing. The promises of their generals were coming true, and there is nothing sweeter than victory after defeat. Fortune, after frowning upon her so long, was now smiling upon the North. The exultant cheer swept through the ranks again, and back came the defiant rebel yell.

A young soldier often feels what is happening with as true instinct as a general. Dick now knew that the North would recover the field, and that the South, cut down fearfully, though having performed prodigies of valor, must fight to save herself. He felt that the resistance in front of them was no longer invincible. He saw in the flash of the firing that the Southern ranks were thin, very thin, and he knew that there was no break in their own advance.

Now the sanguine Northern generals planned the entire destruction of the Southern army. There was only one road by which Beauregard could retreat to Corinth. A whole Northern division rushed in to block the way. Sherman, in his advance, came again to the ground around the little Methodist chapel of Shiloh which he had defended so well the day before, and crowded his whole force upon the Southern line at that point. Once more the primitive church in the woods looked down upon one of the most sanguinary conflicts of the whole war. If Sherman could break through the Southern line here Beauregard's whole army would be lost.

But the Southern soldiers were capable of another and a mighty effort. Their generals saw the danger and acted with their usual promptness and decision. They gathered together their shattered brigades and hurled them like a thunderbolt upon the Union left and center. The shock was terrific. Sherman, with all his staunchness and the valor of his men, was compelled to give way. McClernand, too, reeled back, others were driven in also. Whole brigades and regiments were cut to pieces or thrown in confusion. The Southerners cut a wide gap in the Northern army, through which they rushed in triumph, holding the Corinth road against every attack and making their rear secure.

Sherman's division, after its momentary repulse, gathered itself anew, and, although knowing now that the Southern army could not be entrapped, drove again with all its might upon the positions around the church. They passed over the dead of the day before, and gathered increasing vigor, as they saw that the enemy was slowly drawing back.

Grant reformed his line, which had been shattered by the last fiery and successful attack of the South. Along the whole long line the trumpets sang the charge, and brigades and batteries advanced.

But the end of Shiloh was at hand. Despite the prodigies of valor performed by their men, the Southern generals saw that they could not longer hold the field. The junction of Grant and Buell, after all, had proved too much for them. The bugles sounded the retreat, and reluctantly they gave up the ground which they had won with so much courage and daring. They retreated rather as victors than defeated men, presenting a bristling front to the enemy until their regiments were lost in the forest, and beating off every attempt of skirmishers or cavalry to molest them.

It was the middle of the afternoon when the last shot was fired, and the Southern army at its leisure resumed its march toward Corinth, protected on the flanks by its cavalry, and carrying with it the assurance that although not victorious over two armies it had been victorious over one, and had struck the most stunning blow yet known in American history.

When the last of the Southern regiments disappeared in the deep woods, Dick and many of those around him sank exhausted upon the ground. Even had they been ordered to follow they would have been incapable of it. Complete nervous collapse followed such days and nights as those through which they had passed.

Nor did Grant and Buell wish to pursue. Their armies had been too terribly shaken to make another attack. Nearly fifteen thousand of their men had fallen and the dead and wounded still lay scattered widely through the woods. The South had lost almost as many. Nearly a third of her army had been killed or wounded in the battle, and yet they retired in good order, showing the desperate valor of these sons of hers.

The double army which had saved itself, but which had yet been unable to destroy its enemy, slept that night in the recovered camp. The generals discussed in subdued tones their narrow escape, and the soldiers, who now understood very well what had happened, talked of it in the same way.

"We knew that it was going to be a big war," said Dick, "but it's going to be far bigger than we thought."

"And we won't make that easy parade down to the Gulf," said Warner. "I'm thinking that a lot of lions are in the path."

"But we'll win!" said Dick. "In the end we'll surely win!"

Then after dreaming a little with his eyes open he fell asleep, gathering new strength for mighty campaigns yet to come.